DeVille regarded Kate hungrily yet his manner remained cool and aloof.

'As I suspected,' he said, 'you appear to be unskilled in the erotic arts, despite having the body of an Aphrodite.'

'Does this mean your offer no longer stands?'

She felt both relief and disappointment at the prospect.

'No. To many, innocence in itself is attractive. And you could be taught. But you would have to place your body and soul totally in my care. You would have to do whatever I commanded without question.'

'For how long?'

'Two weeks in May. But two weeks that will change your life for ever . . .'

Two Weeks in May

Maria Caprio

HEADLINE DELTA

First published in 1993
by HEADLINE BOOK PUBLISHING PLC

A HEADLINE DELTA paperback

10 9 8 7 6 5 4

ISBN 0 7472 4229 1

Printed and bound in Great Britain by
Cox & Wyman Ltd, Reading, Berkshire

HEADLINE BOOK PUBLISHING
A division of Hodder Headline PLC
338 Euston Road
London NW1 3BH

Two Weeks
in May

1

The groundsman's hands were big and strong. His fingers totally enclosed her forearm, making escape impossible. Her eyes were large in trepidation as she stared up into his face. His skin was leathered by the sun, and he had a full day's stubble on his chin.

Kate held her unbuttoned blouse together with her free hand. Beneath the thin material, her breasts heaved with the possibility of the unknown.

His dog waited by his side, panting in the heat, a big, brown and powerful Doberman, saliva dripping from its mouth.

She could smell the sweat from the man's body and something else besides; another odour with which she was unfamiliar, but which caused her to catch her breath because of its strong masculinity.

Kate wondered where Gina was and how much the groundsman had seen. She wondered how much he would tell and she flushed at the shame that lay ahead.

But instead of taking her back, he pushed her down on the grass in the clearing, back into the place where she and her friend had been lying. He commanded the dog with a movement of his hand and the beast stood guard over her. The man loosened his belt.

No words were spoken. None were necessary.

Kate knew now that he wouldn't tell, but that his silence would have to be bought at a price. She knew also she was in no position to bargain over the terms of their agreement.

Whatever he wanted to do, she would allow him to do. She would participate to fulfil his desires.

He pushed the trousers down his thighs and she stared in fascination as he undressed. This was the first man she had ever seen without clothes. A real man, whose body was hard, with hair on his chest and over his shoulders, and a rich thatch of black curls between his legs.

There was something else between his legs, too, something she dare not bring herself to look at until he was naked. It was large, much larger than she had ever imagined, and it stood erect and pointed outward from his trunk like the strong branch of a tree.

Her own sweat was causing her blouse to stick to her, and beneath the cotton skirt she was hot and itchy at the juncture of her thighs.

The man knelt by her side and removed her hands that still held the blouse together. He opened the blouse to reveal her large breasts in the white cotton brassiere. His hands moved onto her body and he pushed up the cups of the brassiere to free the soft flesh.

Kate lay spreadeagled beneath his gaze, totally in his

power, unable to do anything but watch and wait.

He moved his hand over the swollen limb that pulsated at his crotch, stroking it intently, and then he leaned forward and took both her breasts in his hands. She gasped and found it hard to breath. He squeezed them, as if weighing their possibilities, before sitting back on his heels and taking hold once more of that swollen limb she dare not name.

The groundsman spoke the first words of the encounter.

He squeezed the limb and pushed his hips forward.

'In your mouth,' he said.

Kate closed her eyes as his bulk straddled her and that strong masculine smell became stronger still and she recognised it as being caused by the lust juices of his loins.

He pushed the limb into her mouth and she had no option but to suck, overcome by his strength and smell and power, and she raised her knees for balance and splayed her legs so that her skirt fell back.

She wore no panties and the breeze cooled the itch between her thighs until the rough tongue began lapping, making her shudder, making her gulp, making her groan in her throat until the groundsman came in her mouth and she lost her senses in an orgasm of total depravity.

Kate opened her eyes and waited for the guilt.

The long grass of the copse that she used in the summer swayed in a light wind that was cooler than the breeze of her dreams. She removed her fingers from her vagina and adjusted her panties before getting to her feet. She peered through the trees at the surrounding fields.

No one was in sight; it was seldom that anyone came here to the bottom meadow.

She zipped up her jodhpurs and smoothed loose grass from her buttocks and went to her horse, the patient grey called Smokey, who had waited, his bridle tied to a branch, and who had watched her solo performance with sad brown eyes.

Kate stroked his neck and sensed his power and embraced him and he pushed his head against her in affection, and to rub his nose against her shirt.

If only all relationships could be so simple, she thought.

She swung herself back into the saddle and headed, reluctantly, for home.

Her fantasies were always wild and remained unspoken. She hardly dare admit them to herself. Her fingers and her imagination were her only means of relief from a loveless and incompatible marriage.

Yet when she indulged herself and gained that marvellous rush of pleasure that eased all tensions, guilt and shame inevitably followed, and made her wonder whether she was abnormal or perverted.

Surely, she thought, other women did not have fantasies? Surely they did not masturbate? Surely they did not, like her, have this yearning to discover a whole area of life that she felt was passing her by?

She supposed, without rancour, that it was all the fault of her mother.

Kate was a 23-year-old English rose who had enjoyed a private education, a privileged upbringing and the claustrophobic attention of a widowed mother. She had been an only child who had been nurtured like a protected species. Boyfriends had been carefully vetted and her husband had been chosen for her.

When her mother died in a car crash, Kate had inherited a country house, a prosperous farming business and a healthy bank balance.

Friends said it was fortunate that she had made such a good marriage, and that her mother had done the right thing in providing her with a man who would look after her interests in the manner to which she had become accustomed.

He ran her life, provided her opinions and told her what to think and she never argued. Unfortunately, not only did he fail to satisfy the desires that lurked beneath the modesty of her tweed skirts and Jaeger sweaters, he was totally unaware of them.

Inside, Kate screamed with frustration that she had never ever been allowed to aspire to be anything other than only half a person. But if she told Roger that, he wouldn't understand. It was something to be locked away with her fantasies.

Kate had natural blonde hair, pale skin and a generous mouth that pouted of its own accord. Her blue eyes appeared to be permanently astonished at the world around her, partly because of her naivety and partly because she was short-sighted. The illusion was enhanced on those occasions she chose to wear large-lensed spectacles rather than contact lenses.

She had wondered whether she was happy with her husband, Roger, although she found it difficult to make a judgement. The other women whom she met socially seemed to have made identical marriages and they seemed happy.

Perhaps her marriage was normal; perhaps it was her who was not.

Happiness, anyway, was hard to identify in an existence that remained cloistered and protected and where the only taxing decision she had to make was whether to ride the grey or the roan.

Emotions had never figured prominently in the household and the most she had felt when her mother died had been yet more guilt at not being overcome with grief. Her death had been a release rather than a loss, but Kate slowly realised she had gained no freedom. She had simply exchanged one jailer for another: her husband Roger.

All her life, it seemed, she had been playing a role for the benefit of other people.

At her boarding school, she had played the role of obedient schoolgirl for the benefit of the teaching staff and to fulfil her mother's ambitions. And yet, although her examination results had been excellent, her mother had not allowed her to go to university.

That would have meant living in a mixed community of young adults who were all eager to explore the

human condition, academically, emotionally and physically.

Instead, Kate had had to return home to protective
custody where the highlight of the social calendar was
a carefully chaperoned hunt ball.

Then she had played the role of dutiful daughter
and aspiring marriage partner, although none of the
young men to whom she was introduced had aroused
any great interest or excitement within her.

But she was so used to role playing that when her
mother decided Roger was a suitable spouse, she
accepted that, too, and became a dutiful and unsatisfied wife, who attended parish church coffee mornings
in the village, and was a pretty hostess at dinner
parties.

Accordingly, when the pressures grew too great, she
hid herself in fantasy.

Even then she had regrets. Because she was of limited
experience, her fantasies were correspondingly limited.
Invariably, they swirled around the same themes, the
same handful of stolen sexual chances and experiments in which she had been involved. Those realities
then became mixed with wanton desires that she knew
were unnatural and forbidden.

But they only happened in her head.

She kept them locked in her dream cupboard so that
they were separate from life and so that she could deny
their existence when shame and guilt were strongest:
they were dreams and therefore not her fault.

The fact that they came whilst she was awake made

no difference. She had no control over them, or herself, when they invaded her mind, and the only way to push them back into the cupboard was through the merciful release she obtained from the ministrations of her fingers.

Kate headed back towards the house, enjoying the feel of the high cut saddle at her crotch. She sensed that if she did not return to the house soon, she would need to satisfy herself again.

There was a great temptation to ride further, to take the itch past common sense and find another quiet place, but that would make the guilt pangs too great when they sneaked up on her later, in those moments when she ran out of distractions and was faced with the emptiness of her existence.

Kate told herself she should be sensible and behave like the respectable young woman she had been brought up to be. Respectability was expected of her; she had a position to maintain.

As she neared the stables, Billy, the stable lad, came forward to meet her. He took the reins and held the horse whilst she dismounted.

'Did you have a good ride, Miss Kate?'

Even though she was married, he still called her Miss Kate.

'Yes, thank you, Billy. Most enjoyable.'

Kate watched him lead the animal away; a big, strong, country lad of nineteen; handsome in an unsophisticated way, with eyes that looked at her, when he thought she wasn't looking, with enough intensity to burn the clothes from her body. She had known him since she was a teenager and he was a boy, but even then he had looked at her in the same way.

He was not unlike the groundsman of her dreams and it occurred to her, and not for the first time, that perhaps she had subconsciously used Billy to flesh out her fantasy, to add reality to the dream.

Kate whacked her boot with her riding crop to send the speculation back into the cupboard where it belonged.

Roger's car was in front of the house, along with another car she did not recognise. Her husband was home and had brought company. She would doubtless be expected to be polite and charming.

It was time to play roles again.

2

When Kate entered the hall she was shocked to hear raised voices coming from the library. Her curiosity overcame any hesitation and she went straight in. Her entrance stopped the argument and the two men present turned and stared at her.

Roger was by the bar to the left, a half-filled whisky glass in his hand. He was tall and, although he was not yet thirty, he already had a stoop and his hair was beginning to thin. His shirt looked crumpled around the neck and his eyes were bloodshot.

Peter DeVille, a business associate she had met twice before, was by the French windows that led into the garden. She was a poor judge of age, but she supposed he would be between forty and fifty years old.

He was of medium height and with a strength in his character as well as his build. Despite being what she would term middle-aged, he wore his thick black hair long and tied at the back of his head in a ponytail. His suit was black and superbly tailored; he wore a white shirt that was buttoned to the neck, but no tie.

DeVille straightened and formally bowed his head towards her in acknowledgement. 'Mrs Lewis.'

Roger was dismissive. 'We're talking business, Kate. If you don't mind.'

She immediately felt chastised. 'I'm sorry. I didn't mean to interrupt.'

DeVille said, 'Far from it. I think perhaps you should stay and hear what we have been discussing.'

'That is hardly necessary, DeVille.'

'I think it essential. After all, it is her money you have placed in jeopardy.'

'Be careful what you say.'

'I always am. Which is why you are the debtor and I am waiting to collect.'

Kate said, 'What is all this about, Roger?' She looked from one to the other, before turning back to her husband. 'Are you in debt?'

'It's nothing that can't be sorted out. Nothing you would understand.'

He gulped the whisky.

DeVille turned to her.

'I apologise for bringing a discordant note into such a charming house and into the life of such a beautiful woman. But I must stress that your husband has come perilously close to losing everything you possess, including this house. I can get no sense from him. Perhaps I could discuss this matter with you?'

She was surprised and flustered at being asked to discuss business.

'I don't know . . .' Automatically she looked to Roger for help.

He said, 'I'll deal with this, Kate. Leave us.'

DeVille said to her husband, 'There is little point in continuing this conversation, Lewis. I shall leave.'

Roger said, 'Talk to my lawyer!'

He turned away to find the whisky bottle.

DeVille began to leave and stopped to shake hands with Kate.

He said softly, 'Please, Mrs Lewis. I urge you to talk to me. If not now, then at my office.' He slipped a business card into her hand. 'Your husband prefers to remain blind to reality. I hope you will not.'

DeVille raised her hand to his lips and kissed her fingers. 'Please call,' he said.

He walked into the hall and Roger shouted after him.

'Get out, DeVille. And don't come back. The only talking I'll do now is through my lawyer.'

The front door closed and Roger drained the whisky and poured himself some more. Kate had never seen him like this before.

'What is it all about?' she said. 'Are you really in debt? Are we at risk?'

'It's business and nothing to do with you, Kate. Stay out of it, and stay away from DeVille. He's a dangerous man. His business is filth and degradation. I won't have you go anywhere near him.'

'But can he really take this house away from us?'

'Of course not.' He did not sound totally convincing. 'I'll sort it out. Trust me.'

His apparent intention to become drunk frightened her and she left him and went to her room. She undressed and took a shower to wash away the sweat of the horseback ride.

Kate avoided him for the rest of the afternoon and did not call him for dinner. Later in the evening she ventured into the library to check on his condition and was relieved to see he had fallen asleep on the leather sofa.

She retired early and locked her bedroom door. More often than not, her husband had taken to sleeping in a guest room of late, but she wanted to take no chance of having him stumble into her room intoxicated or hungover, with the intention of starting an argument about something she did not understand, but about which she had a growing concern.

His condition was unusual and frightened her and she had always shied away from confrontation.

The next morning, when she got up and ventured downstairs, he had already left the house. She sat in the breakfast room overlooking the lawn that swept down to the river, and drank coffee and appreciated the view. She would hate to lose it.

DeVille's threats had been the first that had ever touched her personally. They had been unnerving, an intrusion she had never experienced before, and they had set her pulses racing with the possibilities of what poverty might bring.

Roger had warned her against seeing the man. His business was filth and degradation, he had said. He was dangerous.

He was also fascinating, a man from the real world beyond the confines of her estate and the nearby village, and he had urged her to call.

From the pocket of her dressing gown she took DeVille's card and laid it on the table next to the coffee cup.

The sun was breaking out from the clouds and it glinted on the river. The lawn glistened with dew and there was a mist over the fields beyond the water; a mist that she knew would clear as she rode through it. She really would hate to lose all this.

Kate had never dealt with business in her life but DeVille had said it might be the only way she had of saving her home and possessions. She had to talk to him.

She reached for the telephone.

3

DeVille's office in London reflected his wealth. He had
a suite of rooms in a tower block overlooking the river.
His secretary was a strikingly attractive dark-haired
young woman who wore a tailored business suit, dark
stockings and high heels.

Kate felt under-dressed for the city in a wool dress,
flat shoes and tweed coat.

DeVille smiled when the secretary showed her into
his room but he remained aloof and formal. She took
the seat indicated in front of his desk.

He said, 'Can I get you anything? Tea, coffee, cognac?'

'No, thank you.'

He dismissed the secretary with a nod.

'Then thank you for coming to see me. And, with your
permission, I will get straight to business.' He opened
a file and laid a row of documents in front of her. 'This
is the extent of the damage your husband has achieved.
With your business, your home, and bad investment.'

He touched each document in turn but Kate shook
her head.

'I'm sorry, but I don't understand.' She smiled help-lessly. 'I have never had to. If you could explain, I would be grateful.'

DeVille spread his hands, collected the documents and put them back into the file.

'I'll do my best to summarise. Your husband has changed the policy of the farming business, leading it into loss that will become terminal unless steps are taken to put it back into profit. He has spent a large part of the money your mother left on investments that are proving unsound, and he has used your home and a percentage of your total business interests as secu-rity on gambling debts he has no hope of repaying. In short, Mrs Lewis, he has taken you to the edge of ruin.'

Kate was stunned and could think of nothing to say.

He went on: 'I would not wish you to take my word for any of this but would advise you to immediately appoint a lawyer to investigate the possibility that your husband may have also been guilty of fraud, false pretences and misrepresentation. A lawyer may also be necessary to protect what is left of your property and money. I will be happy to provide you with copies of all these documents, if you wish.'

'Am I really that close to ruin?'

'I am afraid you are.'

'How do you know so much about my affairs?'

'My business interests are extensive. They include a casino where your husband likes to gamble. It is to me that he has signed forty per cent of your business.' He shrugged apologetically. 'Gambling debts are not, strictly speaking, upheld by law, but there are ways around the law. The documents your husband signed acknowledge payment of an amount equal to that which he owed. We had a gentleman's agreement that they would be returned if he repaid the debt. He hasn't.'

'What about my home?'

'He signed that away in a similar deal for a ludicrously inadequate sum to the owner of another casino. If the debt is not repaid by the end of May, you will lose it.'

Kate saw a glimmer of hope.

'But surely, my signature as well as Roger's has to be on these documents, to make them valid.'

'It is, my dear. It is.'

The hope died. She remembered signing several documents for her husband; she had always signed anything he had put before her without question.

DeVille said, 'My forty per cent share in your business means we are partners, which is why my enquiries have been so thorough. I want the business to be rescued and to succeed, just as much as you do.'

'And my home?'

'Ah. To save that, you need to raise two hundred thousand pounds by the end of the month.'

'Oh my god. That's impossible.'

DeVille shrugged in sympathy and said, 'Perhaps . . .' but then shook his head and said no more.

Kate stared at him, her eyes wide behind the spectacles, more astounded at the world than they had ever been before.

'You said perhaps, Mr DeVille. Do you mean there may be a way?'

'No, dear lady. I think not. I came to your home yesterday to reassure myself of your beauty. I was not disappointed: you are, indeed, a very beautiful young woman. But what I had in mind is not suitable for a young lady such as yourself.'

'What did you have in mind, Mr DeVille?'

He shook his head. 'I cannot possibly tell you. Forgive me, but you are too innocent, too naive to even hear a proposal I now realise is totally inappropriate.'

'But if it means saving my home, Mr DeVille, don't you think I have the right to know what it is? The right to make up my own mind on its suitability?'

DeVille got up from behind the desk and went to a drinks cabinet and poured himself a brandy.

'Are you sure you wouldn't like a drink?'

'No, thank you. But I would like to hear your proposal.'

He sipped the spirit and stared out of the picture window at the Thames, as if considering what he should do. At last, he turned away decisively and resumed his seat.

'I have no wish to offend you. But, if you insist, I will tell you. First, let me explain another aspect of my business: I deal in girls. And, if the truth be known, your husband's debt to me was not for gambling. It was for women.'

Kate stared at him in disbelief. Filth and degradation. Her lips went dry and she moistened them with the tip of her tongue. Roger knew because he himself had indulged in the very filth and degradation which he had accused DeVille of dealing in.

The man was staring at her, as if waiting for permission to continue.

He said, 'I'm sorry. But I thought you should know.'

Kate nodded and kept her composure with an effort. 'I still want to hear your proposal.'

'As you wish. I provide girls of breeding for rich clients. Extremely rich clients. I had thought of offering you employment for a limited period in this capacity, to raise the money that you need.'

It was perfectly apt, actually. Her husband had got them into trouble by spending money on prostitutes, and she was being given the opportunity to recoup his outlay by becoming one herself.

The irony eased the shock and made her brain work logically.

'Surely, there isn't time,' she said.

'There could be. Just.' He smiled as if they were involved in a hypothetical discussion. 'Two weeks in May could be just enough time. But of course, the idea is preposterous.'

'When would you need to know?'

Kate felt cold; it was as if someone else had asked the question.

'By tomorrow. But before you consider such a decision, you should know exactly what is involved. I am not talking about making love; I am talking about sex. Providing sex to anyone I nominate, in any manner that is dictated. This is not a role for a beautiful innocent like you, Mrs Lewis.'

'Perhaps it is, Mr DeVille.'

Her voice was distant. For the first time in her life, she was in a position where no one but herself could solve her problems. For the first time in her life, she could feel challenge, instead of cotton wool security.

The blood in her veins was pounding at even considering the proposition that DeVille had rightly described as preposterous. Except that she was well trained at role playing and, already, her dream cupboard had burst its doors at the possibility.

She had led a sheltered existence in all things and her only lover had been her husband; she didn't even know if he was a good lover, or what she herself should feel.

Between them, the sexual act had always been performed with the light out and beneath the covers and had never taken very long. Her only orgasms had been the ones she had provided for herself.

Perhaps this was life's way of providing her with the chance to fill those missing gaps? The chance to make her more complete, to fully discover sex. And if in the process she discovered she didn't like it, she need never do it again.

But could she do it?

DeVille said, 'Forgive me if I seem indelicate, but are you as innocent as you appear?'

'I am not a virgin, Mr DeVille.'

'That is not an answer to my question. Have you had many lovers?'

'Only my husband.'

'Has the sex between you been varied?'

She blushed and dipped her eyes for a moment, but raised them almost immediately in case he took it as a sign of weakness.

'I suspect not.'

'Has it been enjoyable?'

Kate coughed. 'If I am honest . . .'

'We must always be honest, always.'

'I think my husband has gained pleasure from it. But for myself, no. I cannot honestly say it has been enjoyable.'

'As I suspected, you appear to be unskilled in the erotic arts, despite having the body of Aphrodite.'

'Does this mean your offer no longer stands?'

She felt both relief and disappointment at the prospect.

'No. To many, innocence in itself is attractive. And you could be taught. But you would have to place your body and soul totally in my care; you would have to do whatever I commanded without question.'

If she accepted, she would be placing herself in the hands of yet another keeper. The suitability of the role was becoming more pronounced.

'For how long?'

'Two weeks in May. But two weeks that will change your life for ever, Mrs Lewis, as well as providing the chance to save your home.'

Kate hesitated and DeVille smiled.

'Think it over. And do not think too badly of me if you do not feel able to comply.'

He stood up, indicating that the meeting was over.

'On the matter of business,' he said, 'I have taken the liberty of making an appointment for you with an independent lawyer. He will be able to advise you and, if you wish, take immediate action to mitigate the problems created by your husband.'

He handed her the file of documents.

'Thank you,' she said.

'My secretary will give you the address.'

She paused by the door and looked past him, out of the high window and across the river, into a world she did not know.

'And if I decide to accept your offer?'

'Be here at noon tomorrow . . . and convince me.'

4

The grey enjoyed the ride as much as she did and she let him have his head. She enjoyed his power between her legs and her power in being able to control him.

She wondered if it could be the same with men.

The rush of the cool evening air was refreshing after the day in London, and made her realise what she would lose if she was unable to raise £200,000 within the allotted time.

DeVille's choice of lawyer had been excellent and she had placed all her business affairs in his hands, with instructions to remove her husband from any position of authority.

All Roger had been was a manager or director without power. He hadn't needed to be anything else when she had signed anything he asked.

She had nurtured a hope that the lawyer might have seen an alternative way of escaping eviction but he hadn't. All she was left with was DeVille's proposition and less than twenty-four hours in which to make a decision.

The ride complete, she left the grey with Billy at the stables, and walked into the house. She was relieved that Roger's car was absent from the forecourt. When she finally did confront him, divorce would be at the top of the agenda.

One step at a time, was how she was taking things. DeVille had been step one, the lawyer step two. What feelings she had had for Roger had turned to dust with the revelation that he had indulged his own sexual fantasies, not at home, but with a woman he had paid.

It explained why he had been spending an increasing amount of time away, allegedly on business, and why he had taken to using a guest room to sleep in, instead of the marital bed. He had not wanted to disturb her when he returned late from his meetings, he had said.

Perhaps she might find in the guest room incriminating evidence of his amorous liaisons?

She went down the landing and pushed open the door. It was a sparse room with a view over the front of the house. She opened drawers, looked under the bed and pulled open the wardrobe doors. She found a fat briefcase that was locked.

Kate took the briefcase to the master bedroom, in which she usually slept alone, and tried to open it with a nail file, but failed. It was frustrating; briefcases were always easy to open on television dramas. She tried again, using a hairpin, and this time the lock gave a satisfying click.

It was another small step in her integration into the real world. She opened the briefcase eagerly. There was no incriminating evidence. But there was a collection of pin-up magazines.

She took a handful out and spread them on the bed. She recognised the titles and covers from the top shelf at the newsagent in the nearby county town where she shopped, but she had never never seen inside them. The explicit pictures of naked women, women who lay with their legs apart and vaginas spread, shocked her.

There were slim women, curvaceous women, overweight women.

It did not seem to matter what shape they were as long as they were prepared to open their legs and display what was there in technicolour detail.

From disgust, her attitude changed to one of detached curiosity and she began comparing her own body with those pictured. She stripped off her riding gear and stood naked in front of a full length mirror. It had never occurred to her before, but she really was beautiful, as DeVille had said.

Her body was curvaceous and lush without being overweight, her breasts heavy and ripe; her legs were long and shapely, her buttocks firm and full.

The realisation that she was beautiful made her laugh with embarrassment. DeVille had been the only person who had ever told her.

She walked naked to the shower that was ensuite with the room.

When she emerged, wrapped in nothing but a towel,

Roger was standing by the bed. He looked dishevelled and swayed as if he had been drinking.

'What the bloody hell do you think you've been doing?' he said.

Kate felt a sudden tremor of fear. Surely he had not yet discovered she had appointed a lawyer to get rid of him from her life?

'What do you mean?'

'This!' He pointed at the briefcase that lay on the floor and the magazines spread upon the bed. 'Is nothing sacred? You've been rooting about in my bedroom, spying into my private things.'

'They're only magazines, Roger.'

She was aware that behind the towel she held, she was naked. She had never been naked in his presence before in daylight; nakedness was for beneath the bedclothes where it could be discovered with fumbles and grunts.

'I suppose you had a good laugh, as well, at poor Roger's porn collection. Well perhaps I wouldn't have needed it if you'd been more of a woman. At least these naked ladies don't mind if I look at them.'

He glared belligerently and suddenly made a grab for the towel. He caught a corner and pulled and it slid from her grasp. She cried out and put a hand to her mouth, her forearm covering a breast protectively. Her other hand dropped instinctively to protect her pubic area from his gaze.

'Naked as nature intended.' He laughed. 'At last. A naked lady of my own.'

Kate's fear and embarrassment began to turn to anger because he was laughing at her. She had made the comparisons herself and knew she had a better body than anyone in the magazines. The only thing she lacked was the underwear. She pushed her chin out defiantly and lowered her arms.

She said, 'Take a good look. Take a good look at what you've been missing and what you'll never have again.'

His eyes changed and the laughter stopped. He licked his lips and gulped and began taking off his clothes. What had she started?

'Stay away from me, Roger. I don't want you.'

'You're my wife. You're mine.'

He blocked any way out of the room and she felt his tension in the air. She would have to submit; he was in no mood for compromise. Perhaps it would be good training for the next two weeks.

Kate had never seen her husband totally naked before and she was unimpressed. His insistence on darkness could be because he had been ashamed of his own body. It was both thin and flabby, although the part that grew at the juncture of his legs was certainly not flabby. His penis was hard and stubby. It was the first time she had ever seen it and she stared so much he attempted to cover it with a hand.

'Bitch,' he said. 'Where've you been getting it these last three years? From Billy in the stables after you come back randy from a hot ride? Is that what you've been doing, Kate? Have you been fucking the stable lad? Is that where my ration's gone?'

29

He was both dangerous and ludicrous and Kate was surprised that she was more fascinated than frightened; fascinated to discover that her husband had fantasies of his own.

She backed away and felt the edge of the dressing table against her buttocks, and put out a hand to steady her balance. It touched the riding crop she had left there earlier. Her fingers closed around it and she held it sideways from her body as a weapon.

'I said no, Roger, and I'll beat you first.'

'Oh my God.'

His voice was a shudder and his stoop became more pronounced. Kate was confused.

He stepped towards her and she whipped him with the crop, catching a buttock as he turned away. He howled, but through the pain she detected pleasure.

Good grief. Was this what he had spent her money on?

Every time he moved close, she hit him with the crop, and he howled and, despite her loathing for her husband, she felt her own excitement rising.

They were both panting, facing each other naked on the carpet, legs spread and arms wide like wrestlers waiting for an opening. She was conscious of the weight of her breasts as they swung before her. Each time she hit him, his erection quivered and she felt a corresponding tremble through her body.

Then he moved quickly, as if he had been soaking up the punishment on purpose until he was ready for the final act. He grasped her arms and pushed her back on the bed, amongst the open magazines of naked technicolour women.

They fought like children or animals, without inhibition, their limbs sliding in each other's sweat, and she bared her teeth as he forced apart her legs and she felt the stubby erection thrusting at her vagina.

He released her left arm and felt between their bodies with his right hand to direct his penis. Kate stopped struggling in surprise as it slid smoothly inside her. The whole mad scene and the fight had caused her body to react of its own accord and made her wet and accessible.

Roger shouted in triumph with each thrust and she pulled free her right arm, the one that still held the crop. She swung it fiercely and lashed him across the buttocks.

He screamed in pleasure.

'Yes! Oh yes!' he shouted.

She swung again, in time to his thrust, and this time he discharged inside her, bucking and yelling.

In his convulsions he collapsed on top of her, imprisoning her arm and making her unable to hit him any more. His orgasm was interminable and, several seconds after the initial rush, he kept being shaken by shudders, like the following tremors of an earthquake.

Kate lay on her back, unable to move until he had finished completely, feeling strangely closer to him than she had ever felt during their marriage, and yet also loathing him more than at any time they had been together.

Eventually he rolled off her body and she climbed from

the bed and stood by its side, still panting, still unfulfilled; frustrated and angry.

She cracked the crop against the mattress.

'Get out of this room now and never step inside it
again.'

He moved as if in a dream.

'Kate,' he said, in a soft voice, and held out a hand.

She swung the crop and whipped his thigh. This
time his scream was pure pain.

'No, don't. Please.'

'Then get out. I never want to see you again.'

He backed towards the door, bent over to collect from
the carpet what clothes he could reach, moving like a
balding pink spider. He reached the corridor and scur-
ried towards the guest room. She threw the briefcase
after him before slamming her door and locking it.

She dropped the crop on the floor and went back to
the shower and washed him from her body, her mind
confused about the emotions she had felt. It had been
loathsome and exciting and it had made her wet between
her legs and her thighs still trembled at the memory.

Had she been so close to orgasm?

Could it be achieved purely through erotic excitement,
despite a partner's limitations?

Thank god she had not had an orgasm. When she had
her first with a partner, if it ever happened, she did not
want it to be with Roger.

But Robert DeVille . . .? Now that might be a different proposition.

Kate leaned backwards against the wall of the shower

and let the warm water provide a curtain of discretion as her fingers went between her legs to finish what her husband had started.

5

Kate arrived at DeVille's offices at five minutes before twelve. His secretary spoke to him on an intercom.

'Mrs Lewis is here.'

She listened and then said, 'Yes, Mr DeVille.' She replaced the telephone and smiled at Kate. 'He asks if you would mind waiting for a few moments?'

'Of course.'

She took a chair and admired the secretary's legs beneath the open desk. Kate's, too, were now encased in black stockings, and she wondered if they looked as good.

The previous night, she had found two of her husband's magazines beneath her bed and had studied them again. Stockings and suspender belts were the common denominators that linked all the women, that and a predilection for opening their legs. She also remembered how the secretary had looked; cool and in command, elegant and sexy.

DeVille had told her to come back and prove to him she was serious. She had begun her attempt with a shopping expedition before going to the tower block.

Specialist shops that sold underwear had frightened her with their gaudy displays and exotic lines, but she had found what she thought was necessary, if not essential, in Harrods. She had decided upon black because she felt it might endow her with a veneer of sophistication she felt she lacked. At the same store, she bought a two-piece business suit, also in black, and high heeled shoes.

Kate changed in the store and was complimented by the female assistant on her transformation. The assistant said the jacket was so perfectly tailored that it need not be worn with a blouse, but she had suggested two additions: a string of white pearls at her throat, and a black handbag that could be mistaken for a document case.

The new look delighted Kate and her spectacles added to the image of a young professional. It was as if she had taken on a new personality. When the assistant asked her what she should do with the clothes she had taken off, Kate said without hesitation, 'Throw them away.'

This was a new start and she would need nothing of the past during the next two weeks, particularly not a tweed coat and brogue shoes.

She noticed a difference as she walked through the store and into the street. Not only did she feel more confident because of the way she looked, but men's heads turned to stare as she went past. It gave her a small thrill.

Now she was actually in DeVille's offices, some of the confidence was draining away.

Would she be able to go through with it?

Kate had never been a quitter, despite her wealth. She had overcome bullying at school and had become an excellent horsewoman despite a bad fall as a child.

If she said she would do it, there would be no backing out.

The secretary's office was small. It had an outer door, through which entry was only gained after a request through the intercom system, and an inner door into DeVille's spacious room with a view. There was a window, but the view was of other buildings close by. The room also contained filing cabinets, three easy chairs where people could wait, and the secretary's desk and chair.

At precisely twelve o'clock, DeVille opened the door into his inner sanctum. His eyes fixed upon her; they were quizzical. She raised her chin and stared defiantly back.

'Please, come in,' he said.

She went into his office and sat in the chair she had occupied the previous day. He went round to the far side of the desk but did not immediately sit down. He held one elbow in his hand and stroked his chin with his fingers as he studied her.

'I suspected you would be back.'

Kate said, 'I hope you have not changed your mind?'

'No.'

'Or your estimate about the amount that has to be raised?'

'I think it can be done.'

'Well then.' She tried to hide the lump in her throat that made her gulp. 'Then I am ready to begin.'

DeVille sat down.

He said, 'For the final time, I have to warn you about what will be involved.'

'If you must.'

'I am still not convinced that you fully appreciate what you will be undertaking.'

'If it makes you feel any better, Mr DeVille, tell me, and then we can begin.'

'All right, Mrs Lewis. During the next two weeks you will be fucked and you will be sucked; you will have pricks pushed into your mouth and into your body; semen will trickle down your face and down your legs. You will be used and abused by both men and women. And you will obey my every command.'

The directness of his words had slammed the nature of the bargain home more than all her imaginings during the night. This was her final chance to say no and escape back into normality. She probably still had time to go back to Harrods and reclaim her brogues and tweed coat.

His eyes were locked on hers, watching for a reaction.

He said, 'Changed your mind?'

'No.' She heard herself speaking, a distant voice, but firm and clear. 'I haven't changed my mind. I want to go ahead. I'm yours for two weeks.'

He smiled. 'Good.'

DeVille got to his feet and went to the drinks cabinet and poured himself a brandy.

'Would you like one?'

Kate's throat had become dry, her senses tensed.

'I think I would. Vodka and tonic?'

'Of course.'

He mixed the drink and passed it to her. It tasted strong and she drank half of it quickly in an attempt to relax.

DeVille resumed his seat and sipped the brandy.

'Please stand up,' he said.

Kate got to her feet and put the drink on his desk. She felt she was in danger of blushing because he was staring so blatantly at her body, but she controlled herself by staring blatantly back, the spectacles making her eyes appear even bigger.

'Wrong,' he said. 'You should be demure, shy. You should drop your eyes in innocence, or smile softly in allurement. The glare you gave me could offend many men. Worse, it could make them impotent.'

'I'm sorry.'

She dipped her eyes and immediately felt more comfortable being herself.

'Now,' he said. 'Raise your skirt.'

Kate looked up and stopped herself from querying the command. He remained sitting comfortably behind his desk, a smile of superiority upon his lips. He sipped the brandy.

The skirt was tight and she used both hands to slide it upwards. It reached the lace tops of the black stockings and she began to blush but she continued to slide it upwards, revealing the black suspender straps that arrowed across the pale flesh of her thighs. She hesitated because the material was bunching at her buttocks.

He toasted her with the brandy and said, 'All the way, Mrs Lewis.'

She squirmed and pushed the skirt up to her waist, now displaying the tight black panties that were cut high at the sides.

Kate told herself that DeVille was seeing no more than he would if she were wearing a swimsuit. It was just being presented differently.

'Very nice. You have good legs.'

'Thank you.'

Her voice was small and no longer so certain of itself.

'Turn around, slowly.'

She turned, further embarrassed at having to display her body for judgement and approval. Her heart was pounding but mixed with the embarrassment was excitement.

Now DeVille could see her buttocks and the way the panties cut across the curve of the flesh. It was a view of herself she had never seen, and she suddenly wondered if it were faulty, if it might fail the scrutiny.

'Delicious,' he said, and, foolishly, she felt relief.

Kate completed the turn and he indicated with a finger that she could lower her skirt. As the hemline came down, her composure began to return.

'May I compliment you upon your underwear,' he said. 'Most tasteful.'

'Thank you.'

'Now, open your suit.'

This she had been expecting and she unbuttoned the coat and opened it. He stared at her breasts, held by the black brassiere, and shrugged.

'The bra is not right. Far too substantial,' he said. 'Take it off.'

Kate felt like she was back at school and being reprimanded for poor work.

She removed the jacket and laid it upon the chair where she had been sitting, and reached behind her to unclip the garment. As it came away, she realised she would be baring her breasts to DeVille. Her hesitation was only brief. She let the bra slide from her bosom and dropped it on his desk.

Her breathing was slightly ragged but she did not immediately turn to pick up the jacket; instead, she stood before the desk while DeVille stared hard at her large breasts. The situation was surreal; more than that, if she dared admit it, the situation was exciting. She felt her nipples become erect and wondered if DeVille would notice.

He noticed. He smiled.

'You may put your jacket back on,' he said.

Kate fastened the buttons, noticing her fingers were trembling.

'Please,' he said, indicating the chair, and she resumed her seat, reaching for the glass of vodka and tonic which she drained in one gulp.

'Well?' she said.

'You have a glorious body, Mrs Lewis. I know men who would be willing to pay a fortune to own it for a night. But their tastes can be perverse. Are you really willing for the unexpected?'

'Yes,' she said, her voice cracking slightly. She gulped and added in a firmer tone: 'I'm willing.'

'Very well.'

He got to his feet, walked round the desk and opened the door. Kate was confused.

'Have I passed the test?'

'You haven't taken it yet.'

He indicated that she was to leave, and she stood up and went into the outer office occupied by the secretary.

DeVille said, 'You've met Miss Sheldon?'

The secretary smiled.

Kate said, 'We've said hello.'

'Then meet formally. Mrs Lewis will be joining us on a temporary basis, Miss Sheldon.'

The secretary held out her hand and Kate reached out her own. But instead of shaking it, Miss Sheldon grabbed her wrist and pulled her forward over the desk. When Kate placed her other hand down to steady herself, the secretary grabbed that, too.

Behind her, DeVille pulled up the tight skirt; his action was sudden and rough, and she began to struggle. The skirt went past her hips and slid up around her waist. His hands were on her flesh: feeling, groping, delving, and she gasped at the intrusions and the shock.

She could feel the hardness of his erection in his trousers pushing against her, while Miss Sheldon held her wrists and stared up into her face from twelve inches away.

Kate controlled her struggles and stared wide-eyed at the secretary, whose own eyes glinted with an unnatural excitement. Miss Sheldon smiled slowly and moistened her lips with her tongue.

DeVille pulled at Kate's panties so fiercely they dug into her vagina and made her gasp with more than fear. He held them in both hands and ripped the material, tearing the flimsy garment apart at the waist. She felt them slide down one thigh.

Now his fingers were between her legs: stroking, manipulating, opening. He nudged her thighs further apart with a knee, and inserted a finger inside her, making her cry out. He pushed it in and out to create lubrication, and she stared into the face of Miss Sheldon; their eyes locked upon each other. Miss Sheldon released her grip on Kate's wrists and slid her palms down to cover her hands.

DeVille inserted two fingers and Kate cried out again, but she was getting wetter between her legs.

This was shocking, this was madness. It was lunchtime on a weekday in an office in the middle of London and her skirt was around her waist and a man she hardly knew had two, no, three fingers inside her vagina.

The craziness of the situation made it more easy to accept. There was nothing to compare it to, not even her fantasies; and because it fitted no pattern of normal social behaviour, normal rules failed to condemn it.

DeVille was breathing heavily, his fingers making slurping noises as they maintained a steady rhythm, and her body responded by becoming even more wet and loose between her legs. He removed the fingers and her gasp was almost of disappointment. The rasp of his zip made her cry out again, this time in nervous anticipation.

His penis was big, hard and hot against her flesh. He pushed her further across the desk, opened the lips of her sex with his fingers, and inserted the head of his penis inside her.

The secretary's face was now even closer and her fingers curled under Kate's and they held hands.

'Oh my god,' Kate said.

DeVille thrust deep inside her with one motion that momentarily raised her onto the tips of her toes. He held it inside while he adjusted their positions, settling his groin comfortably against her buttocks, gripping her hips with his hands, and she realised she was holding her breath.

It felt as if she had been penetrated by a molten rod of iron but instead of moving out, DeVille squirmed it around inside her. She began breathing again, in gasps and groans. He withdrew almost the whole length, and thrust back inside; a slow motion that he built into a steady rhythm, rocking her body forwards with each deep probe.

Her senses were reeling and she could taste the vodka in her mouth, feel the edge of the desk against her thighs, the gentle fingers of Miss Sheldon stroking her palms, DeVille's power between her legs and the heat of the monster that he controlled, inside her.

She was in a turmoil that had no direction, she was wracked by feelings she did not recognise; with arousal, guilt and a soaring pleasure that radiated from her loins.

DeVille's strokes began to become shorter and quicker and his grip on her hips tighter. She tensed and squeezed the lips of her vagina around his prick, trying to hold it, keep it, milk it, without even knowing what she was doing.

He exhaled with a gasp and buried his penis deep and hard as if attempting to break out the other side. His orgasm shook him, shook her, and his weapon began to pulse its discharge inside her.

All the time she stared into the eyes of Miss Sheldon, who finally bridged the inches that separated their faces by leaning forward and, with parted lips, kissing Kate upon the mouth.

DeVille heaved into her from behind and Miss Sheldon's tongue probed her mouth from the front and Kate was lost in senses she never knew she had.

She was a rag doll, leaning over the desk, when DeVille withdrew and the secretary sat back and released her hands. It took her many seconds to recover sufficiently to take in her surroundings once more.

Miss Sheldon sat back in her chair behind the desk, watching her with a pleasant smile. DeVille was once more fully dressed, no evidence of disarray in his clothing to indicate what had just occurred.

Kate realised she was still gasping, still holding

herself over the desk with both hands, and that her skirt was still around her waist, leaving her totally exposed. She felt incredibly wet between her legs, painfully aware of her indelicate position, and, also, disappointed it was all over.

She stood up, and pushed at the skirt until it became free and slid down over her hips to cover her nakedness. The remains of the panties were still pooled around her right ankle. She bent down, removed them from her foot, and dropped them on the desk.

Kate mustered all her composure, despite the giddiness she felt, and tried to focus on DeVille.

'Well?' she said.

'You've passed. Now I want you to meet my niece. You'll like Chloe. She'll be good for you.'

DeVille opened the door of the outer office and Kate hesitated and looked back.

'Goodbye, Miss Sheldon. I'll see you again.'

The secretary picked up the discarded panties and held them in front of her face.

'I hope so, Mrs Lewis. Enjoy yourself.'

6

They travelled in a chauffeur-driven limousine to a dockland development at Wapping. A uniformed security man checked them into the underground parking area, which was a well lit cavern of coolness, and which was occupied by luxury motor cars.

DeVille led Kate to a lift and they went to the top floor to a spacious penthouse apartment. He rang the bell with three short bursts, which Kate later realised was a warning to the occupant, and let himself in with his own key.

The apartment had a secluded roof-top patio and large windows that provided extensive views over the Thames. Its large living room was littered with cushions, couches and low divans.

DeVille's niece came in from the patio to greet them.

Chloe was a spectacularly beautiful girl with dark hair and brown eyes, and a golden tan from a recent holiday in the sun. She wore a white polo shirt, pleated tennis skirt, white socks and tennis shoes; she was twenty-two, but without make-up and in the sports outfit looked much younger.

DeVille presented Kate to her as if she were a trophy.

'Chloe, this is the lady I told you about. Kate, meet Chloe. I hope you two will be friends.' He smiled as they shook hands. 'Because I certainly intend that the pair of you will be lovers.'

Kate found she could still be shocked, despite what she had only recently experienced, and felt embarrassment for the young woman whose hand she held.

Chloe grinned disarmingly. 'We'll be friends,' she said. 'And don't mind uncle.'

DeVille began to leave the room. 'I have calls to make, so I'll leave you two, to become acquainted.'

As he neared the door, he turned back as if he had forgotten something. He said, 'Oh yes, she may need a bath, Chloe. I fucked her in the office. Come to think of it, she may need an orgasm, too. She never came and she was as tense as hell. Maybe she doesn't know how to come. Maybe you will have to teach her.' He looked directly at Kate. 'In my absence, do everything Chloe tells you to,' he said.

He turned and left the apartment.

Kate blushed, angry at how dismissive he had been about the encounter in the office, and at how accurate was his estimation of her lack of experience when it came to orgasms that were other than self-induced.

Chloe squeezed her hand. 'He's talking like that on purpose. Breaking down barriers. It works, too, you'll see. And don't worry, we really will be friends. Let me show you the bedroom.'

They went down a short corridor and into a bedroom carpeted and draped in soft pinks. It had a kingsized bed covered with a black satin sheet.

Chloe laughed again. 'Looks like a tart's boudoir, doesn't it?' she said. 'Well, it is.'

Kate said, 'Does Mr DeVille live here with you?'

'Sometimes. He has his own house in Chelsea. But he visits quite often.'

'Is he really your uncle?'

'No, but he's known me since I was at school and he always likes me to call him uncle. I think the hint of incest excites him. So do the clothes I'm wearing. I don't play tennis but it fits the other games I play. Makes me look like a schoolgirl. The sort of girl the older man likes to fantasise about.'

Fantasies, Kate thought. Everybody, it seemed, has fantasies.

'But how . . .?'

'No more questions.' She stroked the lapels of the jacket Kate wore. 'This is nice. Very sophisticated.' She began unfastening the buttons. 'Let's take it off.'

Kate was surprised enough to allow the other girl to complete unbuttoning the jacket and remove it.

'Nice breasts. Much bigger than mine.'

Chloe's voice dropped an octave, and she felt Kate's breasts with both hands, weighing them in her palms, stroking their smoothness, rubbing the nipples between her fingers.

Despite herself, Kate's nipples became erect and flutters started in her stomach.

Chloe's voice was now a whisper, words that came on a breath.

'You are tense, Kate. Too tense.' The girl pulled off her polo shirt to reveal her own naked breasts. They jiggled with the movement; small, pert schoolgirl breasts. 'Let's get you out of these things.'

She stood in front of Kate, and stretched her arms around her to unclip the waistband of the skirt, her breasts brushing against Kate's breasts.

The skirt slackened as its zip was unfastened. Chloe had to lean against her to work the zip, and their breasts squashed against each other, nipples rubbing against yielding flesh. Kate's breathing changed.

'Do you like this, Kate? Do you like the feel of another girl?'

To emphasise the question, Chloe deliberately rubbed her breasts against Kate, and ran her tongue gently along her neck.

Kate shuddered.

Chloe pushed the skirt and it slipped over Kate's hips and down her legs to the floor.

'You do like it, don't you?' Chloe said, her hands following the curves from the small of Kate's back down over her buttocks. 'You feel so beautiful, Kate.' She kissed her neck. 'So beautiful.'

Kate didn't know whether she liked what was happening or not. She felt incapable of making judgements and took refuge in the fact that she had agreed to undergo anything that might be done to her. It removed both decision and guilt.

Chloe stroked Kate's blonde hair from her shoulder with her left hand, clearing the pale skin for her lips. Her tongue licked, her teeth nibbled, and Kate quivered in response. She traced Kate's jawline with her tongue, at the same time as the fingers of her right hand slipped between their bodies and picked their way through pubic hair.

The girl's breath was sweet and the tip of her tongue licked for entry at the corner of Kate's mouth. Kate's mind was filled with guilty memories from boarding school, memories that had been rekindled by the kiss of DeVille's secretary; memories that had become so strong they had broken the catch on her dream cupboard.

Was it so unnatural, she thought?

How could it be, when Chloe was so beautiful, so gentle and so soft? How could it be, compared to the undercover fumblings of her husband?

Kate's mouth opened and welcomed Chloe's.

The girls kissed, Chloe taking the initiative, exploring with her tongue as her fingers explored between Kate's legs, encouraging Kate to explore her own mouth in turn.

They broke for breath as Chloe's fingers squelched inside Kate's vagina.

'He did fuck you, didn't he? I can feel it.'

Her fingers dug deeper and Kate felt her body melting against the dark-skinned girl.

Chloe removed the fingers and lifted them until they were between their faces, sticky and glistening. She sniffed delicately, her nostrils flaring in delight.

'Smell,' she said. 'The aroma of love.'

Kate's normal inclination would have been to turn away but this was not normal. She flared her own nostrils and smelled her own most intimate smell mingled with the juices of lust from DeVille.

Chloe said, 'Gorgeous,' and put the fingers in her mouth to suck them clean.

As she removed her fingers, she replaced her mouth over Kate's and they kissed again whilst she delved for more perfumed secretions within Kate's vagina.

This time she pushed three fingers inside Kate, making her groan in pleasure, and when the fingers returned for them to sample with nose and palate like a good wine, it was Kate who opened her mouth and sucked them clean.

They moved to the bed, Chloe directing that Kate lie on her back in the middle of the sheet, her pale skin and blonde hair a startling contrast to the black sheen of the satin.

The dark-haired girl removed Kate's spectacles and pushed off her own skirt and a pair of white cotton briefs, and kicked the sports shoes from her feet. Her tan was complete, unspoilt by bikini lines. She slid onto the bed wearing only white ankle socks.

At first, Chloe didn't touch Kate, but lay alongside her at an angle, only their heads close together.

'Have you ever been with a woman?' she whispered.

'No,' said Kate.

Chloe licked her neck again and cupped a breast with her right hand. She kissed her deeply so that their tongues fought and slithered, and the hand squeezed the breast. When their mouths parted, she continued to lick down Kate's neck to her breasts, taking a nipple between her lips to suck and nibble.

The girl slid across the satin, her head going lower, her hands now stroking Kate's thighs, tracing the straps of the suspender belt from waist to lace stocking tops.

Kate knew what would happen next and held her breath. She had never imagined being subjected to this, never imagined the all-engulfing pleasure that permeated her body.

Chloe's tongue licked along the crease of Kate's groin, between the swell of her stomach and the top of her thigh, getting ever closer to the wetness of her vagina, and Kate could not stop the whimper in her throat.

The lips of the mouth of her sex were already gaping and when Chloe inserted a finger inside, it was almost an anti-climax. It was the other experience, the most forbidden of intimacies, for which she yearned, had always yearned, and never known.

And then the tongue was there, licking gently at her clitoris, like a small animal feeding nervously; so gently that Kate held her breath once more for fear of scaring it away.

The tongue didn't go away but became bolder, and was followed by the wide, pulsating mouth of the girl with dark hair, that suddenly engulfed her vagina, the tongue thrusting like a penis.

Chloe's mouth was lascivious, her lips making love to the lips of Kate's vagina, sucking at her juices and the secretions left by DeVille, mixing a cocktail with her own saliva.

This was pleasure Kate had never experienced before, pleasure that transcended the very word. Her senses felt on the edge of liberation, and she was unaware of the noises coming from her throat, aware only of the mouth at her vagina and the hands that gripped her buttocks and thighs, and a rising panic as even these ephemeral realities began to fragment and she was flung, finally, screaming into orgasm.

Kate briefly lost consciousness and she regained her senses to find Chloe by her side, cradling her head, stroking her hair, kissing her cheek.

She felt different. Relaxed and floating, reborn.

Chloe whispered, 'Was that good?'

It took her a moment to remember how to speak.

'Incredible,' she said.

'Shall we do it again?'

'Oh yes, please. Do it again. And show me how to do it.' She stretched up and kissed Chloe on the mouth, her tongue this time digging into the delicious wet cavern of its own accord, without encouragement. 'I want to make you come as well.'

'You will, darling. You will.'

They remained side by side, limbs pressed together, whilst Chloe used her fingers on Kate's clitoris to bring her to a second orgasm.

The blonde English rose, who until that morning had led a life of reserve, produced her third orgasm herself, her own fingers plying between her legs without shame under Chloe's gaze.

As her spirits gained greater freedom, so did her taste to learn more and indulge more and to give more. She used her fingers between Chloe's thighs, teasing the clitoris, and pushed fingers inside, until her new friend groaned 'enough.'

'Time to use your mouth,' Chloe whispered, and pushed Kate's head down her body.

Kate went willingly, reverently, her hands caressing these fresh new buttocks, her tongue eager for the fresh new taste. She lacked the patience of her teacher but achieved the same result, burying her face between thighs as smooth as the satin they lay upon, her mouth lapping, sucking, demanding.

Her eagerness was an added aphrodisiac and Chloe crossed her legs to clamp Kate's head in place and howled with the intensity of the orgasm.

The girls rested, hands touching, legs entwined, then made love again; Chloe teaching, Kate learning, orgasms flowing into one long afternoon of wallowing pleasure.

In between the sex they talked, exchanged memories, divulged secrets, and became friends as well as lovers.

Kate told Chloe about her repressive childhood, her schooldays and a marriage she had not realised was bad.

Chloe told Kate how DeVille had become her uncle and how he had taken control of her education. She now

combined a career as a photographic model with undertaking occasional and very special assignments for
him.

'I have written it all down,' she said.

She fetched a book from a drawer in the dressing table
and handed it to Kate.

'May I read it?' she said.

Chloe kissed her on the cheek.

'Yes. It will help you understand me and uncle. And,
maybe, teach you a little about sex. Keep it until you've
finished it and then tell me what you think. You rest
now, while I prepare dinner.'

The girl kissed her again before leaving the bedroom
and Kate lay back among the pillows and opened the
book. It was handwritten and on the first page was its
title: *Chloe's Story*.

7

Chloe wrote:

My mother was never married and she never spoke about the past. I never knew who my father was. She worked for uncle; she was the manager of a casino. She was also his lover. I suspected it, even before I met uncle, but at least he treated her better than the other men she had known; he was generous and he sent presents for me, even before we met.

I was fourteen when we did meet, and, I think, I fell in love with him immediately. You know, that childish sort of love that is so deep and intense that it usually burns itself out by the time the next craze or heart-throb comes along.

But this didn't burn itself out. It didn't stay the same, either, it changed and developed. I came to rely upon him.

He was smitten with me as well, although I didn't know it at the time. Within weeks, my mother and I moved into his house in Chelsea. He paid for me to attend a private school, and I was taken there and

back in a chauffeur-driven limousine. The move from
ordinary life to luxury was dramatic and I enjoyed
every minute of it. I called him uncle and he behaved
towards me with the utmost propriety.

My mother also appreciated the lifestyle, although
I guess she must have known where uncle's real interest lay. After a year, he made her an offer she couldn't
refuse: a directorship of the company, on the condition
she went to Australia to run a new entertainment
venture he was opening.

There was another condition as well, of course. That
I stayed in London for the benefit of my education. At
least, that's what my mother told me. Perhaps she
persuaded herself to believe it; perhaps she thought it
was all for the best, and that I would have a better future
with someone like uncle looking after my interests. I
was quite pleased with the arrangement. By now, I
suspected that uncle found me attractive and I was
highly flattered.

During the next year, when I was fifteen, I took
every opportunity to show myself off to him. I would
walk around the house in my underwear, or leave a bathroom naked and walk down a corridor when I knew he
was there. I would sit opposite him reading a book or
watching television and arrange my legs so that he could
see up my skirt.

He never stopped me doing these things, but he also
never touched me. Never took advantage of me, if you
like. He was always the gentleman.

I had a boyfriend at that time, also. He was seventeen, the son of one of the teachers at school. He was called Bob, a good looking boy, but I only really went out with him to make uncle jealous, although he never showed disapproval or jealousy.

Bob and I never made love, but we did get involved in some heavy petting when we were supposed to be playing records or watching a video film. I was quite highly sexed, normal for my age, I guess, and while I got pretty excited with Bob, he never made me come.

And then I became sixteen. Another ordinary day, except that there were cards and presents at breakfast. I was driven to school, picked up afterwards, and driven home.

Uncle was waiting for me and took me into the den, a big, comfortable room with a television and the sort of sofas you can sleep in.

He looked fresh, as if he had just got out of the shower, and immaculate, as always, in a silk dressing gown and Italian sandals. Very European, very sophisticated.

By comparison, I felt very young and foolish, still in my grey pleated skirt, white blouse and school tie, with knee socks and flat brogues. It was a hot day in June and I was also aware that I was sticky with sweat.

Uncle went to the television and picked up a video tape.

'I have an extra present for you,' he said.

He slotted the tape in the video player, switched on the television and we sat side by side on a sofa. When the tape started, I nearly died with embarrassment. It was of me and my boyfriend, Bob, and it had been taken with hidden cameras in that very room during one of our heavy petting sessions.

'Don't worry,' uncle said. 'I'm not angry. I just want you to watch this. It's part of your education.'

We watched.

On the screen, Bob opened my blouse and mauled at my breasts. He pushed me full length on the sofa and climbed on top of me, straddling one of my thighs and rubbing himself against me.

At the time, it had been exciting and I had been aroused as his thigh pushed against my vagina. But looking at it on television, from a different perspective, it appeared foolish and juvenile.

I knew what was going to happen next on the screen and I squirmed on the sofa and put my hand over my face as I watched Bob push up my skirt. The embarrassment was intense, particularly when he took out his penis and pushed my hands around it. I wondered what uncle thought about what we were watching, but I dare not look at him.

As the film got closer to its end, I closed my eyes, not wanting to see any more, but uncle touched my arm.

'You should watch,' he said.

Bob had pushed my panties down until they were around my thighs and he was pushing a finger in and out of my vagina. I remember at the time that what he was doing was both exciting and frustrating, that he was going too fast and touching me only in the correct place by accident. Then he pushed me over onto my stomach and tugged my panties down further and pressed his penis against my bottom.

He shuddered and came and I remembered how hot and sticky his sperm had felt as it gushed into the crevice between my buttocks.

Bob rolled off, red in the face and obviously flustered, and took his handkerchief from his pocket and wiped up the sperm before getting up to fasten his trousers.

Uncle switched the video and television off with the remote control and turned on the sofa so that he faced me. He held my right hand in both of his and looked into my eyes.

He said, 'It is natural that young people should experiment and discover the pleasures of sex. It is also natural that the experiments are clumsy, as we have just seen, and unsatisfying, because the two people lack the knowledge of how to properly satisfy each other.

'But now, dear Chloe, you are sixteen and a woman. The pleasures of sex should no longer be denied you. You should understand and enjoy them fully without shame or embarrassment. You should learn them now, so that in the future you will be able to fill your life with sexual delight. This will be my special gift to mark your sixteenth birthday. Will you let me teach you all about sex?'

I said yes automatically, for I could have refused him nothing. Besides, watching the video in his presence and hearing him talk so openly about a secret which

I longed to know, had made my pulses race.

'Then come to me,' he said, and moved me until I was lying on the sofa.

He lay alongside me and stroked my face and I began to tremble at his touch, my lips quivering. He smiled and bent forward to kiss me and I closed my eyes and felt his mouth upon mine, opening my lips and his tongue pushing inside.

This was something I had imagined happening over the last two years and now it was actually occurring it almost made me swoon. He kissed me for an age, both gently and passionately, until my body ached for his hands to explore more than my face and hair and neck.

At last, they did, moving down to unbutton my shirt which he pulled from the waistband of the skirt. He opened it completely down the front until it was only held at the neck by my school tie. He pushed up my bra without unclipping it, to expose my breasts and I wished they were bigger as his mouth moved from my neck and began to suck my nipples.

My body began to move of its own accord, my hips lifting in an effort to entice his attentions lower. Gasps escaped my lips, along with little moans of ecstasy. Having uncle do this to me made me feel liberated and close to becoming the woman he said I was.

His hands now pushed up the pleated skirt, his palms sliding along my thighs; confident hands, knowing hands. My head was buried backwards in the softness of the sofa, eyes closed to concentrate on the bursts of pleasure he was releasing, my body his to use as he wished.

Uncle moved from the sofa and knelt beside it. His fingers hooked into the top of my white cotton panties and began to tug them down and I raised my hips to help their removal. A hand slid beneath me and gently eased them over the curve of my buttocks. The touch was like an electric current and my flesh quivered; he sensed the reaction and his hand went back and caressed the softness.

Then my panties were being removed, without haste or timidity, but with a sureness, and I felt his mouth upon my legs above the knee, his tongue licking higher.

My thighs parted of their own accord and his hands went beneath me to hold and fondle my buttocks. His tongue licked higher and momentarily I worried because I had come straight from school to this extra curricular lesson without benefit of a shower, and I hoped the aroma of my body would not deter him.

It didn't, and his tongue licked onwards, sliding between thighs that I was now stretching apart, and his mouth finally covered my vagina, nuzzled it, parted its lips and began to feed upon it.

I cried out at that moment and lost control, and my wails would have been an embarrassment if I had been aware of them, and then his tongue found my clitoris, his lips fastened upon it and I orgasmed.

It was the first orgasm I had ever been given and it far surpassed the ones my own fingers had delivered in bed during the past year. I yelled and thrashed and uncle kept on sucking and licking and rubbing at the soft exposed membranes with his face and I kept coming, three, four and more orgasms, all tumbling into one long roller coaster ride of ecstasy.

When I recovered, uncle was sitting on the sofa, cradling my head in his lap. He had covered by breasts with my shirt and had pushed down my skirt.

'Did you enjoy it?' he said.

The question was academic.

'Yes,' I said, still in a daze.

'Are you ready for the next lesson?'

'Yes.'

'Then stand up, Chloe.'

'We both stood up, facing each other. He took hold of the white shirt and ripped it from my shoulders. The act was unexpected and violent and sent a tremor through me that combined fear and excitement.

He tugged again and the buttons at the cuffs snapped and the shirt came off completely. He dropped it on the floor and reached behind me and unclipped the bra, slipped the straps from my shoulders and watched it fall from my body.

All I wore now was a grey pleated skirt and school tie, knee socks and shoes. I felt more naked than if I had been wearing no clothes at all.

Uncle felt my breasts and I closed my eyes and arched my body towards him.

'You like to give, Chloe?'

'Yes.'

He opened the silk dressing gown and let it drop to the floor and was naked before me. I dropped my eyes and saw his erection, big and hard, rising from black pubic curls. It was the first penis I had really seen and it looked strange and alien.

Uncle sat on the sofa.

'Kneel, Chloe. Between my legs.'

I did as I was instructed and his hands fondled my breasts again as I stared at his penis, which throbbed with desire.

'Have you sucked one before?' he asked.

'No.'

'Good,' he said, and taking hold of my head, he pulled it towards his weapon. 'Lick it,' he said, 'get used to its taste and shape and smell, get used to its sensitivities.'

I did so, overcoming my nerves and holding it in my right hand while I licked, becoming bolder until I wanted to put it inside my mouth.

'Do you want to suck it?' he said.

'Yes. Please.'

'Then do it.'

I opened my mouth and sucked the penis inside, and his foreskin slid back with my lips. He groaned and I moved my head up and down.

'Suck and salivate,' he said. 'Don't use your teeth; use the softness of your mouth.'

I complied and gauged how well I was doing by the sounds he made and the way the penis throbbed and pulsed. He allowed me to create the rhythm, his touch gentle on the side of my face as he brushed back my hair to watch my cheeks bulge as I accepted his weapon.

'I'm going to come in your mouth, Chloe, and you are going to swallow it.'

I sucked more wilfully to make it happen, eager for the new experience and eager to please uncle. His breath shortened and he began to gasp.

'Now, Chloe. I'm coming now.'

The penis exploded in my mouth, the volume of sperm taking me by surprise, filling and choking me. I swallowed and gulped but loosened the grip of my lips around his weapon which slipped out, still spurting, and his seed splashed into my face.

I drank what I had received and sucked the head of his penis clean. A dribble escaped the side of my mouth and I used my tongue like a cat to lick it back inside.

His wetness was on my cheek, and I looked up at him, worried in case my performance had not pleased him.

He smiled and reached out to wipe the residue from my skin with a finger which he then offered to me. I sucked his finger as if it were another penis.

'Excellent, Chloe.'

His praise made me smile and made me happy.

'Is there anything else you want me to do?' I said.

'Many things, but we have plenty of time. Sex should not be rushed, it should be explored at leisure.' He stroked my face. 'I shall enjoy being your teacher, Chloe.'

'And I shall enjoy being your student, uncle.'

We went upstairs and shared his bath, washing each other and becoming familiar with each other's bodies: his was strong, dark, firm and hairy; mine was slim and girlish. I kept looking at our reflections in the mirrors in his bedroom as we dried each other with soft towels, the two bodies so unalike that they complimented each other perfectly.

While I was using the towel on his thighs, I couldn't resist taking his penis into my mouth again. It was large but limp, but after a few sucks it began to stiffen and rise.

He led me to the bed and we lay upon it and kissed and stroked and explored each other, my hands timorous at first until he encouraged me. His explorations took his mouth down to my vagina again and we lay head to toe. He began to lap at my juices and I realised his weapon was available for me to suck as well and I squirmed my head beneath his thigh and took it in my mouth.

We sucked each other until I came, releasing his penis from my mouth to moan with the spasm of pleasure. He rolled away and then knelt between my legs and I knew it was time to shed my virginity.

He inserted the tip of his penis between the lips of my vagina and it rubbed against my clitoris, making me shudder with anticipation. He pushed and I tensed and he stroked my face and kissed me gently and I relaxed because of his tenderness and then, when he pushed again, he entered me all the way and I cried out.

I felt no pain but a strange wonderment at the penetration, at the feel of a part of a man's body deep within my body.

Uncle moved his penis inside me, as if widening the

breach. As the strangeness wore off, I could feel him tensing and relaxing his weapon, which, in turn, released appreciative quivers along the tunnel into which he had driven.

Then he slid it partially out, not far, as if worried the wound might heal itself, and back in again; small movements, a short rhythm that he kept gentle until my breathing told him I had become used to the size and feel of the thing inside me.

His strokes now became firmer and longer and the noises I made were of enjoyment. My thighs spread to give him deeper access and he raised them until the soles of my feet were flat on the bed. Then, of their own accord, they curled around his back, my heels digging into him, urging him to ride me harder and faster and deeper until I came.

Uncle eased himself from me and rolled me over onto my stomach. I was still recovering from the orgasm as he positioned me, lifting my hips and re-inserting his penis inside me, but this time from behind. It sank in and he sank down against me, his groin pushing against my buttocks. He moaned at the sensation and moved in and out with quickening thrusts.

'Do you know what I am doing, Chloe?' he asked.

'Making love,' I said.

'No. I am fucking you. We are fucking, Chloe, not making love.' He kept on, his strokes were piston thrusts. 'Making love is for lovers. One day, perhaps, you will have a lover; one day you may fall in love. But you are a student and I am a teacher and this is fucking.

'Do not suffer the misconception that you have to be in love before you can enjoy sex. They are separate experiences. Enjoy sex for the basic, most gorgeous sensation that it is. Enjoy every type of sex, every experience of sex. Receive it, give it, submit to it. Now, what are we doing, Chloe?'

He raised himself on his arms, holding my buttocks as cushions for his thrusts.

'Fucking. We're fucking, uncle.'

Simply saying the forbidden word was a release, another strand of convention broken, and I felt that saying it had excited him as well. So I repeated it, loud and frequently.

'Fuck me!' I said. 'Fuck me, uncle. Fuck me harder.'

The words and the excitement they generated gave me another orgasm but again uncle kept himself under control.

He waited until my turmoil had subsided before slipping from my back. He took my head in his hand, kissed my mouth and pushed me down towards his genitals.

'Taste yourself,' he said. 'Lick me clean.'

I went down without hesitation and licked like a glutton, relishing the combined tastes of male and female sex, wiping his penis against my cheeks and in my hair.

Eventually he stopped me and brought me up to lay alongside him once more.

'One more orifice,' he said, 'before the lesson ends.'

I must admit I didn't know what he meant but I was

willing for him to do whatever he wished. After all, he had used my mouth and vagina, what other place could there be?

Uncle placed two pillows in the middle of the bed and laid me over them, face down. He lay behind me and I felt his mouth again on my inner thighs. His fingers flicked my clitoris and his thumb slipped inside me and I moved my hips and groaned. He licked at the open lips of my vagina, his tongue dipped into the wetness and then trailed, not towards my clitoris, but in the opposite direction, across that short strip of tender flesh, to the rosebud of my anus.

He licked and sucked and I gasped at yet another experience of heaven. His tongue forced a passage and I almost fainted. His fingers all the time were working at my clitoris and vagina and this added sensation was almost too much to endure. My moans were loud and continuous.

A finger probed that sensitive aperture and, after initially flinching, I relaxed and tried to make it welcome. It gained entry and I tried to relax more to entice it deeper, and it slid further inside until I was pierced with fingers from front and back.

Uncle changed position behind me and I shuddered as oil was poured over my buttocks and ran down between my legs. The finger was withdrawn but something bigger was now being presented for entry and, even well greased, it was painful to let it in.

At first, the discomfort threatened to dull my senses to all else, but then the pain mixed with the pleasure.

Even so, when he drove it home I screamed.

As before, when he had taken my other virginity, he simply lay upon me, embedded and motionless, and my body, incredibly, began to adjust to the size that it had accepted.

He moved it slowly, but even the gentlest of thrusts made me cry out, yet it did not stop him. He continued to rock back and forth upon my buttocks as, gradually, the passage became easier. The tightness of the fit was making him groan, and I suspected that this time he would be unable to control himself.

I was right and he pushed so hard that the pillows beneath my hips were flattened and I screamed again and he began to shake and shudder as his penis discharged deep within my bowels.

He lay upon my back until the weapon that had once been so mighty had shrivelled and slipped from me of its own volition. We were both exhausted and, deprived of the sensations and pleasures I had been enjoying, my body began to ache.

I drifted into a light sleep and awoke when uncle picked me up and carried me into the bathroom. He had already run a hot bath and he eased me into the water and washed me with soap and gentleness, dried me and dressed me in silk pyjamas.

We went downstairs and had a birthday tea. Afterwards, we returned to the bedroom for another lesson.

8

Kate shared Chloe's bed that night, and the two girls touched each other, caressed each other, and brought each other to more sensual orgasms before finally succumbing to sleep.

In the morning, DeVille telephoned to say he had arranged an appointment for Kate. He gave detailed instructions to Chloe.

The girl helped Kate dress in black suspender belt and loose-legged black silk panties, shiny black stockings and high heeled shoes, and a black knee-length pleated skirt. Kate also wore a white silk blouse that buttoned down the front, and no brassiere.

Chloe combed Kate's long blonde hair from her face and coiled it high on her head. Her spectacles with the extra large lenses made her look like the perfect secretary from a *Playboy* centrefold.

They giggled together, like schoolgirls, and Kate put on a mock-serious expression when she stared at herself in the mirror.

'I hope your uncle knows what he is doing,' she

said. 'I can't do shorthand.'

Chloe said, 'As long as you can manage dictation, I'm sure you will be all right.'

They laughed and held each other and Kate suddenly bit her lip.

She said, 'I hope I can go through with it.'

'Of course you can. It's only sex, after all. There is no mystique in sex, only pleasure and power.'

'What do you mean?'

'You will find out, Kate. You will find out.'

Chloe kissed her on the cheek and they went into the living room where DeVille was waiting.

He smiled his approval at Kate's appearance and held up a black cape for her to drape over her shoulders which gave her an air of mystery and respectability.

'Come,' he said. 'The board meeting starts at eleven o'clock.'

They travelled into the City by the same chauffeur-driven limousine in which she had been taken to the apartment the day before. Kate was nervous and stared at the back of the driver's neck. She wondered how much he knew about his employer's business.

The chauffeur was a young, well-built man, who wore a grey suit like a uniform and a peaked cap. His profile showed regular features and an open expression. Their eyes met fleetingly in the rear-view mirror from time to time, but she could read nothing in the glance.

Did he know he was driving her to an appointment where she would be required to be sexually compliant in any way her host desired?

The chauffeur negotiated the traffic expertly and stopped in a side street near the Lloyds building. DeVille got out first, and gave Kate a helping hand as she followed. A man in a uniform and top hat opened a discrete door that had no sign, and they entered a dark lobby.

Waiting for them was a matronly lady in a tweed suit and flat brogues, an outfit that made Kate smile despite her nervousness, because it was so like the clothes she herself had worn until yesterday.

No words were exchanged, but the woman led the way to a pair of lifts. The gate of one was open and they entered. There was only one button and the lift rose to the top floor of the building. The woman opened the gates and stepped out into a large room. DeVille and Kate followed.

A long conference table was at one end of the room, and a desk was at the other. Behind the desk sat a large man in his sixties, wearing a dark blue suit. His neck swelled out above the collar of his white shirt and he held a thick cigar clamped in his right hand.

The woman again said nothing but simply left the room by a door at the far end, beyond the conference table. DeVille put his hands on Kate's shoulders and she relinquished the cape.

She felt naked, even though she was fully clothed, for the man's eyes blatantly stripped her. Her breasts reacted of their own accord and her nipples became erect with a mixture of excitement and fear and pushed against the white silk of the blouse.

The man puffed on the cigar and exhaled a cloud of smoke.

He said, 'Are you sure she's new?'

DeVille said, 'This is her first time. Surely, Sir Robert, you can tell?'

Sir Robert stared into her face and slowly smiled. 'Yes. I can tell. You've done it again, DeVille. Bloody surpassed yourself this time. Right. Wait downstairs. When I've finished, I'll put her in the private lift.'

DeVille stepped back into the lift without a word and the doors closed. Kate listened to the hum of the motor as it descended.

She was alone with this stranger and had no idea what was to happen. DeVille had said she should look demure and shy but she couldn't. Sir Robert was leering too much, and he was too old. Sixty-eight, perhaps; maybe even seventy.

Why did he always need new girls? Because he could impress them?

Kate met his gaze and kept her expression aloof. His smile of superiority faltered. Perhaps he needed an audience to show his power.

Power? That was something Chloe had said before she left the apartment. Sex was only pleasure and power. But who had the power here: the elderly man with the cigar, because he had bought her services, or Kate, because she was a highly prized commodity?

The man pressed a button on his desk and she heard a buzzer ring in another room. The door through which the matron had left opened once more. In walked six men, all wearing business suits, all carrying folders of documents. None of them was older than thirty.

Sir Robert waved them to the chairs at the conference table and they took their places, remaining respectfully silent although their eyes were drawn to Kate. They seemed as uneasy with the situation as she was herself.

When her employer moved from behind the desk she got another shock: he was in a motorised wheelchair. He steered it towards the head of the table.

'Come,' he said to Kate, as he passed.

She walked after him.

He stopped when he reached his place at the table and indicated that she should stand alongside him to his right, and she did so, her hands held primly together in front of her.

Sir Robert addressed the men.

'I hope you have all done your homework and are not wasting my time. You were given a problem to solve, a projection to make and a presentation, complete with costings, to deliver. We'll start with you, Bailey. Deliver.'

Bailey was the first young man on the left side of the conference table. He opened a folder and began to present a business proposition.

Kate was confused. Why was she here? This seemed to be a normal business meeting. Bailey was talking high finance that she could not follow and, now that the conference was underway, the other young men were no longer staring at her, but at their own documents, their own reports, some making late adjustments with pen, others listening carefully to Bailey's delivery. She was surplus to requirements.

Sir Robert reached out and put his right hand beneath her skirt. He did it blatantly, with no attempt to hide the movement. He ran the palm along the inside of her leg, up to the stocking top, where it lingered, as if comparing the different texture of nylon and silken flesh.

Then it moved on and discovered the wide leg of the french panties. It caressed the start of her buttock and went beneath the silk and handled the full curves of her bottom.

Kate's mouth opened and her breathing changed. The pressure and demands of his hand made her change her stance and part her legs wider. Beneath the silk of the blouse, her bosom began to heave.

The closest man on the right side of the table had noticed what was happening. His gaze went from the occupant of the wheelchair to the way the skirt was moving, to Kate's face. She stared back at him and he gulped. She parted her mouth wider and touched the underside of her top lip with her tongue. The young man shuddered.

Others had begun to notice and were shifting in their chairs. She gasped softly as the old man stroked her between the legs and parted the lips of her vagina with one finger.

They all knew what was happening, all except Bailey who kept on with his presentation of facts and assessments. From initial shock, their features underwent a change that, at first, Kate didn't understand. Then she recognised it as the same expression she had seen on her husband's face two nights ago when he had caught her emerging naked from the shower: it was lust and desire.

Sir Robert pushed a finger inside her and she gasped again but louder than was necessary. As he pushed two fingers inside, she stiffened and took a sharp intake of breath that everyone but Bailey noticed.

Her employer interrupted Bailey to say, 'What figure was the residue?'

Bailey looked up, momentarily. 'It was . . .'

He stopped as he realised what was going on. His gaze flickered around the table to gauge the reaction of the others, but they were all staring at Kate.

Sir Robert said, 'I'm waiting.'

'Oh, yes.' Bailey fumbled the papers before him. 'Half a million, Sir Robert.' His voice was strained.

'Very well. Continue.'

Bailey did so, hesitantly, finding it difficult to concentrate as Kate groaned regularly and the fingers began to make soft slurping noises.

At last, he finished.

Sir Robert said, 'Grossman, let's hear yours.'

'What? Oh, yes, Sir Robert.'

Grossman began, his voice a mumble because he was bent over his papers in an attempt to block out the visual and increasingly audible distractions.

Sir Robert tugged at the waistband of her panties.

He looked up at her and said, 'Take them off.'

Kate raised the pleated skirt at the back and all the

young men but Grossman stopped breathing, and the one immediately to her right leaned out in his chair in an attempt to see what she might be revealing. She pushed the panties down past her knees and stepped out of them.

Sir Robert held out his hand and she draped them over his fingers. He raised them to his face and held them to his mouth and nostrils with a sigh of pleasure before throwing them into the middle of the table. They lay there, a small wisp of crumpled black silk.

Grossman's mumble became incoherent and stumbled to a halt.

'Berry. You next,' Sir Robert ordered.

Another presentation got hesitantly underway.

Sir Robert moved his wheelchair three feet back from the table and indicated that Kate should stand in front of him. She did so, facing down the table until he turned her so that her back was presented to the young men.

'Sit,' he said.

He moved her hips backwards with his hands to show her what he meant.

She sat on the edge of the table, her feet still resting on the floor, and he moved the wheelchair closer. He reached up and slowly unfastened the buttons of the blouse until it gaped open. He felt her breasts, one in each hand, gently at first, and she tilted her head back and moaned to maintain the spirit of the game.

Then he squeezed hard and she cried out and was aware of the gasps from around the table in the silence as Berry stopped speaking.

Sir Robert said, 'Continue.'

The young man coughed twice to regain his voice.

The old man pushed her onto the table and she was sitting upon it, her legs apart, before him.

In a low voice, he said, 'Lie back.'

Kate lay on the table, her sophisticated hairstyle and spectacles still perfect for the office. But now her blouse was open, and her breasts exposed. She stretched her arms above her, almost as if she were a sacrifice, to heighten the effect of debauchery and to raise her breasts to a more prominent contour.

Sir Robert lifted her legs and place her feet on the arms of his wheelchair. He threw back the pleated skirt to her waist, laying open to the gaze of the young men her open thighs, her stockings and the wickedness of the black suspender straps.

Berry dried up.

'Johnson,' Sir Robert said.

He did not wait for the next man to begin but, gripping a thigh in each hand, he dipped his head between her legs and began to lick greedily at her vagina.

Another voice presented another report, despite the sights and sounds. Sir Robert licked and sucked in obvious enjoyment and, although he was much less skilled than Chloe, his tongue and nose did occasionally rasp against Kate's clitoris, causing her to cry out and moan.

Pleasure and power, she thought, and here I am in the middle of it.

She was amazed at how she had so easily slid into

this role, how easily she had allowed her body to be displayed, and how she enjoyed taunting the young men, who could watch but could not touch, with her cries and pretence at ecstacy. The experience might fall short of ecstacy, but it was pleasurable in a most peculiar way.

The old man's tongue dug deeply into her and she raised her hips against it and the thought suddenly occurred to her that after he had finished, he might easily turn her over to all six of them.

It sent a shudder through her that started as trepidation but changed to anticipation.

What if he did? This was part of her bargain and she was guiltless. All she had to do was lie back and endure whatever happened.

She was very wet between her legs and the old man was making a great deal of noise and had begun to lick her with a particular rhythm as if he wanted to make her come.

If that was part of the game, too, the least she could do was fake it.

Kate moved her hips in response to his ministrations and her moans grew in intensity and, as they became shrill, the anonymous voice shambled into silence and she felt she had won another victory. With surprise, she slipped over the edge into a real and prolonged orgasm.

The flesh of her thighs shook in the grasp of the old man and her lower abdomen fluttered like a butterfly as the pleasure subsided.

Sir Robert lifted his head and stared into her face.

He said, 'You can get up now.'

He took her hands and helped her sit up and stared into her eyes with appreciation, his face glistening with her juices. He moved the wheelchair back until he was two yards from the table and she got shakily to her feet.

'Wainwright,' he shouted down the table.

Another voice began another delivery.

It started hoarsely but gained in strength because the distraction had been removed.

Sir Robert spoke to Kate. 'And now, you do it to me.'

He opened his jacket and unfastened the waistband of his trousers and she knelt at his feet, and prepared to undertake an act she had never done before.

She unfastened the zip and opened the trousers. Something lay curled inside white underpants. She pulled them down and saw his penis. It seemed asleep, not rampant and angry like her husband's had been, but lethargic and peaceful.

Kate looked up into the old man's face for confirmation.

'Go on, suck,' he said.

His voice was louder than he had intended and, down the table, Wainwright began to stutter.

Kate took hold of the limp weapon and tried to remember what she had read in Chloe's story. She stroked it, and lifted it upright, and felt it begin to twitch. She dipped her head and kissed it delicately and it reacted again, twitching and losing its apathy.

Now she licked its length and it began to gain strength of its own. She was fascinated at its progress and how she was affecting it and she was impatient to see if she could make it fully erect.

Kate held it around its base with her forefingers and thumbs and looked up into Sir Robert's face. His power had gone now and his eyes pleaded. She opened her mouth and licked her lips slowly and felt the prick harden further; she smiled at him and dipped her head.

She sucked it into her mouth and he groaned and the penis stiffened. It was a weird sensation, but one she was determined to get right, and she put into practice what she had learned from Chloe's writings and adapted her own technique from the reaction she was getting.

The experience was one of discovery and, she realised with surprise, enjoyment. Behind her there was silence and she was aware of Sir Robert issuing another order but she was no longer interested in what he said or what the voices said: she was totally immersed in perfecting the sucking of a prick.

Kate shuddered as the words came into her mind, for she had never used such language, never been subjected to obscenity. Never been subjected to anything interesting, she thought ruefully, until now. And even the words, unspoken but in her mind, were another shedding of inhibition.

The penis was short and fat, shorter than her husband's and, judging by the depth of penetration she had felt the day before, shorter than DeVille's. Three pricks in three days. Another thought to shock and delight her.

Pleasure and power.

She continued sucking and, as she lifted her lips away, she licked the head with the tip of her tongue. Down her mouth went again, and on the up stroke she slurped, as the old man had slurped when he had been between her legs, and she flicked again with her tongue and made him groan.

He began to breathe more heavily, began to moan more regularly, and he took hold of her head in his hands and she realised he was close and she hoped she would be able to swallow what he discharged.

Sir Robert's yell brought the room to silence.

He came, and each of five spasms was accompanied by a loud rasp of air from his throat. There was little sperm but what there was, Kate held in her mouth.

She put the now limp penis back into its nest inside the underpants, zipped up and fastened the trousers, and he nodded his thanks.

Kate got to her feet and stood alongside him in her original position, facing the table and the six young men. All were silent; the bottom lip of one trembled, the face of another was bright red and Kate wondered if, perhaps, he had been unable to contain his excitement.

Her blouse remained open and her breasts hung free, again providing an odd contrast with her neatly pinned-up hair and the large spectacles that gave her such an air of innocent professionalism.

She smiled at the young men and opened her mouth to let them see the strands of sperm. With great deliberation, she licked her lips and swallowed it.

Berry closed his eyes and shuddered, and another,

whose name she had forgotten, trembled and shook.

Sir Robert said, 'Get out, all of you.'

They gathered their papers. Wainwright dropped his and caused the two men behind him to collide when he bent to pick them up. They shied away from each other at the contact, as if they had touched an electric current.

Then they were gone and the door closed.

Sir Robert said, 'The most that can be said about that lot is that there isn't a pouf among them.' He gave Kate a long look. 'Young woman, you were bloody marvellous. The best I've had, and I've had plenty. I hope you didn't mind being part of my little experiment in composure.'

'It was fascinating.'

'Good. Now, let's have a drink before I return you to DeVille.'

9

DeVille took her back to Wapping in the same chauffeur-driven limousine.

Kate again tried to see if the driver showed by his expression that he was aware of the nature of her employment, but his face remained neutral.

They did not speak in the car, and when they arrived at the underground parking area at the apartment block, the chauffeur got out of the car with them, took several packages from the boot and accompanied them in the lift to the penthouse suite.

The lift was small and, with the parcels as well as two men, Kate felt cramped. She was also aware that the aroma of lust still clung to her body.

No words were exchanged until DeVille unlocked the door of the penthouse. This time, he had not rung the bell.

'Chloe is out,' he said. 'She will not be back until this evening.'

He pointed and the chauffeur carried the parcels into the bedroom.

Kate dropped the cape over a chair. She was still bemused by the conference she had attended.

She said, 'Does Sir Robert always do the same thing?'

'I don't know. What did he do?'

The chauffeur returned and waited by the door, his peaked cap beneath one arm and his hands held together in front of him, as if in relaxed prayer.

His presence made Kate uncomfortable and she did not know how best to respond to DeVille's question.

She said: 'He . . . used me, while six young men attempted to present reports.'

'What do you mean by "used me"?'

'You know what I mean.'

'Can't you bring yourself to say the words? Even though you've done the deeds?' DeVille smiled. 'Does an audience inhibit you? Even though you have had an audience of six?'

Kate realised false modesty was out of place, and that DeVille was using the chauffeur's presence as a further step in her education.

She said, 'He pushed fingers into my vagina. He removed my panties, which, by the way, he did not return, and he lay me on the table in front of the young men, and licked me until I came. Then I knelt in front of him and sucked his penis until he came in my mouth.'

DeVille smiled. 'Very good.'

'Now. Does Sir Robert always do the same thing?'

'No. His immobility restricts what he can do physically, so he likes to invent situations. It sounds as though this was a particularly good one. Did you enjoy it?'

'Yes, I did. I'm surprised.'

'There will be more surprises to come. And I think you will enjoy them all. Was that the first time you have sucked cock?'

Kate was trying to watch, in her peripheral vision, for a reaction from the chauffeur, but she could detect none.

'Yes.'

'Remove your blouse.'

'What?'

'Do it.'

'I thought . . .'

'For two weeks you do not have to think. All decisions are taken for you. Remove your blouse.'

Kate was surprised again. She had begun to look upon DeVille in a non-sexual role, as a guardian who was guiding her new career. His assault upon her in his office, she had assumed, had been dictated more by the need to test her reactions than by his attraction to her or desire for her.

He had seemed to enjoy it at the time, although he had been dismissive of the incident afterwards, when he had introduced her to Chloe.

Was this another test, in the presence of the chauffeur? Was he going to command her to perform sexually for his driver? The young man was good looking and his stare was now appreciative; it would not be a difficult command to obey.

But then she saw the look in DeVille's eyes and realised she had aroused his desire. She was flattered.

Kate unbuttoned the blouse and dropped it on a chair.

'And the skirt.'

She removed that, too, and threw it on top of the blouse.

DeVille and the chauffeur both stared at her body with appreciation and she remembered the looks of lust she had evoked from the six young men and a different butterfly began in her stomach; this time one of need.

After the conference room scenario, Sir Robert had been civilised and gracious, which had helped her subdue her feelings of arousal. But being half-naked again, being under scrutiny again, stirred the dormant embers of desire which had remained unfulfilled.

She stood with legs apart, her arms by her side, making no attempt at innocence or modesty.

DeVille said, 'You really do have a magnificent body, Mrs Lewis. Lush, voluptuous. And a face that you stole from an angel.'

He stepped closer and weighed her breasts in his hands.

'Beautiful,' he said.

DeVille bent his head and sucked each nipple in turn into his mouth. He licked and suckled them.

Behind him, the chauffeur remained in the same position, although he was watching their every move.

DeVille stepped closer still, so that she could feel the clothes he wore against her nakedness, and he stroked her face and guided her mouth onto his. Her lips parted for his tongue and her eyes closed because she wanted to enjoy the sensations without distraction and she forgot the chauffeur.

As he kissed her, his arms went round her body, one in the middle of her back pulling her to him, the other grasping the softness of her buttocks, sliding over them, between the curves, his fingers reaching from behind to open her other lips and discover the wetness between her legs.

Her own arms circled him, her fingers digging into his shoulder, while her mouth continued to masticate against his.

DeVille moved his face away and she opened her eyes.

He stared into them. 'Do you want fucking, Mrs Lewis?'

'Yes. I do.'

'Then ask.'

'Please, fuck me, Mr DeVille. Fuck me until I come.'

He pushed her backwards to a couch.

'Sit,' he said.

Kate sat on the edge of the cushion while he stood before her and unfastened his trousers. He pushed them and his underpants down around his thighs, and took his penis in his hand. She had been right, it was much bigger than Sir Robert's weapon.

'Suck it,' he said.

She opened her mouth and took it deep inside with no preliminaries and was gratified to hear him gasp. Her fingers circled its base and held it tight whilst her head moved upon it. His fingers reached into her hair and released the clips that held it in place so that the long blonde tresses fell to her shoulders.

'You are a swift learner, Mrs Lewis,' he said, and pulled her mouth from his now throbbing prick.

He knelt between her legs and pushed her back onto the couch. He pulled her thighs towards him so that her bottom slid off the cushion, which now supported only her back. The fingers of his right hand slid beneath her to hold apart the lips of her vagina from below.

'Ask me again, Mrs Lewis,' he said.

He stared down into her pale face that was wide-eyed behind the spectacles; the beautiful, innocent face that was framed by cascades of blonde hair.

'Fuck me. Please fuck me.'

Her voice was hoarse, and the need that she detected in it shocked her, almost as much as her words.

'Again,' he said.

'Fuck me. I want your prick inside me.'

DeVille lurched forward and drove his penis deep into her vagina and she screamed. His hands cupped the globes of her buttocks and he rocked backwards and forwards on his knees, and he fucked her.

It was pure lust that had no finesse and it was exactly what she wanted. She gasped and shouted and urged him on and throughout the coupling they stared into each other's faces: his intense and sweating, his mouth pulled back to bare his teeth in a grimace; hers now the face of a demented and debauched angel that screamed, 'Fuck me! Fuck me!'

It could not take long, their feelings were too hot for

it to take long; it needed a swift conclusion.

Kate's eyes began to widen more and her mouth opened in silent anticipation and DeVille pounded more fiercely still to meet her at the gates of orgasm.

His penetration was total, she was impaled on a spear of pleasure, and when the wail of her crescendo began, he screamed at her and twisted and thrust deeper still and they came together; bucking, limbs jerking, throats moaning.

He extricated himself and got to his feet to fasten his trousers whilst she remained slouched upon the floor, back resting against the couch.

DeVille said, 'I will call you tomorrow, Mrs Lewis.'

Kate nodded and was aware again of the chauffeur, still waiting patiently in the same position by the door, although his eyes were now riveted to her body. She made no attempt to cover herself or close her legs but stared back noncommittantly.

Kate soaked in a bath after DeVille had gone, and tried to come to terms with the speed of all that had happened, to assimilate all she had experienced and learned.

Were the lessons worthwhile? Were they simply the means to an end – the saving of her home and lifestyle – or was the real reason she had accepted DeVille's outrageous proposition because her life had been so empty?

She became confused and angry at her self-examination.

The reasons didn't matter; her acceptance of the

terms of spending two weeks in May in the custody of a man whose business was filth and degradation had removed right or wrong.

There was no guilt, she told herself, because she was under someone else's orders. If there was any guilt, it was because she was enjoying having to obey the orders.

Was that so wrong?

She climbed out of the bath and dried herself and walked around the bedroom naked to inspect the contents of the wardrobes and to marvel at the variety of underwear, dresses, outfits, shoes and uniforms they contained.

In the drawers next to the bed, she found five vibrators of various size and shapes. They lay in open boxes, like chopped trophies taken on an expedition by female warriors from the Amazon.

One of the vibrators was black and bigger than the rest and she wondered if any man really did have a weapon that size. She took it from its box and fingered the smooth contours; she pressed a switch and it vibrated in her hand. But she needed Chloe to help bring it to life, or a fantasy she had not yet experienced.

She replaced it in its box until she and her new girlfriend had the time to explore fully the possibilities of love with an inanimate object. For now, she preferred more interesting stimulation.

Kate turned to the next part of Chloe's story.

10

Chloe wrote:

Uncle said: the secret of sex is that there is no secret.

During the two years after my sixteenth birthday, I learned what he meant.

My body was something to be proud of, not to be ashamed of; to be enjoyed, not denied. At the same time, it was not to be flaunted without reason; not to be given haphazardly.

Some people find pleasure in food. There were two girls at school who were severely overweight. They were conscious of their size, and were always excused the sort of physical activities I enjoyed, because they were incapable of doing them.

They were nice girls, but unattractive, and lacking in self-confidence because of their appearance. Their parents, too, were unprepossessing and overweight, and they had followed the example they had received at home and made the choice to take their enjoyment from food, with little regard to what damage they were doing to their bodies.

My choice was to take my enjoyment from my body without causing it damage: by healthy sex under the guidance of uncle, or at my own instigation.

But first, the veils that society drapes across the subject had to be lifted and thrown away. I had to learn to give, to control, to take, to accept and to submit. It was an exciting time and uncle was expert at arranging the unusual.

I left school and attended art college. I had no academic aptitude in the sciences and no desire to pursue my education through sixth form studies and university. The sort of education I preferred was the one that uncle could provide.

Art college was interesting and I was able to pursue the subject whilst continuing to live in Chelsea. I also took modelling courses, at uncle's suggestion. It proved to be an excellent all-round basis for the future: I have an arts diploma, I am enrolled with an excellent photographic model agency, and I am considered an expert in the ways of love.

Although I was always more mature than others of my age, I was able to mix and make friends with students easily. Uncle taught me the social graces and I learned to be a chameleon. I had the ability to wear sophistication like a dress and was comfortable in any gathering, in London, Paris or New York; places to which I went with uncle. Then, when it suited either of us, I would shed the dress of sophistication and become the perfect schoolgirl.

Uncle kept me for himself for a year, during which

time we travelled, attended social occasions, and entertained. And yet, he did not interfere with any relationships I formed on my own account with students at the college: they were something apart, something which he insisted were mine alone.

Within those terms, he kept me for himself, and, although I indulged in my own experiments on rare occasions, I was content for him to control my sexual development, for him to enjoy my body and for me to enjoy his expertise.

After my seventeenth birthday, uncle began arranging encounters to broaden my education still further, and to explore the ocean of pleasure that was there to be discovered by anyone adventurous enough to try.

On this particular day in summer, uncle dressed me in a thin cotton dress with pleated skirt. I wore a white suspender belt and tan stockings, with flat shoes; no make-up and my hair was pulled back into a ponytail.

'We are entertaining a friend,' he said. 'Someone less fortunate than ourselves. It is time that your beauty was tempered with humility.'

I had no idea what was in store, nor what my role would be, although uncle instructed me to be careless in the way I sat, so that I accidentally displayed my legs to our guest.

And who was this person less fortunate than us? A poor person? A leper? I had no need to worry and, indeed, had to suppress a laugh when finally our guest arrived, for his misfortune was to be small.

'Chloe, my dear, this is Mr Derek. Mr Derek, this is Chloe.'

He entered the living room hesitantly. He was, perhaps, no taller than five feet, and, like the two girls I had known at school, he had compensated for his physical shortcomings by over-indulgence in food.

While not obese, he was certainly fat, and wore a thin moustache to give him added dignity, which it didn't, and platform heels on his shoes to give him added height, which succeeded, instead, in making him appear top heavy. He was about thirty years old.

We shook hands and he accepted a whisky and soda from uncle, who purported to talk business, while I sat on the couch opposite like a teenager who had become bored.

I picked up a magazine and changed my position, so that my legs were up on the couch too, and my skirt inadvertently rucked to the side to provide Mr Derek with a clear view of stocking tops and the white triangle of my knickered crutch.

Uncle was unsighted and continued talking but I noticed over the magazine that Mr Derek had observed my indiscretion and was intensely gazing up my skirt.

As the conversation continued, uncle walked around the room and saw the way I was lounging.

'Chloe!' he admonished. 'Sit properly.'

I put my feet back on the floor, but when he moved away, I changed position again. Now I sank down in the couch and crossed my legs high so that my skirt gaped. Mr Derek's gaze once more peered beneath my skirt.

'Chloe!'

Another admonishment and another adjustment.

By the side of the couch was a low table that contained magazines. I dropped the one I had been pretending to read and leaned over the arm of the couch to ponder the titles, knowing full well that Mr Derek's view from behind would reach almost as far as my bottom.

'Chloe!'

I sat upright.

'Yes, uncle?'

'This is too much,' he said, in mock exasperation. 'I apologise, Mr Derek, if Chloe has embarrassed you.'

'No, that's quite all right,' said Mr Derek.

He coughed nervously.

'It is almost as if you have been deliberately provocative towards our guest, Chloe. And provocation deserves punishment. I think a spanking is called for, don't you agree?'

I replied, 'Yes, sir. If you say so, sir.'

'I do indeed.'

My stomach was now bubbling with excitement at the prospect of taking the show further for the unfortunate Mr Derek, when the telephone rang.

Uncle excused himself and went into the hall. When he returned, he said, 'I apologise again, Mr Derek, but I have been called away urgently on another matter. Please, stay and finish your drink, and do me one favour, if you will. Punish the girl for her provocation. I believe a spanking is in order, but whatever you feel is necessary, I trust you will inflict.'

'But . . .'

'Please do not refuse me. Punishment should be dispensed immediately. I would be obliged if you would do this on my behalf. Chloe, you will obey Mr Derek totally; you will do everything he says.'

'Yes, sir.'

'When you have finished, Mr Derek, Chloe will see you out and I will be in touch further, about the possibility of the business which we have discussed.'

Uncle shook hands with the startled little man and left the house.

Afterwards, he explained the telephone call had not been quite so well timed as I had imagined, but that he had an electronic device in his pocket which had enabled him to trigger the ring.

The silence stretched after the slam of the front door and I sat, hands in my lap, eyes lowered to the carpet, and waited.

Mr Derek coughed. 'Is there anybody else in the house?'

'No, sir.'

'Then, I think, perhaps, I'd better be going.'

He heaved his rotund little body out of the chair and stood up.

'Oh no, sir. Please. Uncle will be even more angry if you don't punish me.'

I stared up at him, at his red face that was beginning to sweat, at the glint in his eye that reflected the possibilities in his mind that he was trying to control.

'I've never spanked anybody,' he said. 'I don't know how.'

'I can show you, sir.' I got to my feet and tried not to look down on him. 'If you will sit in the middle of the couch?'

He sat on the couch, his feet dangling above the carpet. I knelt on the cushion next to him and positioned myself across his lap, resting myself at first on hands and knees, until I was correctly in place. Then I pulled my skirt up to my waist, and lowered myself onto him.

The little man groaned at the contact and the sight presented before his eyes of my bottom, tightly encased in white panties, of the taut white suspender straps and the way that the tan of the nylon stocking tops melted into the tan of my thighs.

'I hope I'm not too heavy, sir?'

'No, not at all. Not at all.'

He sat and stared without taking any action and I squirmed tentatively and identified his erection.

'Sometimes,' I said, 'uncle pulls down my knickers.'

'What? Oh, yes. Of course.'

His hands touched my thigh and stroked the curve of my bottom all the way to the waistband of my knickers. His breathing was irregular and his erection throbbed against my hip. He tugged at the knickers and I raised myself so that he could push them down until they were around my thighs.

'Dear God,' he said.

'Please don't hit me too hard, sir.'

'No, no, no.'

He caressed my buttocks again, as if in a dream, and then, as if he remembered why I was lying in such a state, he smacked me.

I moaned and pushed my hip against his prick, and he groaned, too.

He smacked again and, as he discovered that each smack upon my quivering flesh caused me to press against him, his strokes gained vigour until we were both panting and the blows began to hurt.

'Please, sir, no more.'

'What?'

It was as if my words had broken a dream.

'Don't spank me any more. I'll do anything if you don't spank me any more.'

He gulped and attempted to get his breathing under control.

'Anything?'

'Yes, sir.'

'Such as what?'

The question was a rasp, as if he dare only ask it in secret.

'Sometimes, after a spanking, my uncle soothes my buttocks.'

'How does he do that?'

'You promise you won't tell anyone?'

'I promise. What does he do?'

'He fucks me.'

'What?'

The man moaned loudly and shuddered and I felt his prick erupt in an involuntary orgasm. I lay against it, pressing hard, whilst his hands gripped my buttocks and thighs, as if he was frightened he might shudder himself away if he did not have something to cling on to.

I was disappointed at bringing our little play to such an abrupt conclusion, except that I hadn't. When his shaking had subsided, his breathing became almost normal. I remained lying face down across his knees.

'Tell me again,' he said. 'Tell me what your uncle does?'

'He fucks me.'

'Does he now? And did he also tell you to lead me on this way?'

'No, sir.'

'It's all a game, isn't it? You and DeVille have set this up?'

'I don't know what you mean.'

'All right.' His voice was tinged with anger, but also fresh excitement. 'Let's play the game some more. DeVille said you were to do anything I said, didn't he?'

'Yes, sir.'

'Then kneel on the floor.'

I slid from his lap and knelt before him on the floor, my knickers still around my thighs. He unfastened his trousers and pushed them open at the front and peeled down his underpants. They were sticky with his orgasm and his penis was still half stiff.

'Suck,' he said.

So I sucked; sucked it clean of the sperm he had so recently shot, and within a minute his prick was big again, a large and potent weapon for such a small man.

'He fucks you, does he?'

The question was rhetorical as he heaved himself from the couch and pushed my head into the cushions. He knelt behind me and pushed his penis between my legs aggressively but aimlessly, as if he had never done it before and did not know how.

My feelings had been changing all the time, from the enjoyment of teasing him, of leading him on, of enticing him and daring him to touch and fondle. I had felt a slight shame at being found out, and had been pleased to suck him clean and erect in compensation.

And all the time, my own juices had been flowing, my own excitement building. One of the reasons I had been so forward was because my vagina needed satisfying.

I reached between my legs and opened myself, and twisted to meet his lunges, but in such a way that it was not a comment upon his incompetence. The head of his prick slid against the wetness and I caught it with my hand and guided it inside in a movement smooth enough for him to believe he had achieved the entry himself.

Mr Derek cried out and gripped my hips and shuddered and shook inside me until he discovered a rhythm. It was fortunate he had only just ejaculated, for it enabled him to last for two or three minutes before he came again.

His hands stroked, grabbed, pulled and touched as he drove towards his second orgasm. The weight of his stomach flattened me against the couch, but I did not mind, as the edging of the cushion rubbed against my clitoris.

I came first, murmuring my pleasure into the cushions, and, as he increased the power of his thrusts with the imminence of his discharge, my libido was incensed afresh, and I managed a second coming. Then, as he shuddered on the brink of shedding his sperm inside me, the thought that this was probably the first time he had ever fucked a woman, enraged my pleasure buds still further.

As he came, I rode the residue of his passion and came again for a third time.

Afterwards, the little man asked no more questions, and I remained head down in the cushions, a suitable sight of ravishment to feed his memory, while he adjusted his clothes and prepared to leave the room.

At the door, I heard his footsteps falter and he stopped and said, 'I don't know why. I don't care. But thank you.'

It is one of the sweetest things anyone has ever said to me.

11

Kate prepared a salad in the well-stocked kitchen and defrosted a large bag of prawns. She thinly buttered brown bread and set the coffee percolator bubbling so that its aroma permeated the apartment.

She was looking forward to being with Chloe again and wore blue silk lounging pyjamas that draped around her curves seductively. The colour of the pyjamas complemented her blonde hair, which she wore loose around her shoulders.

When Chloe arrived, she commented on the smell of the percolating coffee.

'Delicious,' she said. 'It's making me hungry.'

'Good. Dinner is ready when you are.'

Chloe showered and Kate resisted the temptation to join her. The dark girl eventually emerged wearing only a pink silk shirt, which she had omitted to fasten.

They shared a bottle of chilled Chablis with the meal and discovered they had made no mistake about their liking for each other. Their conversation was intimate and they touched frequently and Kate wanted an excuse to suggest they go straight to bed.

Chloe eventually laughed, came round the table and kissed her on the lips, her breasts excrutiatingly close.

'It's very flattering,' Chloe said.

'What is?'

'That you want to fuck me.'

'No. I want to make love to you.'

Chloe's smile softened and she leaned over her again and this time kissed her properly, with an open mouth and a tongue that made promises.

They went to bed and undressed each other, and licked and touched, and kissed, and caressed; they didn't need the collection of vibrators in the bedside drawer.

Much later, as they lay side by side naked on the satin sheet, Kate asked about them.

'Do you use them?'

'Sometimes. Men like to watch.'

'But do you ever use them for yourself? When you are alone?'

'Yes.'

'Why?'

'I enjoy penetration. I enjoy being taken. The man can be as ugly as sin, but if I'm in the mood to be taken, I don't care as long as he can fulfil a function and fill me and make me come.'

'Is there such a thing as sin?'

'Oh yes. But sex, freely given, is not sin.'

'DeVille does not provide it freely. He charges.'

'The money is incidental. The sex is freely given.

Neither you nor I have to do this. You may lose your farm and your home if you break your agreement, but you will not lose your life. There are other jobs, other ways of making a living. Personally, I like satin sheets. I like good clothes, and I like this arrangement. Of course, it helps if you like sex.'

'What about the men?'

'The ones we meet are harmless creatures who are ruled by their pricks. They may want to spunk in your face but so what? It washes off. And why do they want to do that? Because they are frightened of us and excited by us at the same time. I enjoy making their pricks go stiff simply by looking at them; I enjoy making them moan and lose control. I enjoy using them for my pleasure.'

Kate touched her hand.

'Have you been with many women?'

'Some.'

'Do you enjoy that, too?'

'Being with a woman is always special.' She rolled onto her side and kissed Kate on the mouth. 'You are very special.'

They lay side by side in silence for a while before Kate said, 'You asked me if I'd ever been with a woman before. I said I hadn't, but that's not strictly true. I had a friend at school. We were very close.'

Chloe looked at her, and said, 'Have you seen her since?'

'No. But I think about her quite often.' She laughed nervously. 'Until I met your uncle, I could count my sex life on the fingers of one hand. These fingers, to be precise.' She held up her right hand and extended her first two fingers. 'My sex life was restricted to my memory and imagination, and the two fingers with which I masturbated.'

Chloe said, 'What about your husband?'

'He was useless. Worse than useless, because being married to him stopped me from discovering myself. I knew so little about sex that even my fantasies were blurred because I didn't know what really happened between men and women.'

She turned her head to stare at Chloe. 'Do you ever fantasise?'

'Doesn't everyone?'

'I didn't think so. I thought there was something wrong with me. I thought I was abnormal and perverted.'

'Are your fantasies that bad?'

'I don't know.'

'Worse than yesterday's board meeting?'

'Different to that.'

'Tell me.'

'I couldn't.'

'A few days ago, there were many things you couldn't do. It didn't stop you doing them when you were told to.'

'But this is different.'

'It is no different. Uncle said that in his absence, you have to obey my orders. Well, I'm ordering you to tell me your fantasy.'

Chloe said it softly, using her power to coax from Kate a fantasy that she suspected might also be a burden upon her conscience.

Both girls lay on their backs, their eyes closed, not touching. At last, Kate began talking.

'It's not always the same one, although it follows the same lines. Usually the same people are involved. The situation is always similar.'

She let the familiar fantasy start and, hesitantly at first, she began to describe it.

'I'm in the woods with my friend Gina. It's summer and the grass and the trees are very green and lush, and it's very hot. We are at school, the boarding school I used to attend. We are sixteen and we know a little about sex. We would like to know more, but what we know we like.

'There is a spot in the woods that we go to. A secret clearing that we have made our own, a clearing that no one else knows about, where the trees and bushes ensure privacy and where the grass is soft as a bed.

'We go there hand in hand, the touch of our fingers making us nervous: skin on skin. We know why we are going there but our thoughts and hopes have to remain unspoken. When we get there, we are hesitant and embarrassed, even though we have done this before. Even though the desire is making us shake. We feel guilty.

'I sit on the grass and Gina lies back and I am very conscious of her body next to mine; I have the urge to roll on top of her, to grab her, to have her totally, even though I don't know how.

111

'Instead, I pluck a daisy and lie on my side and tickle her nose with it. She laughs and tries to push my hand away and, suddenly, we are touching and pretending to fight. We have the excuse our guilt and embarrassment needed, to roll our bodies against each other.'

The fantasy began to work, as it always did, and Kate slipped her hand between her legs.

'Then I'm lying on top of her and we stop pretending and I kiss her. It's a proper kiss, a deep kiss, with our mouths open, and it releases all our inhibitions.

'Our legs are intertwined and we push our vaginas against each others' thighs and the excitement in my tummy is intense. I have opened Gina's blouse and my skirt is around my waist. Her hands are pulling at my panties.

'Soon, we have discarded our panties and both our blouses are open. I suck one of Gina's nipples while my hand is between her legs. My fingers are inside her and I can hear the noise they are making and it excites me even more. I have one of her legs trapped between both of mine and I'm rubbing the wetness of my vagina against her velvet skin.

'Gina comes and makes so much noise that the birds stop singing in the trees. I feel marvellous as she comes in my arms, marvellous because my fingers have made her come. At that moment, I feel I am in love with her.'

Kate paused at the intensity of the images in her mind and held herself back from the brink of orgasm.

'And then, suddenly, we are aware that someone is watching us. We roll apart in a panic and a man comes crashing from the undergrowth. Gina runs off in the opposite direction. I try to run, too, but the man grabs me. It's the school groundsman, a big, strong man, and I can't escape.

'I'm terrified of the trouble I'll be in and the shame I'll feel when he takes me back to school and tells the headmistress. But instead of taking me to the school, he lays me on the ground. For a moment, he simply stares at me while his dog, a big, brown Doberman, stands guard to prevent any attempt at escape. Then the groundsman begins to remove his clothes.

'I realise he is not going to tell anyone but that he is going to have sex with me. I'm frightened, but excited at the same time.

'He strips naked and I stare at his body. It is the first time I have seen a man naked. He is powerful and his body is hairy. He smells of sweat and lust and his hands are dirty from working in the fields. His penis is huge, bigger than anything I have imagined, and I'm frightened that if he puts it inside me, he will split me apart.

'And all the time I'm watching this big, rough man, his dog is watching me, panting in the heat, saliva dripping from its mouth.'

She paused and timed the movements of her fingers.

'He kneels down next to me and opens my blouse. He pushes up my bra and releases my breasts. They have always been large and I am very conscious of their size as he grabs and mauls them. His hands are exciting me and so is his smell, that is so much stronger now

113

that he is naked and kneeling next to me on the ground.

'His dog stands by my feet, still breathing heavily, watchful and intimidating.

'The man says, "In your mouth." And I'm relieved, disappointed and shocked: relieved he is not going to split me in two, disappointed I am not going to lose my virginity, and shocked that he is going to put his huge, smelly penis in my mouth.

'He straddles me and first rubs it between my breasts, which he lifts and holds like cushions. Then he pulls my head forward and I open my mouth and suck him inside.

'As he fucks my face, I raise my knees. My feet are flat on the ground, my legs splayed and my skirt falls up to the top of my thighs. My vagina is exposed and I can feel a breeze between my legs.'

The words were getting difficult to say now, and her fingers were working faster, in time to the tempo of the fantasy.

'And then, I feel hot breath between my legs and a tongue. A rough tongue, licking at my open vagina.' The words were forced out in gasps. 'It's the tongue of the groundsman's dog. The dog is licking me between my legs. The man comes in my mouth, and I come as well.'

Her legs clamped together and stiffened and she went into orgasm.

Afterwards, Kate and Chloe again lay in silence and Kate felt the familiar guilt and wondered how she could have confessed such thoughts.

Chloe said, 'I came, too.' Her hand slid across the sheet to find Kate's and take hold of it. 'That is now a fantasy shared, and one I'll use myself when I'm alone, picturing you in your secret place in the woods, imagining that I am Gina. That you make me come and I run away, but that I stay to watch while the man uses you.'

'But aren't you shocked?'

'No.'

'But it's, it's not normal.'

'It's fantasy.'

'It's perversion.'

'You mean the dog?'

'Yes. I mean the dog.'

'The dog is just another part of your submission. You like the idea of being powerless and being forced to submit, but you didn't suffer any pain, only pleasure. Involving the dog is different, but I wouldn't call it a perversion. Unless you actually tried to turn your fantasy into reality.'

'The thing is, the dog part is reality.'

Chloe did not say anything immediately. She let go of Kate's hand and traced the outlines of the blonde girl's face with her fingertips, assuring her of her understanding with the gentleness of her touch.

'Do you want to tell me about it?'

'Yes.'

'Tell me.'

Kate took a deep breath and said, 'It happened when I was sixteen.'

She hesitated and bit her lip. This was another secret she had never divulged to anyone.

Chloe squeezed her hand and said, 'Go on.'

'It was during the school holidays and I was at home, alone as usual. It was a hot day and I had been out for a walk with my dog. He was a labrador, called Jason. When we got back, I was feeling tired and lethargic so I went inside to have a shower.

'In my bedroom, I took off all my clothes and then flopped backwards onto the bed. My feet were still on the floor, my legs apart, and I lay back with my arms flung wide and relaxed.

'I began to think about my friend at school, Gina, and I touched myself between my legs and made myself wet. But I was too lethargic even to make myself come, so I stretched my arms again and tried to summon up enough energy to go for the shower.

'Jason was in the room with me. He was restless as he waited by the end of the bed. I was hot and my fingers had probably released odours from my vagina. When he nuzzled my leg, I stroked his back with my foot and thought nothing about it. He pushed his head between my thighs, and I still thought he was playing. Then his tongue began licking me between my legs.

'It was a shock and my first reaction was to laugh out loud. Then I realised I liked it, that it felt good. No one had ever licked me between my legs before and it was a strange and delicious sensation.

'I don't know how long it lasted, probably no more than a few seconds, when I had a sudden visualisation of what was happening and I felt utter disgust. I pushed Jason away and told him he was a bad dog and I ran into the shower.

'The warm water didn't help. My legs were unsteady and shaking and I felt loathing at what I had allowed to happen. Yet, at the same time, I was still terribly excited by it. My legs were shaking and my thoughts were making no sense.

'My fingers went between my legs and I began to masturbate. At first, I didn't want to, but I could not stop myself. Then the pleasure took over and I didn't care. I came three times in the shower, imagining the tongue had been Gina's or that of a male lover.'

Kate paused and remembered the intensity of the orgasms she had had in the shower. They had left her sitting splay-legged on the tiles as the water cascaded around her.

'I never allowed it to happen again with the dog, and I eventually convinced myself that it never did happen, at least, not quite the way it had. I told myself that Jason had licked me and made me tingle but that I had stopped it immediately. It was the guilt of those few seconds when I had allowed it to continue that I attempted to hide, that I attempted to bury somewhere in the back of my mind.

'Then, after I was married and needed diversions, the memory came back, but as fantasy instead of reality.'

Chloe said, 'And you've felt guilty ever since?'

'Yes, I think I have.'

'Let me put it bluntly, Kate. Do you want to fuck a dog?'

'No! Good heavens, no!'

'Whose tongue do you prefer between your legs, mine or that of a labrador?'

Kate turned her head and saw the twinkle in Chloe's eye, and she laughed; at herself and at the guilt she had felt all these years.

'Oh Chloe, you're so good for me.'

She rolled over and the girls embraced, giggling.

Chloe said, 'You still haven't answered.'

Kate raised herself on her elbows so that she was staring down into Chloe's face, and this time it was her eyes that twinkled.

'Well,' she said. 'It depends. How good looking is the labrador?'

Chloe was up at five the next morning for a modelling assignment that started at six.

Kate murmured sleepily, 'I thought modelling was glamorous?'

'It is. It is also hard work. The photographer wants to use the morning sunlight.' She smiled. 'He says it is virginal.'

Chloe emerged from the bathroom looking beautiful and fresh. She took Kate a mug of tea in bed along with the morning newspapers.

'I will not be back until this evening.' She smiled. 'When I get back, perhaps we can share some more secrets?'

She gave Kate a kiss on the forehead, and left the apartment in a swirl of fresh perfume.

Kate did not bother with a shower but remained in bed and enjoyed being unwashed and lazy. Besides, she could still smell Chloe on the pillow next to her.

Her thoughts remained centred on the dark, vibrant girl who had become her lover, and she drifted back to sleep to dream erotic dreams.

When she awoke again, around midday, her body was aroused, even though she could not remember the substance of the dreams. She knew only that they had been about Chloe and she wished her friend would return so she could turn them into reality.

Until Chloe did return, Kate would have to find some other way of pleasurably passing the time: she reached for the book in the beside drawer.

12

Chloe wrote:

Uncle did not discourage me from having relationships with people my own age, outside the very special relationship we shared together. I could entertain my friends at home with complete freedom, although I guessed after my first lesson with uncle that some of the rooms at home might be under the scrutiny of concealed cameras.

I divulged this to no one but it added a piquancy to my own modest experiments, for experiment I did, although not with completely satisfactory results. Eventually, I chose to keep my student friends simply as acquaintances; they stopped interesting me as lovers or potential partners.

When it came to serious sex, uncle was able to provide a far more varied and enjoyable menu.

At art college, I had an occasional boyfriend. He was tall and handsome and blond; he was eighteen years old and his name was Tim. When I was with him, I allowed him to make sexual advances at his own pace;

I was careful not to allow anyone to realise that I was, in fact, already an expert at most forms of sexual activity.

Tim enjoyed kissing and feeling my body; he enjoyed rubbing his erection against me when we were both fully clothed; but he was slow at pushing back the barriers of acceptable sexual behaviour between us. I decided he needed help.

I held a party. About thirty or forty teenagers attended. There was an abundance of food and drink and uncle abandoned the house to us. He placed no restrictions upon us but did let it be known that he would return at midnight.

When I was at college, I wore jeans and sweatshirts like everybody else, but the party gave me the chance to be more sophisticated. I wore a black silk cocktail dress, black underwear and lace-topped stockings, and high heeled shoes.

Tim had never seen me dressed like this before and he was both aroused and jealous because of the attention I was getting from the other male guests.

We used one room with the lights turned down for dancing and indiscretions, although the rest of the house was available if couples wished to find somewhere more private.

During the early part of the evening, I danced with Tim and could feel that his penis was stiff in his trousers. But when we were alone together, he was still reluctant to go further than we had gone before, and simply touched me through my clothes.

To provoke a reaction, I danced with other young men, relaxing in their arms and moving close against them, counting it a victory every time I caused an erection to grow against my belly.

I also pretended to drink a great deal and, under the guise of being intoxicated, I became even more friendly and accommodating whenever I danced with anyone, using my stomach and abdomen in a more blatant manner against their eager hardness.

Two of the men I picked for this special attention were Richard and John, who were slightly older than the others and who I did not know very well, as they had arrived in the company of other friends.

Tim was in the kitchen whilst I danced with Richard and, in the dimly lit room, his hands wandered down my back and over my buttocks. He kissed me, open-mouthed, and his hands went further down my legs and discovered the suspender straps through the silk of the dress.

I pushed against him, as if only half aware of what he was doing, and he gripped my buttocks again in both hands, pulled me against him and rubbed his erection against me.

When the music stopped, we moved to the edge of the room. His friend, John, was waiting for us and claimed the next dance so I went back into the throng once more and allowed this new body to push against me. All the time, I subtly encouraged him with movements that could have been inspired by drink or by lust or by accident.

His hands, too, moved over my dress, and he cupped

a breast and kissed me before sliding his hands down the material and over my hips. He traced the outline of my underwear and I felt his penis grow against me.

'Stockings?' he whispered.

I smiled and kissed his neck.

'They make me feel sexy,' I said.

The music finished and I said I felt a little dizzy with the heat and all that I had had to drink and he became solicitous. He and Richard escorted me from the room.

'I think perhaps I should go to the bathroom,' I said, and stumbled against them. 'There is one upstairs that will be quieter.'

They helped me up the stairs and along a corridor but instead of going to the main bathroom on that floor, I pointed to a bedroom door.

'In there,' I said. 'Nobody will bother me in there.'

We went into uncle's room and switched on the bedside lamp. They waited hesitantly while I went into the bathroom that was attached to the room. I ran the taps and splashed water and emerged a few minutes later.

I bumped into Richard and mumbled that I was feeling sleepy. When I stepped away from him, I deliberately fell onto the bed. I gave a sigh, rolled over, and pretended to fall asleep.

My intake of wine was sufficient to relax me and make me carry off the ploy with believability. I was curious to see how they would behave and my insides began to churn in anticipation.

Richard said, 'Chloe? Are you all right?'

I said nothing.

He said, 'Maybe we should make her more comfortable?'

I heard them move into position and I was pulled gently by my shoulders until I was lying on my back in the centre of the bed. Then my feet were lifted and placed on the mattress and, perhaps inadvertently during the manoeuvre, my skirt slid up my thighs.

The two boys remained by the side of the bed.

'Chloe?' Richard said.

'Chloe?' said John.

A hand shook my shoulder.

I made no response; I remained unconscious.

My skirt was lifted, but not to cover my exposed thighs; rather to afford the two young men a better view of what was beneath.

One of them whispered, 'Oh, my God!'

The skirt was placed about my waist and I felt the first hand on my leg. It moved tentatively along the nylon but hesitated when it moved onto the flesh above the welt of the stocking. When I did not move, it progressed further, the palm dipping beneath me to feel the flesh of a buttock.

A second hand began climbing the other leg, but this one went between my thighs at the front. I moved lazily in my pretend sleep and opened my legs. Fingers stroked my vagina through the silk of my panties.

Richard said, 'I want to fuck her.' His voice was hoarse.

John said, 'What if she wakes up?'

'I don't care. I want to fuck her.'

'But she'll know. I mean, she'll realise when she wakes up.'

One hand was removed but the other, the one between my legs, continued stroking, a finger now pushing aside the silk to touch my wet opening.

Richard said, 'She's ready for it.'

'You can't. It's rape.'

'She's not objecting.'

The panties I wore had loose legs; I had dressed with care and with accessibility in mind.

I heard Richard fumbling with his clothes.

John said, 'What if someone comes looking for her?'

'Stay by the door. Don't let anyone in.'

He parted my legs and knelt on the bed between them. His fingers moved the silk of my panties to one side to expose my vagina. His next move was unexpected and I almost cried out in surprise: he crouched down and licked the open lips of my sex.

His tongue was inexperienced but eager to taste my forbidden places and he lapped at my juices for several seconds.

From the door, John said, 'Come on, for chrissake. Get on with it!'

Richard lifted his head and positioned himself above me and tried to enter me with his penis. Again, he was inexperienced and too eager. He reached between us with his right hand and tried to guide his weapon into the opening, and his face was so close to mine that I could smell myself upon his breath.

He pushed but the head of his penis missed the portal and slid, instead, along the channel of my vulva, brushing deliciously over my clitoris. He pushed again, and this time it slid the other way, down between the cleft of my buttocks.

Little yelping noises of frustration were coming from his throat. Again, John spoke from the door.

'Hurry up!'

His inability to satisfy his lust overcame his caution and he moved from the bed, pushed my legs together, and tugged down my panties. He took them off, parted my legs again, and climbed back between them.

It was almost as if he did not care any more if I awoke or not, for now he knelt up close to my vagina and spread my thighs. He lowered himself yet again, found the entry and pushed and went inside with a deep sigh.

My insides were aflame and the membranes of my sex enclosed and sucked his prick. Richard cried out and began to come almost immediately.

His orgasm took him by surprise and he tried to withdraw. The first burst of his sperm shot inside me but the rest splashed upon my inner thighs and around the mouth of my aching sex.

He crawled from the bed and I heard him trying to catch his breath as if he had been running.

John gulped. 'We'd better go,' he said, but in a voice that cracked with his own desire.

Richard said, 'Your turn. I'll keep watch.'

'I don't know . . .'

'Go on. You've got to.'

I heard John approach the bed. 'God, you've made a mess.'

'So turn her over.'

He straightened my legs and rolled me onto my stomach. My skirts were once more pushed up to my waist and he took a moment to feel my bottom and part my legs.

It was Richard's turn to say, 'Get on with it!'

I heard him unfastening his clothing and then the mattress dipped as he climbed upon the bed. He was kneeling between my legs and he lay forward so that his penis was in the crease between my buttocks. It was only semi-erect but contact with my softness made it stiffen.

He gasped and moved it between the pillows of flesh.

'Put it in!' Richard urged. 'Fuck her!'

I suspect John had never had full sex with a girl before but he raised himself and pushed his penis between my thighs that were slippy with the ejaculation of his friend, and thrust hopefully. It slid along the groove without penetrating but the heat and wetness that it encountered there was enough to make him come.

He gasped, and tried to push himself away, and his sperm deluged over my bottom.

'Quick!' Richard said. 'Someone's coming!'

John got off the bed with a yelp and Richard moved from the door.

'The bathroom,' he said. 'In the bathroom and keep quiet.'

As the bathroom door closed, the bedroom door opened.

'Chloe!'

It was Tim and he sounded shocked, as well he might, considering the sight that confronted him. I lay face down upon the bed, my skirts around my waist, my panties missing and my legs open. Glistening snail trails of sperm traversed my buttocks.

'Is she okay?'

I recognised the second voice as that of his friend, Philip, a small, thin, studious boy who was the exact opposite to Tim in build and temperament. Philip was shy and withdrawn, happier working on a project than in the company of girls.

Tim said, 'You'd better wait outside.'

'Good grief!'

Philip had obviously seen me, too.

'Outside, Phil.'

The door closed and I heard Tim come across the room.

'Chloe! Are you awake?'

His hand shook my shoulder but I remained unconscious. He rolled me over and as my skirt was still around my waist, he gasped when he saw the creamy juices that covered my thighs and pubic hair.

'Who did this?' His voice was an angry whisper. 'Who did this, Chloe?'

I continued to remain asleep, but breathing gently so as not to cause him serious concern about my health.

His anger changed and his hands began to touch me in a way he had never touched me before, groping my thighs, rubbing the sperm into my skin, pushing his fingers between my legs and inside me.

'Chloe,' he whispered hoarsely, 'what did they do?'

My legs opened as a result of the work of his fingers and I lolled my head sideways and moaned gently.

And then I heard his clothing being unfastened and he, too, was on the bed and kneeling between my legs and the penis I had only ever felt through his trousers was exposed and pushing at my wetness.

But Tim, too, was inexperienced, and did not know where to direct his thrusts and the head of his weapon slid in the trough of my sex that was running with juices. At last, it discovered the entry, pushed deep inside, and the heat was enough to bring him off.

He held himself above me, on his knees and arms, so that there was no contact between us except where his weapon pierced me, and he discharged its contents.

Tim got off the bed and pulled my skirts down to at least give me the appearance of respectability. I heard him fastening his clothing and then he left the room. As the door opened and closed I heard him speak to Philip.

'I'll find them and make them pay!'

The door closed and I remained supine and content at causing so much turmoil and lustful urges simply with the power of my body, and waited for the bathroom door to open.

Richard and John came out and I listened to them cross the room and pause by the outside door.

'Now,' Richard said, and the door opened and they left quickly.

I remained on the bed: I realised that to make the game continue to work my recovery would have to be gradual, and besides, I was tired with the alcohol I had consumed and the tensions of the recent situation. What I really needed was an orgasm and I was considering giving myself one, when the door again opened.

Someone crossed the room and stood by the bed and my curiosity was burning to find out who it was and their motive for being there.

The person knelt on the floor and leaned on the mattress. I could feel their breath on my face.

'You're so beautiful, Chloe,' Philip said softly.

I was flattered by the remark and to discover I had a secret admirer in the studious young man who was too shy to get a girlfriend. But why was he here?

Had Tim sent him to stand guard over me until he returned, to make sure no one else took advantage of my body? If he had, he had made a mistake.

Philip's hand felt my breasts through the dress. Perhaps it was expecting too much for the young man not to be tempted after what he had seen, and what he suspected Tim had done.

The hand moved lower, down to my knee, and began to slide up my leg, taking the skirt with it.

'So beautiful,' Philip said. 'So beautiful.'

His hand crossed onto my flesh and he groaned and used both hands to pull my skirt up and expose me completely.

'Ooh, Chloe.' He pushed a finger in between the swollen lips of my vagina. 'They've all done it to you, haven't they?'

His tongue began to lick my leg, following the skin alongside the arrow of the suspender strap, and two fingers and then three went inside me.

I had remained still while three young men had thrust upon me but now I could not help my hips moving against his hand.

He stopped what he was doing immediately, his fingers motionless inside me, and I moaned and snorted softly as if in sleep and in the midst of a deep dream.

'You like it, don't you?' he said, and resumed using his fingers.

I again moved my hips gently against them and this time he did not stop for quite a while. When he did, I heard him standing up and unfastening his clothing. I would never have thought he would have had the nerve, but shy Philip was to be my fourth conquest.

He climbed on the bed and parted my legs, rubbing the juices that he found there into my skin and into my vagina. His fingers took their time at locating the entrance, and when he moved closer, he guided his penis inside at the first attempt.

I moaned sleepily and raised my hips against him and he lay upon me, his weight slight in comparison with the other three, but his penis a respectable size and solidity. He exhaled as if he had been punctured. He did not attempt to move his penis straight away but wisely allowed it to adjust to the heat and myriad sensations that surrounded it.

After a while, he shifted his weight and began to move it in and out, taking his time with the rhythm so as not to go too fast and precipitate his orgasm before he had taken his full measure of pleasure. He seemed oblivious to the possibility of someone walking in or of me waking up, oblivious to anything but my body and what he was doing to it.

His rhythm was easing my frustrations and I could not stop another groan escaping from my lips. The fact that he had elicited such a response from me made him thrust with more determination and purpose, as if attempting to push more moans from my throat with the depth to which he plunged his shaft.

I rewarded him with another moan and by opening my legs even wider to allow him to push deeper. He gasped and his rhythm became faster and went out of control.

'Oh Chloe,' he whispered, and he came inside me, and I twisted my hips and caused my own orgasm, my vagina clamping around his penis to drain it.

I disguised the tremors of my body and swallowed the noises that wanted to escape my lips and I am sure he did not suspect I had taken my pleasure from him, as he had taken his pleasure from me.

And then he, too, climbed off the bed, rearranged my limbs and dress so that it looked as if I had been sleeping undisturbed, fastened his clothes and left.

Tim returned thirty minutes later when I was in the bathroom. When I eventually emerged, I told him I had drunk too much and upon awakening had felt a strange tiredness and that my thighs had been aching. I told him I had simply climbed into the shower fully dressed and disrobed beneath the hot water in an attempt to sober up and ease the aches.

I now wore one of uncle's silk dressing gowns, my make-up washed from my face, my hair sleek to my head with the water. Tim wanted to touch me again, as he had earlier without my permission, but I pushed him away playfully and told him to behave.

When uncle returned after midnight, the party broke up and the revellers drifted away. Richard and John had left early and I had not seen them since emerging after my shower, and Tim said nothing about finding me stained with the sex juices of other men in deshabille on the bed.

Perhaps he did not know how to tell me, perhaps he was overcome by his own guilt, by the shame of giving in to his dark desires. When I kissed Tim goodnight, I also kissed goodbye to our casual relationship.

Philip went with him, looking back with piercing eyes to capture and keep every detail of the night in his memory.

Uncle closed the front door and put his arm around me.

'Enjoy yourself?'

'Sort of.' I snuggled against him. 'But I think the evening may just be getting interesting. Did you have a camera in your room?'

'But of course.'

'Then let's play the film back. I think you might find it interesting.'

We both found it interesting and arousing and I finally received total satisfaction.

13

The day was hot and the lack of wind made the evening sultry. Kate prepared a dinner of chicken and salad and put white wine to cool in the refrigerator.

She had showered but had not bothered with make-up; she wore a silk shirt that buttoned down the front and which came to her mid-thighs.

When Chloe returned she was sticky with perspiration and tense with the hectic business of the day. She threw her clothes off and took a shower and when she came back into the room, her hair was wet and slicked back and she wore a silk robe.

Kate smiled because the way she looked reminded her of the latest chapter of Chloe's story she had read earlier that day.

They ate on the patio, looking down at the river, above the noise and pollution.

Chloe said, 'I could get used to this.'

'To what?'

'Being looked after. Coming home to a friend.' She laughed. 'It's almost like being married.'

As the evening cooled, they cleared the table and went inside. They sat together on the thick rugs on the floor, content to be close without actually touching. That would come later.

Kate said, 'What you said, about coming home to a friend, was nice. It may sound sad, but you're only the second friend I've ever had.'

'It's not sad. You're selective. I'm wary of people who say they have lots of friends. They might have lots of acquaintances, but friendship is something else.'

'No. It is sad. I never had the opportunity to make friends.'

'Who's the other friend?'

'Gina. The girl at school.'

'Were you very fond of her?'

'Yes.'

'Were you lovers?'

'Yes, although we didn't know enough to make love the way you have taught me.'

'Tell me about her.'

Kate smiled as she remembered, and lay back, her head resting on a cushion.

'Gina had long auburn hair; it hung in ringlets like a Pre-Raphaelite Madonna. Her eyes were large and dark and always seemed to be half closed. She had a smile that was slow and knowing and a body that was slim and curving. We shared a room at school.

'Relationships between girls, I mean physical relationships, were inevitable at boarding school. The teachers were supposed to discourage it but they could never

138

stop it. Some of the teachers were themselves lesbian.

'I moved into the room with Gina when I was sixteen. Until then, I had been in a dormitory where the opportunities for relationships were less and the dangers of getting caught were greater. I had avoided any involvement.

'At first we didn't touch, but we watched each other. We confessed this afterwards. If I were in bed first, I would watch while Gina undressed. Often, she would not look towards me when she took off her clothes, so I could watch without embarrassment. At other times, I would undress and hope she was watching me.

'We both wanted to become involved with each other, but we did not know how to start and we both feared rejection. It would have been very embarrassing if one of us had made a sexual advance only to be turned down.

'It got to the point where my insides would churn with desire. You know, those nervous, flickering feelings in your stomach? And if I were under the covers, I would touch myself while I watched her walk around the room, wearing only white panties; imagining her slim body under the covers with mine, her small breasts pushing against mine.

'I used to touch myself until I was excited, but I never went all the way to orgasm. At that time, I didn't know what it meant to have an orgasm or how to achieve one.

'One hot evening, when it was still light outside, I had undressed first and lay on my bed above the covers, wearing only my panties. I was pretending to read a book.

'Gina began to remove her clothes slowly, almost as if she were attempting seduction, which she was. Her body glowed in the soft light that came through the window and I watched.

'She lowered her skirt and stepped out of it; her legs long, slim and tanned. The curves of her bottom were hidden beneath the white blouse and I held my breath as she unbuttoned it. Finally, she removed it, letting it slide down her back and holding it, for a few tantalising seconds, across her buttocks, before she discarded it.

'Her body was beautiful. So young, so graceful. She stood with her back towards me, her legs apart, and reached behind her to unclip her brassiere. Between her legs, I could see pubic hairs that had escaped the white cotton panties.

'She removed the bra and threw it across the room, showing me her jiggling breasts in profile. They were small, high and pert; the nipples were hard and erect.

'Gina now wore only white knee socks and panties. She looked towards me, as if only just aware of my presence, and caught me looking at her. She smiled and came and sat on the edge of the bed. There was a tension between us, an expectancy that something was going to happen.

'She asked about the book I was reading. She asked jokingly if it was full of sex and debauchery, and I went along with the suggestion, and said that it was. She asked me to show her and I held the book away and she reached for it and suddenly she was lying on top of me and we were fighting for the book.

'And then we weren't fighting any more. All I was aware of was the feel of her body upon mine, of her breasts pushing against mine as I had so often imagined, of her open thighs that entwined mine, and of the rising excitement between my legs.

'I let the book drop to the floor and touched her hair. Her face was above me, her mouth open. Her breathing was ragged, even though the pretend fight had not been severe or lengthy. Our eyes met and we knew. I felt myself melting into her and I licked my lips. She lowered her head and we kissed.'

Chloe had moved closer to Kate and her fingers unfastened the buttons of the shirt and her hand slipped inside and caressed Kate's breasts.

'That first kiss was exquisite. It was tentative and soft. It was a kiss with which we were exploring our emotions as well as our mouths. We sensed we felt the same way and the kiss became more urgent, more lascivious, and our mouths spread saliva across our faces, our tongues licked teeth and gums.

'The kiss ended and Gina raised her head, her mouth still open, her eyes now dazed. We looked at each other. I was stunned by the inner turmoil caused by her kiss and her body. It might have ended there, in embarrassment, but I didn't want it to. I ran my hand down her back and followed the curve of her spine, all the way to her bottom. My fingers slipped beneath the panties and I slid my palm around the softness of a buttock.

'Now there was no going back. This was no longer a

game and something inside of me had forced me to declare my intentions. Gina responded by pushing herself against me. Her legs were open, her vagina was against my thigh, and she pushed it against me and made a soft noise of pleasure in her throat.

'My hand had been gentle and caressing but now it became demanding. I gripped her buttock and pulled her even harder against me and she lowered her head and we kissed again and she thrust her vagina against me, again and again. I reached down with my other hand and now held both her buttocks and helped and encouraged her rhythm as our mouths made love.

'It was all new to me, but it seemed so natural that she should relieve the itch between her legs by rubbing herself upon me. And then she came.

'Gina raised herself and stared wide-eyed into my face. Her vagina was hot and clamped against my thigh and she shuddered as if in a fit. Groans came from her mouth and her eyes flickered and shut and, at last, she fell back upon me.

'I had never experienced an orgasm and I had never seen anyone have one before and I was panic-stricken at what had happened. I kept asking her if she was all right and she nodded and kissed my neck and slid from my body. She lay alongside me, a leg still across me, and she held one of my breasts.

'She said she had come and I immediately felt relief and wonder. I had heard other girls talk about orgasms and coming but what they actually meant had been a mystery to me. Gina said she had been taught how to make herself come by an older girl the previous term and had been wanting to come on me ever since we had moved into the room together. Now, she said, it was my turn to come.

'Gina raised her hips from the bed and removed her panties. She said it was best without them and pushed the waistband of my panties down. I took mine off reluctantly, because I was confused and excited, and also worried in case I couldn't achieve an orgasm.

'She touched my breasts and enticed me to lie on my side and touch her. I thought her breasts were beautiful because they were small and I rolled them, one after the other, in my palm. She pulled my head down to her face and we kissed again and clumsiness and reservations disappeared.

'I straddled one of her thighs with my open legs; I lay on top of her, my breasts pushing against her breasts, our mouths wide and wet and clamped together, our tongues fighting and delving.

'The feelings that surged within me were overpowering and felt so right, so natural. Gina's hands moved down my back and onto my bottom and I pushed my vagina against the hardness of her thigh and released a thousand explosions of sensation.

'Her hands guided my movements, her thigh twisted into just the right position and my vagina opened and became wet and I moaned into her mouth as our tongues wrestled lazily.

'This was the sensation I had had when I had touched myself without knowing what I was doing, and now I had gone past that point where, before, I had always turned back.

'With Gina's hands and body and mouth enveloping me, there was no turning back this time, and I thrust against her and pushed the sensations higher and higher, until my head and body and my whole being seemed to explode and I rode into my first orgasm.'

Chloe pushed the shirt from Kate's shoulder and kissed her neck. She slid down to lie alongside her and gently rubbed herself against her thigh.

'Was it good?'

'It was shattering. Marvellous. After that, I would bring myself off every night. Often with Gina, but also by myself. Gina enjoyed it when I pushed my fingers inside her and she could orgasm that way, but I never could if she did it to me. I would come by using my fingers on myself, or by rubbing myself against her.

'I also enjoyed kissing her, but as we became more familiar with each other's bodies, somehow, we stopped kissing and concentrated on rubbing or using fingers.

'After the incident with the dog, I wondered what it would be like to be licked between my legs, and I wondered if Gina would like to be licked there, but I never had the nerve to suggest that we do it.'

Chloe said, 'In your fantasy, you told me about the groundsman. Did he exist?'

'Yes, but not in the way I told you.'

'Tell me about him.'

'Gina and I went to the secluded place in the woods. That really did exist. We removed our panties and we touched each other and Gina came on my fingers. In our room, we had to be quiet and discreet but outside, she liked to let her feelings overflow and she made a lot of noise.

'The groundsman had been watching us from the undergrowth and after she came, he stepped out into the clearing. Gina saw him first, scrambled to her feet and ran away. By the time I realised why, it was too late to run.

'I was lying in the grass, too frightened to move. My blouse was open and my bra unfastened and my skirt was around my thighs.

'The groundsman was not the man in my fantasy. This man was about sixty. He was small and his belly was fat. He had a thick moustache and a balding head. He was dirty and he was not well built.

'This man had no dog with which to frighten me, but he had a mean look and a spiteful nature. None of the girls at the school liked him; we suspected him of spying on us at games or in the changing rooms.

'He said, "You'll be in trouble if I tell."

'And all the time, his eyes were moving over my body, and I knew what he wanted: he wanted me.

'Watching Gina and me touching each other had excited him and I could see his desire in his eyes, in the heaviness of his features, in the way he breathed through his mouth and licked his lips nervously.

'And yet, he wanted me to make the first move, to provide him with the opening to make a bargain, to offer my body for his silence.

'"Please don't tell," I said.

'"Why shouldn't I?"

'"Please," I said, knowing exactly what he wanted to hear. "Please. I'll do anything."

'It was strange, because I knew that was what he wanted me to say and because I wanted to say it. My senses had first been excited by Gina. The knowledge that someone had been watching us aroused me further. The fear of being exposed before the whole school for an elicit sexual liaison added to it. Also, I was consumed by a burning teenage curiosity about sex.

'This was a poor specimen of a man, but the situation was still highly exciting and frightening. This man did not excite me, but the thought of being in the power of any man did.

'He stepped closer and I could smell him. It was a smell like putrid sex, as if he had not washed his private parts for weeks, as if he had spilled his seed a hundred times inside his clothes and never changed.

'"Take off your blouse," he said.

'I did, more frightened now that I had allowed our discovery to develop into something else. I put the blouse on the grass next to me and, as my bra was hanging loosely from my shoulders, I removed that as well.

'He stared and gulped and licked his lips some more and fumbled with the belt of his trousers. He unfastened it and put his hand inside. From his movements I could see he was masturbating.

'Then he knelt by my side and his smell was revolting and yet I welcomed it because it added to my degradation and punishment. He groped my breasts, harshly and without regard to me, pulling and squeezing the flesh, rubbing my nipples between his thumb and fingers so roughly that he made me cry out.

'"Lie on your front," he said suddenly, as if he had just made up his mind about what he was going to do.

'I lay down on the soft grass and rolled onto my stomach and immediately he pulled my skirt up to my waist, revealing the nakedness of my bottom. His hands gripped my flesh again, as rough as before, kneading it with fingers that dug into my buttocks. Then I heard the rustling of clothes and, a moment later, he rolled on top of me.

'His smell was all around me and I buried my face in the grass. His hands pushed beneath me to hold my breasts and, in the channel between my buttocks, I felt his manliness, hard and hot and urgent.

'He rubbed it against the softness of my flesh and I felt it getting wetter, creating dampness there in my secret crease. And then he moved slightly and pushed again and it went between my legs and his wetness rubbed against the wetness of my vagina and I bit the grass to stop myself from moaning.

'The sensation for him was too much and he moved again, replacing his prick between my buttocks. He removed his hands from my breasts to grip the softness of my bottom and push it closer around his hardness.

'His movements became shorter and quicker, his thrusts more and more urgent, and then his upper body arched away from me and he came. He made strange, strangulated noises and I felt hot wetness splash across my skin. He stayed above me, holding his upper body away from mine on straightened arms, for a few seconds more, and then rolled away.

'He fastened his trousers quickly, suddenly in a hurry, and got to his feet. He began to walk away, as if someone might catch him in this secluded place, and hesitated at the edge of the clearing.

'"I won't tell anybody," he said, "but don't do it again."

'His face was red and he could not look me in the eye and then he turned and went. I remained lying on my stomach and wondered about what had happened. I had not been raped and I had not been required to carry out an unnatural act. My contribution had been to lie face down in the grass while he had jerked himself off against my bottom.

'I reached behind me and touched his sperm. It felt like glue and its odour was not unpleasant: a purer version of his filthy smell. I licked a small amount from my fingers but it did not taste of anything.

'The incident had been brief. The way in which it had occurred had been more exciting than what had actually happened. While the man had been doing it to me, I had felt disappointment, cheated, if you like, at not being able to see his penis.

'I was also unsatisfied sexually. Both Gina and the man had gained their satisfaction, and now they had gone and I was still there, alone and aroused.

'I wiped the fingers of my right hand clean of his juices

and put my fingers between my legs and closed my eyes and imagined a groundsman bigger and stronger and more masculine than the grubby little man of reality. My fingers worked well and it did not take long, and I came, alone in the soft grass.

'Gina and I never went back to the clearing in the woods and we avoided going anywhere near the groundsman. He, for his part, avoided us, probably out of fear that we might tell about him.' She turned her head to smile at Chloe. 'And now you know all my secrets.'

Chloe touched Kate's face and they stared into each other's eyes.

'What wonderful innocence,' Chloe said. 'I wish I had been Gina; I wish I had shared your room and been the first to discover your body. I wish I had been there in the clearing and shared your grubby little man.'

Kate said, 'You've got me now. And all these memories have made me wet.' They kissed. 'Close your eyes and be Gina and we will make innocent love.'

14

DeVille telephoned the next day, to compliment Kate because of the favourable report he had received from Sir Robert. She took the call in bed, Chloe lying alongside her.

'He was very pleased,' DeVille said.

'Good. I liked him.'

'Your next commission will not be so ordinary, Kate. Are you ready for it?'

The board meeting had been ordinary?

'Of course, I'm ready.'

'I have two Japanese gentlemen who want to meet an English lady. Do you have any strong feelings about the Japanese?'

'Race or nationality are immaterial.'

'Good. The Japanese enjoy bondage and rape. It is something of a national hobby. Not that they indulge in it seriously, of course. Japan is a very cultured nation, but they like to practise their pastime in a safe environment. Tonight, you are to be the victim. Do you have any problem with that?'

'No problem.'

'Very well. I'll send the clothes round and pick you up at six.'

She replaced the telephone and lay on her back and stared at the ceiling.

Chloe said, 'Well?'

'Rape and bondage,' she said. 'With two Japanese gentlemen.'

'Lucky you.'

Kate turned her head to look at her. The apprehension showed.

Chloe smiled gently. She said, 'Are you worried?'

'I don't know. I don't know what to expect.'

'Don't try to anticipate. Just let it happen. It's another fantasy and you get to play the lead role. But this time without guilt.'

Guilt.

It was an emotion that had always shadowed Kate's sexuality. But now, at last, she was beginning to understand the misconceptions upon which it had been built. The guilt was falling into a perspective that was receding fast towards the horizon.

DeVille's deal had started the process towards freedom but it was the conversations and friendship with Chloe, as well as the insights she was gaining from the girl's diary, that had helped her rationalise past fears and begin to gain control over her own sexual destiny.

Chloe helped Kate with her make-up and her hair, which she again piled on top of her head.

'Much more sophisticated,' Chloe said. 'Much more aristocratic.'

'If you make me look too aristocratic, it might turn them off.'

But then the clothes chosen by DeVille arrived by messenger. They were a costume for an uncompromisingly erotic production: a red silk cocktail dress, black underwear and black spike-heeled shoes.

No matter how aristocratic her hairstyle, the outfit was calculated to incite rape.

Kate was shocked at her reflection in the mirror when she donned the underwear.

The basque was delicate; the bra only a quarter cup so that her large breasts were projected from her body; and at the back it was cut high and curved to accentuate her buttocks and provide extra long suspender straps that cut across her flesh like whiplash marks.

The panties were a G-string, a triangle of black webbing at the front, another strap at the back, that added to the image of sexuality.

She didn't recognise herself. It was getting easier to assume a role.

Chloe said, 'You look sensational. Those spectacles are the perfect accessory: so wanton and yet so untouchable. I wish you didn't have to go out.'

Her hands stroked Kate's exposed flesh and the two girls embraced.

Kate said, 'There isn't time.'

Chloe said, 'There's always time.' She pushed Kate down onto the bed. 'Lie back,' she whispered. 'Let me.'

Kate lay on the bed, her arms outstretched, her feet in the spike-heeled shoes, resting on the floor. Chloe's hands parted her thighs and her head went between them, directly to the source of pleasure. She pulled aside the G string, opened her vagina and began to lick her clitoris.

Her juices began to run immediately. The unexpectedness of the situation had accelerated her arousal. Chloe's mouth was magical and enticing; her tongue expert and loving. Her fingers added to the pleasure, delving into her vagina and gently probing her anus.

Kate came with a groan of surprise and delight.

Her friend got to her feet, licking her lips.

'I enjoyed it, too,' she said. 'And you might need a little damp start for your Japanese friends. I'll wait up for you, and you can return the pleasure.'

Kate put on the dress, which was waisted. The bodice was thin and transparent and buttoned to the neck, the skirt was knee length and full. Even with it on, she felt undressed because it was so flimsy, because her body was so accessible.

DeVille arrived on time.

Kate said, 'Am I supposed to be demure in this?'

'You look as sexy as hell. Try to look haughty, English, inscrutable.'

'I thought the Japanese were supposed to be inscrutable?'

'The Japanese will be horny. Shout at them, treat them with disdain, but don't expect to be understood.

They speak no English. Then they'll take it from there.'

He slipped the same black cape around her shoulders that she had worn before, and escorted her to the car. The same chauffeur drove them to Belgravia.

She tried to hide her nerves by looking out of the window. It didn't help. People out there were leading ordinary lives, doing ordinary things. That was her alternative but she had had enough of being ordinary.

The car was driven through a set of high gates and stopped outside an impressive house. Four wide steps led up to a front door that was framed by doric pillars.

DeVille said, 'I'll collect you in four hours. Don't worry, you will not be hurt.' He smiled into her face. 'Simply well fucked.'

15

Kate got out of the car and climbed the steps. Before she could touch the bell, the door was opened by an elderly butler. She was obviously expected.

Behind her, she heard the car pull away, but she did not give DeVille the satisfaction of looking round. She walked into the house.

The man led her through a hall, along a corridor and down a winding staircase. He opened another door and stood back to allow her to pass.

He said, 'Please help yourself to a drink, madam.'

Then he left and closed the door and she was alone in a large room with no windows. She guessed the room was underground. There was a bar in one corner, low couches and a pile of large cushions on the thick carpet, and heavy beams across the ceiling from which hung chains and straps.

The decor was in reds and blacks. It looked like a romper room from hell and Kate's nerves began to fray.

She saw the cameras positioned high on the walls and she composed herself. She had to be haughty, she had to play the game. With a sweep of the hand, she removed the cape and threw it carelessly across a chair.

Full length mirrors were fixed to two walls and she practised her gaze in them and speculated on it being two-way glass. Perhaps the Japanese gentlemen were standing behind the mirrors, staring back at her.

She licked a hint of lipstick from her teeth with the tip of her tongue and felt herself slipping into character.

For good measure, she turned her ankle and studied her stocking and then slowly slid her hands up her leg to smooth away a non-existent wrinkle, taking the hem up above the lace top to show an inch or two of white flesh. She adjusted a suspender strap and let the dress drop back into place.

It was a relief to turn away from the mirror and go to the bar. Had that really been her being so deliberately provocative? She poured herself a large vodka and tonic and added ice from a silver bucket and took a long pull at the drink.

Music started playing from concealed speakers; oriental music whose rhythms she had difficulty following. She finished the drink and poured another. It was helping her submerge herself deeper into the role.

The door opened and the two Japanese gentlemen entered. They were not, as she had expected, small men. One was of medium height; the other tall and heavily built. They wore kimonos and wooden sandals.

Kate took another drink before placing the glass on the bar.

They crossed the room towards her and stopped to assess her. They spoke to each other in Japanese, obviously discussing her merits.

'I have been brought here against my will,' she said. 'I demand that you send for my chauffeur and allow me to leave at once.'

One smiled at her words and said something else, that caused his companion to also smile.

'Perhaps you do not understand what I am saying,' she said, articulating as clearly as possible, making her voice as English as possible. 'Perhaps you should send for your butler and I will explain the situation to him.'

The tall one spoke to her, but still in Japanese. The manner in which he spoke suggested the prelude to their performance.

Kate blinked at them, wide-eyed behind the spectacles, and began to walk past them towards the door.

Her arm was grabbed by the tall one who pulled her back with some force, causing a strand of her hair to be dislodged.

'How dare you!' she said.

He reached out with his other hand, grasped the neck of the dress, and ripped it open to the waist, the buttons bursting from their stitches like shrapnel.

Kate was aware of her breasts, heaving because of the action and exertion, and hardly contained in the quarter cups of the flimsy basque.

The man spoke again in Japanese and licked his lips. There was no mistaking his intention.

She pulled free and backed to the bar and the man

159

followed. Her drink was where she had left it, and she picked it up and threw the contents at him.

His face darkened and his eyes glinted at what he was going to do, and she hoped she was not playing the game too well.

'Please, leave me alone,' she said. 'Don't touch me.'

He grabbed her arm again and she tensed and he slowly raised his other hand and removed her spectacles. The action made him laugh for some reason, and he placed them carefully on the top of the bar before, abruptly, hurling her towards a couch.

Kate fell onto it and her skirt flew up, exposing the tops of her stockings. She pushed it down to cover herself and stared wide-eyed and unclearly at them, and watched as they opened the kimonos and dropped them on the floor.

They were both big men. Even the one she had thought of as being of medium height was well built. And they had big erections.

'No!' she said. 'No, don't!'

They moved leisurely and in conjunction with each other, as if they had practised the moves. The large one came directly at her and, as she raised her hands to fend him off, he grasped her wrists and pushed them above her head. He sat astride her on the couch, holding her down with his bulk, his hairless chest against her face.

His body was oiled and she tried to hold herself away, to stop her breasts from coming into contact with his naked flesh, conscious of his weight and the hardness of his penis that pressed against her stomach.

The second man fastened her wrists in soft leather handcuffs and they pulled her into the middle of the room below a beam from which hung a chain. Her hands were hooked above her head onto the chain.

Kate was helpless and at their mercy. But what could she suffer apart from sex?

One of the men stepped behind her and unfastened her hair so that it tumbled around her shoulders. He covered her eyes with a blindfold.

The sensation of helplessness was increased by one hundred per cent. She had been deprived of sight and mobility and she began to panic, and struggled against the handcuffs and the chain, and heard the men laugh.

They were enjoying the game and she was the game. There would be no enjoyment without her. It was her body that was making them breathe so heavily, making their laughter so brittle with desire.

She was aware of her breasts, further accentuated by the position of her arms, heaving in the basque; she felt the sweat of fear and excitement at her armpits and on her back. She felt an itch between her legs and pulled her wrists in the handcuffs to confirm the confinement and spice her growing anticipation with a touch of pain.

Hands felt her breasts, with firmness but without brutality, and her skirt was raised from behind and other hands cupped her buttocks. The men had stopped talking now, their throats too dry for words, they were now only interested in exploring her body.

Behind her, the man moved closer and his penis

pushed against her softness and she attempted to move away, but her hips came up against the hardness of his accomplice.

They moved from her, briefly, and the dress was ripped away completely, shards of the material digging into her waist and making her cry out with welcome pain. A finger gripped the G-string and ripped that off, too, and this time the fleeting pain dug deliciously into her vagina.

Kate was now hanging from the hook, blindfolded, her voluptuous white body clad only in the basque and stockings. Her thoughts were jumbled, her memories confused. She felt she was in danger of losing her identity.

The hands roamed her body, taking their pleasure, pulling her flesh, groping and feeling. Her breasts were sucked and fingers delved between her legs. Then her upper body appeared to be abandoned, and she felt the breath of both men as they approached her vagina and buttocks.

Two mouths now licked and sucked, and fingers parted flesh. Tongues probed both her vagina and anus and her mind felt ready to implode. Instead, she orgasmed, amazed to hear the echo of her own scream as she partially recovered.

A penis now pushed at her vagina and hands lifted her thighs to enable it to slide in. She was off the ground, the man holding her on his hips as she hung from the chain, his penis deep and effective. Her gasps were ragged but they sharpened when a finger went into her anus, lubricating it with grease.

'No,' she said. 'No.'

The word was not a refusal but a suspension of belief. She had even forgotten her name; she was simply a sensation.

A penis followed the finger, as she had known it would, and as it pushed, she bucked and pulled at the handcuffs for more pain in her wrists. She was already full with the prick in her vagina, and her mind said there was no more room, but the second prick was persistent and gained an inch and she yelled and wanted more and pushed down against it, and it went inside.

She had no identity. She was simply She. She was Sex, and She loved it.

Her eyes were closed behind the blindfold, her mouth open, each breath a wail, and through the totality of their locked bodies, she felt orgasm approaching, not necessarily her orgasm, for she was no longer a separate entity, but one that belonged to them all.

She started coming and did not know when she stopped, as both her partners also came, the twin spears within her threatening to burst her membranes, as they spurted and shook.

Kate became aware of herself again only when the two men had slipped from her body and she hung slackly from the chain. Her legs no longer supported her weight.

Somebody held her and she was lifted from the hook and laid upon a couch. A tongue licked gently at her clitoris and she spasmed with pleasure. The handcuffs were removed, her hands put behind her back, and the handcuffs replaced. She lay on her back, her breasts jutting forward, her legs carelessly spread.

Her blindfold was unfastened and she blinked at the intrusion of a sense she had learned to be without. The two men were still naked, their pricks now limp between their legs. One held up what appeared to be two ping pong balls on a string, opened her legs and inserted them into her vagina.

They were heavier than ping pong balls and the feelings they aroused were peculiar. Kate flexed herself gently and they moved inside her and made her gasp.

The larger of the men pressed a bell on the bar and, a few seconds later, the door opened and the butler entered carrying a silver tray. He placed it on a low table and began to leave the room, without once looking at Kate. She tried to change position to watch him go and the balls moved and she groaned again, and began to enjoy their sensation.

She wondered how long she had been here and what else would happen to her and was filled with wonder at feeling so free, despite her hands being tied behind her.

Her captors opened champagne from the bar and drank and ate raw fish and ignored her as she lay, available and beautiful, squirming gently against the pleasure of the balls.

When they had finished eating and drinking, the large one stood in front of her and stroked his penis back into life. He moved closer and moved it across her face, and she tried to capture it with her open mouth, and he laughed.

He positioned a cushion on the floor and they moved her so that she knelt before it. The large man sat on the cushion, his back resting against the couch, and he pulled her head down onto his penis. She took it in her mouth and sucked, and the other man knelt close behind her, removed the balls, and replaced them with his penis.

The men remained motionless but rocked her, so that her mouth sucked as she went down and her vagina sucked as she was raised up. Kate found it an uncomfortable position but the men enjoyed it for a considerable time, taking turns at each end.

At last, they unfastened her wrists and lay her on the floor. They spread-eagled her, and the large man lowered his bulk upon her, and began to fuck her with slow deliberate strokes.

His partner sat alongside them and held up a long silk scarf for her inspection. He tied knots along the length of the scarf, tight knots so that when he had finished it looked like a thin silken rope.

The man on top of her rolled over, taking her with him, so that she now straddled his bulk, his penis still deep inside her. Behind her, the other man parted her buttocks and she tensed for another double assault, but it was not to be. Instead, he inserted the silk scarf, knot by knot, into her anus. It was a strange but not an unpleasant experience.

She remained on top but the large man changed his

rhythm, pushing harder, digging deeper, pulling her thighs wider and she responded. He was getting close to orgasm and she did not want to be left behind and worked her hips to bring herself closer.

Kate was on the brink of coming, small yelps in her throat announcing the imminence of the occurrence, and the Japanese gamesman timed his own orgasm to hers, burying himself inside her.

As she yelled, he pulled from her body the silken rope as if it were a ripcord of pleasure, each knot producing a sharp burst of sensation. Her yell became a scream.

This time she passed out.

When she regained consciousness, she was lying face down upon the couch, and the smaller Japanese was taking her from behind. Her presence was not required and so she let her mind slip away while he used her for a long time before he came.

The men drank more champagne and, this time, offered her some, too. She gulped it greedily, and they poured her more, and the bubbles added to the sense of unreality.

They continued to drink and to use her, periodically requiring her mouth or vagina or breasts or buttocks, and she was adrift on a sea of alcohol and total sex.

She was abandoned briefly, while the men fetched a new device that was shaped like a trestle. It was padded on top and hanging below it was a curved piece of gnarled but polished rubber, like the handle of an inverted walking stick.

They bent her over the device, her stomach resting

on the padding. Her ankles were strapped to the legs of the trestle and her wrists were strapped to the legs on the other side. She was bent forward, rather than bent double, and totally disorientated.

She moved her hips to make her position more comfortable and discovered that the curved piece of polished rubber fitted between the lips of her vagina. It was an irritation, for she felt her body was no longer capable of reacting to any further sensations.

But then the smaller of the men produced a cat o' nine tails, and her attention became focused once more.

He stroked its soft leather thongs across her buttocks and her flesh quivered and her throat went dry. She moved her hips to escape its attention and the rubber protrusion rolled against her clitoris.

The thongs were lazily twitched over her exposed nakedness and the tips brought life back into her deadened senses. She rolled her hips and pushed her clitoris against the rubber device and yelled with delight and pain. The whip cracked and speckles of fire burst across her bottom and she rubbed against the rubber prick and cried out.

It cracked again and the fire intensified, and again and again, and she screamed because she was ablaze and because her clitoris was taking her over the brink into yet another orgasm.

Before she had subsided, the bigger of the men was taking her from the rear, heaving and panting, his sweating oiled flesh a balm against the tenderness of her raw bottom. The whip cracked and she saw the smaller man still using it, but this time upon the shanks of his companion.

The blows made her lover yell and push his penis deeper still inside her, making her, in turn, push her clitoris against the rubber prick, bringing together her senses once more for another orgasm.

She passed out again.

Kate awoke briefly. She was no longer strapped to the tressle but was unfettered and lying on a couch, still in the basement room.

The Japanese had gone; they had apparently exhausted themselves and abandoned her. She, too, was exhausted, and drifted into a light sleep.

Later, she became aware she was being used again. She was lying face down upon the couch, more naked than naked in the black basque, stockings and spike-heeled shoes, and her body was being explored. But the touch of these hands was different to the ones of her recent lovers.

Was she dreaming?

Had she had such a surfeit of sex that she could no longer differentiate between reality and fantasy?

She remained in the same position and she maintained the regularity of her breathing until she could work out what was happening.

The hands that now roamed her flesh, feeling her buttocks, and sneaking beneath her body to caress her breasts, fluttered like the butterflies that invaded the pit of her stomach when she was aroused. They were gentle because they were feeble: they belonged to the butler.

That aged and respectable and very British retainer, who had met her at the door and shown her into this room of pain and pleasure, was groping her body.

Kate made no protest and gave no indication she was awake and aware of what was happening. She remembered Chloe's story and was content for the surreptitious fondlings to continue to a conclusion. It was, after all, another experience and another facet of erotic enjoyment.

Although she was too tired now to respond, the memory of being taken by an old man in her sleep would arouse her in the days ahead, particularly when she shared the memory with Chloe.

When she gave no indication of waking, the butler's hands became bolder. They opened her legs and probed between them. Kate was so wet and gaping from being so thoroughly used, that all four of his fingers slid inside her with ease, to slurp around in her juices.

She could hear him groaning to himself and hoped the excitement would not prove too much for his heart, and then she heard buttons being unfastened and a zip being opened.

Even though her senses had been dulled by total usage at the highest intensity, this scene was arousing her because it was, again, so unexpected and unlikely.

How old, she wondered, was the butler?

How old, she wondered, did men get before they

could no longer have an erection?

Perhaps the old man simply wanted to masturbate while he looked and touched and remembered his prime in another age.

But she was wrong. He approached closer still, and, with difficulty, knelt between her legs upon the couch. He lowered himself and she could suddenly feel his penis upon her bottom.

This was no shrivelled weapon of another age, it was huge and swollen, and Kate imagined that it contained the unused sperm of many years.

It was difficult, now, to remain immobile, but she knew she had to, she knew she could not break the spell. She stayed prone, her breathing regular, and felt him manoeuvre. He guided the penis between her legs, and then pushed slowly forward with great deliberation.

Her passage had been well used, but she still felt filled with the immensity of the butler's penis. She moaned, as if in sleep, and raised her bottom against it.

He held it in position for several seconds until he was convinced she would not awaken, and then he began a regular but short rhythm, gaining as much pleasure from flexing it inside her as he did from pushing it in and out.

When he came, he did so without warning, simply pushing deeper inside with a slow grind so that he flattened her buttocks, and leaving it there whilst it pulsed its sperm; his breath as dry as death upon her cheek.

The butler climbed from her back as carefully as he

had climbed upon it, and she let herself drift back into a semi-conscious state whilst he adjusted his clothing.

When she finally opened her eyes, it was at the insistence of his hand that was shaking her shoulder. Her throat was dry and her body ached. Once she moved, she could smell sex upon her like a rich perfume.

The butler was his bland, polite self.

He said, 'It's time to go, madam.'

It was an effort to sit up. Her head, and most other parts of her body, ached.

The butler handed her a glass of liquid that bubbled.

'What is it?'

'Lemonade, madam.'

She sipped it suspiciously and then drank it greedily. It was cold and tasted finer than the finest champagne.

The butler handed her the spectacles that had been placed upon the bar and she put them on, wondering how incongruous they looked now.

Five empty champagne bottles lay on the carpet, and a few pieces of raw fish remained on the silver tray.

Kate got shakily to her feet and the butler steadied her with a white-gloved hand. Beneath them, she knew, they would smell of her sex.

But now, the elderly retainer had reverted to character, and he kept his gaze discreetly lowered from her face. He stared, instead, at her buttocks and those whiplash suspender straps which he had been feeling so recently, and the real whiplash marks upon her bottom.

Her cloak was on the chair by the door where she had left it when she had entered light years before, and he picked it up and placed it about her shoulders to provide her with immediate modesty.

She climbed the stairs slowly, each step taking her closer to a bath and a bed, went down the corridor, and crossed the hall.

The butler opened the door and helped her down the steps to the waiting limousine that was driven by the chauffeur. The rear door was open and, in the glow of the interior light, she could see DeVille waiting in the far seat.

Kate paused, to regain some composure before facing his probing eyes.

'Thank you,' she said to the butler, smiling at him in such a way that she caused the mask of his face to slip.

Understanding flickered in his eyes; understanding that she had been aware of what he had done and yet was not objecting.

'You're welcome, madam. And thank you,' he said. 'Goodnight.'

'Yes, it has been, hasn't it.'

She got into the car and slumped back against the leather upholstery and the butler closed the door. DeVille looked at her and she smiled in return.

'Are you all right?' he said.

'I'm tired.'

'Any problems?'

'None. They were perfect gentlemen. In fact, they were perfect.'

16

Chloe brought her breakfast in bed the next morning: cornflakes, orange juice, toast and marmalade, fruit and a pot of tea.

Kate propped herself up on pillows.

'How marvellous,' she said. 'It's ages since I was so pampered.'

When she had finished, Chloe cleared the things away and sat beside her on the bed.

'Still aching?'

'Yes. How can having so much put into you take so much out of you?'

'Any regrets?'

'None. I think I needed this, regardless of what state my financial affairs are in. Perhaps, in a way, I owe my husband a vote of thanks for putting me in such a position.'

'It's only sex. There's no mystery.'

'But there was. I mean, to some people, sex remains a mystery all their lives. It was for me. I found pleasure in the company of Gina at school but she could never make me come. The only pleasure I gained from sex, I gave myself.

'I came to believe that there was something wrong with me, or that all those films and books about how sex was a great shared experience were all lies; all made and written by men. Sex was a male preserve and women were there to be used. I would not have minded that, but my mother's protection kept me unsullied and my husband failed to use me.'

Chloe said, 'Sex doesn't suit everybody. With men, yes, it probably does. My experience is that the male has an obsession with sex all his life. His prick says it all. It rears its ugly head, whether asked to or not, at the sight of any pretty woman. All men need is an opportunity. Women need a reason.'

'You mean, the sort of reason I have?'

'That is one reason. And there are a lot of women playing the game who basically do not like sex, but they do like the money.

'But in general, if a woman chooses someone with whom to go to bed, there has to be a better reason than that the man is available. She'll pick a partner because of his looks or brain or sense of humour, or because she has fallen in love. But a man is not so choosy. When he wants sex, all he is looking for is that magic three letter word: yes.'

Kate said, 'You sound cynical.'

'I don't mean to. After all, men can't help the way they are. They're different to women.' She smiled to ease the philosophy. 'That's what makes sex fun. But women are better equipped, emotionally and physically, to take it or leave it.'

'Do you enjoy it?'

'If I didn't enjoy it, I wouldn't do it.'

'Have you ever been in love?'

'I love uncle, in my own way, but I'm not in love with him. Up to now, I haven't been in love with anybody.' She shrugged. 'Maybe I never will be.'

Kate said, 'Don't you think DeVille might be the reason why? That he has influenced you too much, from such an early age? Maybe, if he hadn't assumed the role of your guardian, you would have met someone by now. Maybe you would have an ordinary life, a family.'

Chloe shook her head. 'I would not like an ordinary life. I was never an ordinary child. At school, I was one of those girls who were always sexually aware, more interested in men than ponies. The reason I didn't experiment more with boys was because I guessed that uncle would one day show me how. In that way, I suppose he was an influence: I was always interested in men rather than boys.

'But I certainly don't regret what I have done. I was shown a direction and was pleased to take it. Uncle never coerced me. He saved me from the boredom of an ordinary life.

'I often think that those happy couples who walk down the aisle together fall in love out of convenience rather than anything else. They mix in the same crowd, they pair off, and they follow tradition and set up home to share expenses and to have someone convenient to screw.

'That is not for me. That is not falling in love. When it happens to me, if it happens to me, it will be different.'

Kate said, 'Your uncle is using me. Don't you think he used you?'

Chloe took her hand.

'You have discovered already that it is a two-way thing. Uncle's greatest business assets are the beautiful women he can supply to extremely wealthy men. We are his assets. We are the business. Without us, he is nothing. You can turn the whole thing around and say we are using him.'

Talking so intimately with another woman was another part of Kate's education. Perhaps, when the two weeks were up, she would have had a surfeit of sex and would not be interested in it for a long time. But for the moment, it was good to be a first class passenger on an odyssey into the unknown.

As DeVille had said, for two weeks she did not need to think. All decisions would be taken for her.

Kate remained in bed and slept until lunchtime when Chloe brought her soup and a baguette still warm from the oven. She dropped a couple of magazines on the bed and gave her a kiss on the forehead before leaving for a modelling assignment.

After lunch, Kate soaked in the bath and felt the aches in her body easing. She walked back to the bed naked and pushed the magazines to one side. She would rather read Chloe's story.

176

17

Chloe wrote:

Uncle chose my clothes as usual: a white dress, white underwear. He didn't tell me where we were going but drove to a suburb thirty miles away. It was after nine-thirty in the evening when we got there.

The street lights were orange, the pavements wet from rain. The people we saw seemed to be heading from one bar to the next, heads down and scuttling like crabs to escape the weather.

We stopped in a quiet street outside an Asian restaurant. The rain stopped as we did, as if uncle had arranged it. Like he arranged everything. He came round and held the door while I got out and he led me into the restaurant. Only two tables were occupied but we hadn't gone there to eat.

The Pakistani manager, who had a heavy black moustache and wore a dinner suit, smiled at uncle and stared at me. He opened a door at the rear of the room and uncle ushered me forward.

The manager went first, up a steep flight of unlit stairs

to a landing. The carpet was worn, the wallpaper peeling. At the end of the landing, he opened another door and I heard Asian music and voices. The voices stopped. I hesitated but uncle's hand was in my back, an indication that I should enter.

Inside, three Pakistanis waited. They were middle aged; two wore suits, the other the loose cotton suit like pyjamas that is their traditional dress. One was thin with a sharp moustache, the other two were over-weight. The one in the cotton pyjamas had a beard that was dyed red with henna. They were sitting in old armchairs and on a settee and they were smoking cigarettes. The smoke from the tobacco hung in clouds in the stillness; it seemed as if they had stopped breath-ing.

The room was small and claustrophobic and the music from the cassette player made it crowded. An elec-tric fire threw out heat from the fireplace; two lamps provided light and a red silk scarf had been thrown over one to give the room a glow, as if to shroud what was to happen with mystery.

Behind me, the manager closed the door. Uncle switched off the tape recorder and moved me to the centre of the room, so that I faced the men. He took the lamp without the scarf from its table, removed the shade and placed it on the floor behind me so that the men could see the outline of my body through the dress.

Uncle said, 'Do they know the terms, Nasim?'

The manager said, 'They know, but they think it is expensive.'

Their eyes were fixed upon my body. I could feel their tension, smell their desire. One gulped, another licked his lips. They would pay whatever uncle told them to pay.

'If they wish, we can leave now.'

Uncle stood in front of the lamp and blocked the light that was providing the silhouette of my body, and they moved restlessly. The thin one spoke in Urdu to the manager.

'They ask you to explain again.'

Uncle moved out of the light and removed a cassette tape from his pocket.

'I will play this tape. It will cost five pounds for a dance that will last for the duration of one song. During that time, they can hold her as close as they like and touch her over her clothing.'

Nasim translated before uncle continued.

'For ten pounds, the dance will also last for the duration of one song. They can touch her as before, but they can also take out her breasts.'

The manager translated again and the thin one asked a question.

'He says what can they do with the breasts?'

'They can touch them, lick them, suck them.'

He provided the translation and the thin man nodded.

Uncle said, 'For twenty pounds, it is the same, the dance lasts as long as the song, but this time they can put their hands beneath her skirt and can touch her anywhere they please.'

Nasim told the three men in Urdu and then turned to uncle.

'What for thirty pounds?'

'Nothing.'

'Forty pounds?'

'Nothing.'

'Fifty? They pay no more than fifty.'

'For fifty pounds they can have one dance. They can take out her breasts, they can lift her skirts. While they do this, they can themselves be naked, and they can put their pricks upon her body but they cannot put them inside her.'

'They can spill their seed?'

'They can spill their seed anytime they like, but not inside her. It is also forbidden to kiss her on the mouth.'

Nasim spoke to the men again and they discussed it amongst themselves. The one with the beard shook his head and Nasim turned to uncle.

He said, 'They would like to hear her speak. They do not believe she is an English lady.'

Uncle smiled at me. 'Speak to them, Chloe. Let them know you are a lady.'

'What should I say?'

'Anything you like. They don't understand English, but they do understand an English accent.'

The three men were staring harder, as if they wanted confirmation that I was a flower of the empire.

'Good evening, gentlemen,' I said, aware of how correctly English was my voice. I could think of nothing appropriate and trivial with which to fill the void. Shakespeare rescued me.

'Shall I compare thee to a summer's day?
Thou art more lovely and more temperate:
Rough winds do shake the darling buds of May,
And summer's lease hath all too short a date . . .'

The thin man was convinced. He stood up and took a five-pound note from his pocket and held it out.

Uncle took the note from him, put the lamp back in its place, and removed the tape of Asian music from the cassette. He inserted the cassette he had displayed to them.

'You may begin,' he said, 'when the music begins.'

Nasim spoke and everyone, myself included, watched uncle press the play button on the cassette machine, and listened to the hiss of the tape.

The thin man stood before me. He was salivating and kept gulping to get rid of the excess moisture in his mouth. He stared into my face, his eyes glazed with lust. Yes, it's true, men's eyes do glaze with lust.

I kept my features composed and blank but I couldn't control my nerves and I, too, had to gulp and lick my lips. This dingy room above a restaurant was a lot different from the luxury we lived in.

The thin man shuddered at the sight of my tongue and then the music began. It was a Buddy Holly song; plaintive and slight. It would last no more than three minutes.

The man hesitated before putting his arms on my waist; I put mine on his shoulders, and swayed with the music. For a few seconds we remained apart and he gulped several times more and I could smell the spices on his breath. A man on the settee shouted encouragement and he moved closer and discovered I did not pull away.

He let out his breath and pushed slowly against me, and still I did not move away, but complied with the contract he had taken out with a five-pound note. I continued swaying to the music, my legs slightly apart, and felt his erection stiffen against my thigh.

His hands moved down over my buttocks and gripped the flesh, and he thrust his pelvis against my crotch, moving my legs apart with his knees. I looped my hands behind his neck and rested my head on his shoulder as he manoeuvred and pushed his prick between my legs. His breath came in shudders.

The music matched his movements and I swayed against his thrusts which were against my most sensitive parts and I felt the lips of my vagina part. His hands felt my thighs and, belatedly towards the end of the song, he palmed a breast aggressively, and then the music stopped.

Uncle switched off the cassette player.

'That's enough!'

It was an order that cut through the thin man's passion. I pushed him away. He stood before me, his composure ragged, the air rasping through his teeth. I could not help smiling sweetly at him. My body had brought him to this condition.

Another man in a suit paid five pounds and uncle pressed the switch on the cassette player. It was another

Buddy Holly song, the timing guaranteed.

My new partner was more forward, understanding the concept better after watching the first man. His hands brushed my breasts but did not linger when they confirmed they were relatively small. He went, instead, for my buttocks and thighs, feeling and groping and pulling me against his belly and the erection that filled his trousers.

I moved against it, opening my legs of my own accord, enjoying the feel of him shaking as I rubbed my crotch along the hardness.

The music stopped and uncle had to shout twice before he relinquished his grip on my bottom. He had been, I knew, extremely close to orgasm. He slumped back into his seat and the man in the cotton pyjamas, whose face now matched his red hair, got to his feet.

He took twenty-five pounds from a purse and spoke to the manager, who translated.

'He says, one dance for five pounds and one dance for twenty pounds.'

The music started again, and he put his hands on my hips, slid them down over my buttocks and pulled me against him. Because he wore only thin cotton, I could even feel the heat of his penis as it pushed against me.

Causing the men to become aroused had had its effect on me, too, and I pushed against him more willingly than I had done at the start and was rewarded by hearing him groan.

There was now little pretence at dancing, and we stood in the centre of the room and rubbed our bodies against each other. The tension was finely tuned and I was aware of the other three Asians, watching our every gyration.

The song ended and another began, and the man lifted my skirt and his hands slid up the backs of my legs, across the tops of my stockings, onto the flesh and upwards to push beneath the white nylon panties and cup my buttocks.

Around me, the other men were moving, going behind me and crouching to get a better look up my skirt. One of them shouted to the red haired man and he grunted and obliged them by raising my dress to my waist with one hand so they could have a clear view.

I was gratified by the gasps and pushed harder against the erection and, in his concentration, he let the skirt drop. He, too, seemed to be close to an orgasm when the music stopped.

The manager, Nasim, now took his turn and handed thirty-five pounds to uncle to pay for a natural progression through three dances.

Nasim smiled as the music started and took me in his arms. I put mine around his neck and pushed against him. The smell of the restaurant below was on his clothes, but there was another smell present, too, the smell of sex which had been provided by the first three men, and by myself.

He felt my buttocks leisurely whilst moving his penis against my crotch, tracing the suspender straps through the material of the dress, spreading his palm around my thigh and over the curves above.

I was turned on by the situation, particularly as it had not been explained to me in advance, and my stomach was molten with desire.

One song ended and another began and while we maintained the contact of our hips and thighs, I leaned away from him to allow him the freedom to unfasten the front of the dress all the way down to my waist.

Beneath it, I wore no brassiere and my breasts seemed to have swollen with the excitement and protruded high and firm, the rosebud nipples erect. He palmed them, felt both nipples with his thumbs, and dipped his head to suck one into his mouth. I moaned and moved harder against him.

The song changed for the last time and his hands slid confidently beneath my skirt, not bothering to raise it for the benefit of anyone else, eager only to find his own pleasure. One hand cupped my buttocks while the other went between the front of my legs and found the dampness at my groin.

He rubbed his erection against my thigh, holding me close with the hand that gouged into my bottom, sucked a breast and pushed the panties to one side to push a finger inside my vagina.

My head was tilted back and I was groaning in time to the music as well as miming copulation.

The song ended and left us both gasping.

In the silence, the loudest noise was the heavy breathing of the men. Only uncle appeared to be in control as he rewound the tape and waited for the next offer. I tried to calm myself by concentrating on rebuttoning the front of my dress, but my legs were shaking.

The three Asians who had danced with me first talked together while the manager, Nasim, leaned against the door and gazed with lustful appreciation at my young body. The talk became an argument until Nasim intervened and they fell silent to listen to him.

Nasim looked at uncle.

He said, 'They want the fifty-pound song, but they want conditions.'

'What conditions?'

'They want to do it in private.'

'Impossible. I have to be present to ensure they abide by the rules.'

'But these are important men in their community. It would be unseemly for them to disrobe together.'

'It has been unseemly for them to dance with my niece.'

'But this last thing, the spilling of their seed, is too much. They have dignity.'

'Nasim, their dignity is between their legs and very hard. If they want to use it, it will be on my terms. And I will not allow my niece to be alone with them.'

The manager translated what had been said so far, and placated them with a raised hand.

Turning back to uncle, he said, 'Okay. But one other request.'

'What is that?'

'That the young lady remove her dress before we start.' He shrugged his shoulders. 'It would save it from being stained if anything were spilled upon it.'

Uncle considered the proposition and nodded.

'All right. I agree to that.'

Nasim collected the money and paid it to uncle.

Uncle said, 'Remove your dress, Chloe.'

I unfastened the buttons at the bodice once more and pulled the dress over my head. Uncle took it from me and draped it over a stiff-backed chair.

The men had fallen silent again as they stared at me, now dressed only in white suspender belt, panties, stockings and high-heeled shoes. My breasts were still heaving from the recent encounters and the anticipation of this latest development.

Uncle said, 'Who is first?'

The thin man got to his feet and stepped forward.

'Remind him, Nasim. He stops when the music stops.'

Nasim spoke to the man in his own language, and he nodded his head impatiently and began to unfasten his trousers.

Uncle said, 'I will begin when he indicates he is ready.'

Nasim again translated and the man hesitated, holding his belt and open waistband in his hands, and looked at the others who were watching intently. I waited, legs apart, apparently impassive, but tense inside. The man looked at me, his eyes travelling down my body, and stepped forward.

Uncle switched on the music.

The man reached for my body and let go of his trousers, which dropped around his knees. His hands pawed at my breasts and went between my legs, and he whimpered when he felt the dampness at my crotch. He pushed down grey flannel underpants and pulled me against him.

As the music went inexorably on towards the end, he rubbed his penis frantically against my thigh and groped my buttocks. I felt sorry for him. I slipped my hand between us and took the end of his penis in my palm and squeezed gently and rhythmically. I was more concerned for his condition than my own and moaned softly in his ear to coax his orgasm.

It worked and he began to shudder, although he tried to stifle his groans, and his sperm splashed onto the insides of my thighs and over my hand. The music stopped and I stepped away and wiped my hand across my stomach.

The man appeared confused, slowly pulled up his trousers and backed away with them still unfastened.

So much for dignity, I thought.

That must have been the conclusion reached by the second man, for he removed his trousers and underpants completely, and stepped forward, fully dressed down to the waist and with his shoes and socks on. His legs were brown and thin below the belly and I suppressed a smile.

One smile, I thought, and that impressive piece of dignity between his legs would shrivel.

Instead, I put my hands on my hips and licked my lips.

He moved towards me and uncle started the music.

Unhampered by trousers, he pushed his penis

between my thighs and I rocked against it, glad of the harshness of his pubic hair which rubbed against my clitoris through the thin panties, glad of the hotness of his weapon against my ever dampening vagina.

He held my buttocks and we mimed flagrant copulation and I began to think he would miss out but he had been timing himself perfectly: he came in the same position, his juices soaking and staining my panties between the legs and on my bottom.

The man staggered away and picked up the clothes he had removed. He looked neither left nor right, but went to the door and left the room.

Uncle said, 'Next.'

It was the red-haired man in the pyjamas whose hotness I had enjoyed. He did not take his trousers off but went and stood behind me. I heard a rustle and looked backwards and saw that he had unfastened the cord of the loose trousers, and they had fallen around his ankles.

The music started and he took my hips and pulled me backwards. He wore no underpants and his erection slid between my thighs from behind, greased by the sperm of his predecessors, until my buttocks were hard against his groin.

It was another experience I could enjoy, and I arched backwards into him, and dropped one hand to touch the end of his prick. He squeezed the flesh of my bottom around his weapon, which throbbed and pulsated, and began to come well before the music was due to finish.

His thrusts of orgasm were wild and jabbed me most

sensitively and I cried out with him and almost came, too, but held back at the brink.

When he had finished, he pulled up the pyjama trousers and went straight towards the door, the thin man who had been first following him.

The manager, Nasim, was the only one left.

He stared at my stained knickers and body and took out his wallet.

'How much to fuck her?'

Uncle said, 'Not for sale.'

'I pay two hundred.'

'Not for sale.'

He licked his lips, never taking his eyes from my body, and opened his wallet.

'Okay. I pay five hundred pounds for fuck.'

'Nasim, you can offer me your restaurant and I will still refuse. You know the terms.'

Nasim took several deep breaths and I considered whether he might call upon the help of the waiters who were below serving curry to come upstairs and incapacitate uncle and hold me down while he had his fuck for free.

I licked my lips. It was a prospect I thought I might enjoy.

'Okay,' he said. He took another fifty pounds from his wallet and handed it to uncle. 'But I buy two songs.'

'Just tell me when you are ready.'

Nasim took off his jacket and his tie and I realised he was seriously intent on getting value for his money.

I watched while he stripped completely, even removing his shoes and socks.

He was a well-built man, the hair on his head and at his groin thick and dark and curly, his body a gleaming brown, sweat making it glisten. His chest was broad and his thighs powerful. Without the suit and the veneer of respectability, he was a tribal warrior from the North West Frontier.

His penis was erect; thick and long. It throbbed its own rhythm, lifting and weaving with lust.

Nasim placed an upright dining chair nearby and stepped close. We were inches apart and I stared into his eyes, my lips open, my breasts thrusting in search of contact.

'Ready,' he said.

The music started and Nasim pulled me on to him, his prick sliding between my legs and into the wet, his hands ranging down my back, his nails softly scratching and making me cry out, his fingers massaging my buttocks and pushing down my panties. His mouth was on my neck, licking and kissing, his tongue moved up from my jaw and slid into my ear.

I moaned and realised I was moving of my own volition, without direction or encouragement, doing my utmost to give him pleasure.

He pushed me down onto my knees and his hands cupped my breasts around his prick and he fucked the tunnel of flesh that he made. I dipped my head but remembered I could not use my mouth and instead I rubbed my face against it.

Nasim pulled me to my feet and I arched backwards over his left arm while he sucked my breasts and his right hand dipped into my panties, his fingers pushing through my wet bush and into my vagina. I curled against his hand and came, yelling and limp and useless and realised, dimly, that the music had stopped and was starting again.

He turned me and I rested my hands against the back of the chair as he pushed against me from behind. My panties had been pushed down around my thighs and I could not remember whether this was allowed or not, but I also didn't care, as his penis slithered between thighs that were now soaking with sperm and my own juices.

He held my hips and, spooned in behind me, he worked into a rhythm that pushed his weapon along the open lips of my vagina all the way to the button of my clitoris. When the rhythm was secure, his left hand moved over my body, tugging in my hair, kneading at my breasts, while his right dipped into the valley of my groin and his fingers pushed deep inside me.

I yelled and groaned and he licked and nibbled my neck and shoulders and his fingers went onto my clitoris and I came again, convulsively, and in my throes I felt his surge and his weapon discharged powerfully between my legs. I pushed a hand down to catch it and felt the hot liquid splash into my palm.

As he staggered backwards, and as the music stopped, I pushed his sperm deep inside me with my fingers.

Nasim flopped onto the couch and I remained holding

onto the chair with one hand.

Behind me, I heard uncle remove the tape and replace it with the one that had originally been playing. He switched on the player again and the Asian music crept delicately around the room.

Uncle walked up behind me and pulled up my panties, and helped me to put on my dress but I was unable to button it. He fastened the bodice for me, brushed my hair from my face and wiped the sweat from my forehead with his handkerchief.

I reached for it to wipe my hands but he withheld it. 'No. Wear the stains with pride, Chloe. You earned them, you enjoyed them. Later, I will enjoy them too.'

As we prepared to go, Nasim, still naked and sitting on the couch, said, 'Do we do this again?'

Uncle said, 'No, not again. I never repeat experiments. I hope you enjoyed it?'

Nasim shook his head. 'Enjoy? I would kill for her.' He laughed softly. 'Think yourself lucky I am a civilised man, Mr DeVille.' He stared deeply into my eyes. 'In my country, she would already be mine.'

We left, retracing our steps down the stairs and out through the restaurant. In the car, on the way back to Chelsea, he lowered the window and threw out into the night air the money he had taken from the men, the money I had earned.

He smiled at me. 'It wasn't for the money,' he said. 'It was for you. To give you enjoyment, to teach you restraint, to show you the power of sex and the pleasure of the journey.'

I looked at him but didn't fully understand.

He said, 'You came twice?'

'Yes.'

'And yet you were never penetrated. If you had been, if Nasim had had his way, the evening, the event, would be over. But he didn't and you still have desire between your legs. You want fucking, don't you, Chloe?'

'Yes.'

'You see, the night is just beginning and, when we get home, I will fuck you until dawn.'

18

It was three days before DeVille called round to the apartment, three days in which Kate rested and recuperated and bathed away the aches.

'Are you ready to earn some more money, Mrs Lewis?'

'Of course.'

'Then you have an appointment at the Dorchester this afternoon. Wear what you judge to be appropriate for the job. The man who has bought your services is an American. He is a millionaire but he has a problem: his son Bobby.

'Bobby is sixteen, very shy and a virgin. His father is worried that Bobby may be homosexual. He wants you to seduce his son, take his virginity and introduce him to the delights of the opposite sex.

'How you do it is your business. It may be simple, it may not. But if the father is convinced you have done a good job, he will pay well. I will collect you at two o'clock.'

Kate left her hair down and wore a simple blue cotton dress with a drop waist, white cotton panties and bra, white ankle socks and low heeled shoes. She wore minimal make-up. Her intention was to look as young as possible so as not to intimidate the young man.

DeVille accompanied her in the car to the Dorchester and up to a suite on the third floor.

Cyrus J Prentzel opened the door himself. He was a big, middle aged man who wore cowboy boots with his suit and carried a whisky glass in one hand.

'Come in, come in,' he said, and they entered a reception room.

DeVille said, 'This is Kate, Mr Prentzel. I'm sure she'll be satisfactory.'

Prentzel did not shake hands but stepped back to appraise Kate.

'She's pretty enough, I'll grant you, but she don't look red blooded enough to capture my boy's cherry.'

DeVille said, 'I have every confidence in her abilities.'

Prentzel said, 'How about you, little lady? You hot enough to fuck my boy?'

He said it as if to test her, to see if she was as innocent as she appeared.

Kate said, 'I'll fuck his brains out, Mr Prentzel. And yours, too, if you want.'

She stared at him with wide eyes behind the glasses, wondering where she had got the words from on the spur of the moment. But they seemed to have the desired effect. Prentzel nodded his approval.

'Okay, Kate. You got a shot at the title. The little shit's through there.' He nodded towards a door to his left. 'Bobby has his own set of rooms. Mine are over there.'

He nodded to a door on the right. 'If you want anything
– ropes, Spanish fly, or anything, just shout.'

'I will not need any help, Mr Prentzel. As long as we
are not disturbed.'

'I'll see to it. Take as long as you want. All day, all
night, all week. Just give me some good news when it's
over.'

'What have you told him about me?'

'What could I tell him? I hadn't met you.'

'Did you tell him you were going to pay a woman to
fuck him?'

'No. Christ, no. If I'd said that, the little shit would've
gone missing.'

'Then what did you tell him?'

'I said someone was coming to see him about his
problem. I used jargon to make it sound okay. You
know, I said it was a sex therapist who would talk
some sense into him.'

'Very subtle,' she said, and wondered what the millionaire used for brains.

Kate went to the door that led to the young man's
rooms and knocked but there was no reply.

'He's shy,' Prentzel shouted behind her, disgust
evident in his tone.

She opened a door and let herself in, closing it behind
her. It was dark, with the curtains still closed, but she
could make out that she was in a large and expen-
sively furnished sitting room.

'Bobby?' she said.

There was no reply.

197

Kate crossed the room slowly, checking the armchairs and settees, but they were empty. She left the curtains closed and entered a short corridor. On one side of it was a bathroom with a jacuzzi, on the other a small service kitchen where drinks or simple meals could be prepared.

The door at the end of the corridor was closed and she knocked on it and tried the handle. It opened.

She stepped inside and stopped. Bobby was on the bed wearing pyjamas and watching television. There were no lights on in the room and the curtains here were also closed. The only illumination was from the television screen which was showing an old black and white film.

'Bobby?' she said.

The boy ignored her.

She closed the door and walked hesitantly across the room until she reached the side of the bed, where she waited, holding her hands in front of her and playing with her fingers as if she were nervous.

'My name is Kate.'

Bobby wore glasses and was skinny. His features looked too big for his face, as if they were waiting for him to grow into them. His lips were big and fleshy and pouted. He didn't look at her, but continued to stare at the screen.

'Please go away,' he said.

'Oh?' She sounded hurt. 'Do I have to? Can't I stay a little while?'

'I'm watching a movie.'

'Can I watch it with you? I like movies.'

He shrugged.

'It's an old one. Bogey and Bacall. You wouldn't like it.'

'Oh, but I love them. Is it the one where she teaches him how to whistle?'

'Yes.' He sounded surprised that she knew. *'To Have and Have Not.'*

She stared at the screen and was aware of him looking at her.

'Look,' he said, 'I don't want to be rude, but I don't feel like talking and I don't have a problem.'

'That's okay.' She sat on the edge of the bed, still staring at the screen. 'I don't want to talk.' She looked at him briefly and smiled. 'And I don't have a problem either.'

Kate returned her attention to the television.

Bobby said, 'I don't need a therapist.'

'Neither do I.' She turned to look at him again. 'Why do you say that? Who says you need a therapist?'

Bobby looked confused. 'Look, who are you?'

'I told you, my name is Kate. My father does business with your father. They've gone out to a meeting and I've been left here until they get back. I hope you don't mind?'

'So you're not . . .?'

'Not who?'

'It doesn't matter.'

'I'm just a girl who keeps getting in the way of business. I spend a lot of time waiting around in hotel rooms.'

199

'How old are you?'

'How old are you?'

'I asked first.'

'You shouldn't ask a lady her age.' Kate attempted to blush and put her head on one side like a schoolgirl.

'I'm eighteen,' Bobby lied. 'Nearly nineteen.'

'I'm eighteen, too.'

In the darkened room and without make-up she was sure she could pass for being a teenager.

Bobby ran out of things to say and they watched television. After a while, Kate moved further onto the bed, kicking off her shoes and edging closer until she was lying alongside him, although not touching.

The film was on a video cassette and when it finished, he got off the bed and removed it from the machine. He knelt by the bottom of the bed and switched on a lamp while he put it back in its cover.

Kate sat up on the bed, her back against the pillows, her knees raised to give Bobby an innocent view up her skirt if he looked that way. He looked that way.

He immediately put his head down again and looked through a stack of videos that were on the floor.

'You want to watch another?'

'Sure. My father is going to be hours, yet.'

She tipped her head back on her shoulders to stare at the ceiling and to give him the opportunity to look up her skirt again without fear of being caught.

'What sort?'

His voice was cracked and she guessed he was looking. He didn't sound as if he were homosexual, just shy.

'Something scary, something grown-up. Adults only, that sort of thing.' She moved her head to look at him and he dropped his eyes to the cassettes. 'My father is over-protective, he never lets me out of his sight. It means I'm a bit retarded when it comes to, you know.' She shrugged and pulled a face. 'He still thinks I'm a little girl and he's worried somebody will seduce me. Chance would be a fine thing.'

Bobby picked up a cassette and read the sleeve for a moment.

'But he let you come in here with me?'

'Your father told him I would be safe with you.' She pulled another girlish face. 'I guess he meant you were a gentleman, or something.'

Bobby snorted.

'Or something.' He held up the video. 'You want an adults only? This is an adults only.'

'Okay.'

He put it in the machine and got back on the bed.

Kate said, 'Is it scary?'

'My father says it's educational.'

'Oh?'

On the screen, two men walking down a city street met a girl guide. The dialogue was German but the plot line was international. The three of them went to an apartment where the men began to kiss and fondle the girl. They removed most of her clothes and pushed down their trousers. The girl knelt down and took a penis in her mouth.

Kate began to cry and hid her face in her hands.

Bobby said, 'You said you wanted something for adults.'

She continued to cry and he used the remote control to switch off the video and television. The dark surrounded them.

'I'm sorry,' he said. 'I didn't mean to upset you. I thought that's what you meant.'

When she still didn't speak, he put an arm hesitantly onto her shoulder and she put her head into the crook of his neck. His arm went all the way round her shoulders and she cuddled against him.

'I'm sorry,' he said.

'It's all right. It's not your fault, it's mine. You're used to these things. You jet around the world and you've had lots of girlfriends. But I don't know anything. I'm so ashamed at not knowing.'

'It's not quite like that.'

'You're just trying to make me feel better. The video didn't shock you. You've done it all before. But I don't even know how to kiss properly.'

Kate looked up into his face. He seemed confused at being expected to play the role of the experienced man of the world to her unsophisticated girl. Life, it seemed to Kate, was a series of roles.

'Kiss me, Bobby. Show me how?'

She closed her eyes and pursed her lips and, after long seconds of hesitation, Bobby pushed his big, fleshy lips against hers and they kissed.

He was as inexperienced as she was supposed to be, but he had watched a lot of movies and used an open mouth and his lips seemed to be everywhere over her face.

When they broke, they were both breathless.

'Should I use my tongue, this time?' she asked.

'Yes,' he said. 'Use your tongue.'

They kissed again and she managed to contain his lips and pushed her tongue deep inside his mouth, enticing his tongue into her mouth in return. She could feel his excitement tremoring his body and it made her excited, too, to be leading him in the first steps of his sexual awakening.

Kate lay back on the bed and looked up at Bobby.

'Oh, Bobby, you kiss so good. Touch me. Make me feel like a woman.'

She removed her glasses and dropped them over the side of the bed before putting his hand on her breast; she groaned and twisted against it. He gripped it harder, squeezing it, kneeling up to use his other hand on her other breast.

Kate reached up to his neck and pulled him down on top of her to kiss him again, moving her legs to guide him between her thighs. She could feel his erection and pushed against it, causing him to grunt in surprised pleasure.

'Oh, Bobby, you feel so good.'

She raised her legs so that her skirt fell back and, almost inadvertently, pushed his right hand down below her waist. His palm came to rest on her naked thigh and she gasped and gripped his wrist.

'Oh, you've got me on fire. No one has touched me

there before.' He seemed inclined to remove his hand but she held it firmly in place. 'I can't stop you touching me, I want you to touch me, you're turning me on so much.'

She guided his hand higher along her thigh, beneath the skirt and under her bottom.

'Bobby,' she whispered. 'You can do anything to me. But be gentle, don't hurt me.'

'I won't hurt you,' he grunted.

His hand discovered the softness of her flesh, his erection pushed hard against her vagina.

They kissed some more and rolled about the bed, sometimes Kate on top, sometimes Bobby, and all the time he delved a little further and became a little bolder, groping the globes of her buttocks and the softness of her breasts, all the time encouraged by her squeals of fear and moans of delight.

Her dress slid from her shoulders almost of its own volition and she broke apart from him briefly to push it down and kick it off completely, as if frustrated by its restrictions. She removed her bra, as well, and knelt on the bed, dishevelled, her breasts swinging heavily in front of her.

Bobby lay on his back, the jacket of his pyjamas open.

Kate said, 'I'm sorry my breasts are so big and ugly.'

'They're not ugly,' he said, reaching up to hold them, his eyes wide in wonder. 'They're beautiful.'

She lay on top of him in gratitude, pushing her breasts into his face. He licked and sucked at the nipples and rubbed his face in them so that his glasses became dislodged.

Bobby dropped his spectacles over the edge of the bed and Kate tugged at the pyjama jacket.

'Take it off,' she said.

He relinquished it with reluctance, probably because his chest was so thin, but he forgot his embarrassment when he felt Kate's flesh against his own.

They rolled about the bed again, kissing, rubbing themselves against each other, his hands exploring everywhere they could reach. But they still had not delved into her vagina, and she was frightened in case he came in his pyjama trousers before they had established a first base from which they could later start again.

She, too, was highly aroused and she recognised he needed the release of an orgasm, but it had to be orchestrated correctly.

'Bobby,' she murmured, 'you're so sexy, you know just how to touch me, how to make me feel so wonderful.'

'You are wonderful, Kate. You feel wonderful.'

'But I'm still learning, and there is so much to learn.' She was lying on top of him and she raised herself on her arms so that they could talk. 'Please, will you do something for me?'

'What do you want me to do?'

'I've never seen a boy's . . . thing. You know, his prick. Will you show me yours? Please, let me see it?'

Without waiting for a reply, she slid down his body and felt its outline through the thin material of the pyjamas.

'It's so big!' she whispered, unfastening the trouser cord and pulling open the material.

It was an uncircumcised penis of reasonable size and it throbbed with the passion of being on display for the first time.

'Can I touch it?' she asked.

'Yes,' he said, hoarsely.

Kate took it in her hand and stroked it and he groaned. Her head was by his thigh and she looked up his body to his face.

'Bobby, can I watch you come? I've heard about it but never seen it. Please let me watch you come?'

She squeezed the prick and rubbed it as she spoke and Bobby simply grunted because he was beyond words.

Kate massaged it gently with both hands and sensed he was on the verge. One more gentle but firm movement and he cried out and began to come. She held the prick around its base and watched his virgin sperm burst like shellfire, one, two, three spurts arcing through the air and onto his stomach, the rest bubbling slowly from the head of the already softening weapon.

She put her hand in the pool of his juices and smoothed it into his skin and slid back up the bed to lie against him and prevent the possibility of him leaving for the bathroom.

'That was marvellous, Bobby. Thank you so much.' She kissed his cheek softly and moved her hand onto his thin chest. 'There was so much!'

They rested for a few minutes until he had got used

to lying there almost naked in her arms and his breathing had returned to normal.

Kate said, 'I have to do something for you, now. It's my turn. But I don't know what to do. You must tell me what you want me to do, what you like.' She widened her eyes as if she had just had an idea. 'The girl in that film took the man's prick in her mouth. Do you like that? Do you want me to do that?'

She was already sliding down his body again, her fingernails scratching through his pubic hair to the base of his half-erect penis. Bobby said nothing but appeared to be nervous.

First, she tugged off the open pyjama trousers and threw them on the floor. His legs were long and thin and hairy. She took hold of his penis and it twitched in her fingers and she put her mouth close to it and the smell and the power she had to make it stiff caused her abdomen to flutter in a spasm of excitement.

'I've never done this before,' she whispered. 'You must tell me what to do.'

Her open lips enveloped the head and sucked it into her mouth and Bobby moaned. The penis stiffened with each suck and his hips began to rise and fall in time to the movement of her head. She held the penis around its base and lifted her mouth to ask, 'Am I doing it properly?'

'Yes. You're doing it properly.'

'What do you want me to do?'

'Suck. Keep on sucking.'

Kate dipped her head and took his penis back into

her mouth and continued sucking. One of his hands gripped the cover of the bed, the other held the back of her head with an increasing boldness and pressure.

She slipped her free hand between her legs and inside her panties and stroked her aching clitoris, matching the rhythm of her fingers with the rhythm of her head.

His breathing was becoming ragged again and she sucked deeper and more strongly and he began yelping in his throat and his hips began to buck and he came in her mouth.

Kate pressed demandingly upon her clitoris and came too, her throat constricting with her moans, so that she did not swallow all of the sperm.

She raised her head and moved back up the bed towards him, her lips apart, the stickiness apparent around her mouth, a dribble escaping to run down her chin. Her tongue flicked out to catch some and she wiped the rest with her finger, which she put into her mouth to suck like a lollipop.

'Oh, Bobby, you're teaching me so much and I'm so grateful.'

His eyes closed and he held her in his arms, almost protectively.

After a while, she began to move herself surreptitiously against him, rubbing her vagina against the boniness of his hip.

'Teach me more, Bobby. Teach me more.' She lay on her back, lifted herself on her shoulders, and removed her panties. She took his hand and placed it over her vagina. 'I'm all wet and hot. I've never felt like this before. There. Can you feel it? Ooh. That's so good when you put your fingers in there. Oh yes, push them in and out. Do it, Bobby, do it. Oh, Bobby, you are going to make me come! Don't stop, don't stop! Oh, Bobby, I'm coming, I'm coming!'

Kate did not need to fake an orgasm, the situation was enough. Her vagina was on fire and she had held his fingers in place whilst she fucked his hand. She held nothing back and moaned and yelped as she jerked around the fingers that were buried inside her.

As she once more cuddled up against him, and thanked him for his expertise and his patience, her fingers played with his fresh erection.

'You've taught me so much. Will you do one more thing before I have to go? Promise me you will? Promise?'

'What is it?'

'No, promise first!'

'Okay. I promise.'

He squeezed her shoulders and kissed her forehead.

'Make love to me. Properly, I mean. Put your prick inside me and make love to me.'

His body stiffened in alarm. Coming in her mouth was one thing, but actually discovering where to put it in her body was another. She sensed he was unsure that he would be able to accomplish the task.

'I don't know,' he said.

'You promised.'

'But your father thought you'd be safe with me.'

'I am safe with you. I feel very safe with you. And you

promised.' She rolled onto her back and tugged at him to follow. 'I promise I'll try not to be awkward and make it difficult for you. But please, fuck me. You promised.'

He allowed himself to be rolled on top of her and she positioned him between her open legs. She put her hands between their bodies, as if investigating, and stroked his erection which, after two orgasms, was back to full size.

'It's still so big,' she said. 'But I'm so wet. Feel me, Bobby. Feel how wet I am.'

His right hand went between them and she guided it to the open lips of her sex, all the time stroking his penis in the palm of her other hand.

'Put it inside me.' She guided the head of the penis between the lips that he held open. 'That's it. Oh, Bobby. Do it to me.'

She removed her hands, leaving him in control now that his weapon had found her sheath.

He guided the rest of its length inside and then lay upon her, almost holding his breath at the intensity of the experience. If he had not come twice already, Kate guessed he would have come upon first entry.

Bobby tried a tentative stroke and Kate moaned for him and moved in response. He did it again with equal pleasure and success, and started his first rhythm of love.

'Fuck me,' Kate whispered in his ear. 'Fuck me, fuck me!'

He speeded up and his strokes became bolder. He

pushed himself away from her on his arms and stared down into her face as he continued to thrust in and out of her body. She opened her mouth in ecstasy and rolled her eyes and groaned continuously, and raised her legs so he could gain deeper penetration.

Bobby was totally in control now and pounding her body like a piston. She stared into his face and saw him getting closer to the edge and she squirmed her pelvis against his bones to keep in synchronisation.

He came, heaving a discharge of sperm inside her, surprise and shock at his achievement showing in his expression, his mouth open in wonder, and Kate came with him, carried over the edge by his virginity and innocence.

Afterwards, they got between the sheets and Bobby slept. Kate looked at his profile in the darkened room and felt tenderness for this thin boy with a bully for a father. Shyness, an underdeveloped physique, but most of all those unrelenting paternal expectations, had kept him away from girls.

But now he knew how to do it.

Kate dozed off and was awakened by Bobby, who lay at her back, pushing a fresh erection against her bottom and feeling her breasts.

'You're marvellous,' she whispered over her shoulder to him. 'Insatiable. A real man.'

She rolled onto her stomach and he lay on her back.

'I love you,' he whispered.

'I love you, too.'

His penis was resting in the groove between her

buttocks and she opened her legs and twisted slightly and it slipped between her thighs.

'Mmm,' she murmured. 'Is this another way of doing it?'

His fingers were between her legs, seeking her opening, and she raised herself so that he could find it. He slid two fingers inside and they squelched and when he pushed his penis there, she arched and manoeuvred and sucked it in with a slurp.

Bobby started by taking his time but this new sensation of lying upon such a succulent bottom swiftly incensed him. His strokes became harder, faster and more demanding; his hips slapped against her buttocks. He alternately groped her breasts and gripped her hips, he licked and suctioned the arch of her back with his lips, and she responded with groans and yells of encouragement.

He lasted for ten hectic, non-stop minutes, pounding against her buttocks, before he came for a fourth time. He sighed as if he had drained himself of all his juices.

He rolled off, stroked her back and fell asleep again.

Kate waited until he was snoring gently and regularly before she slipped out of bed. She collected her clothes and took them into the sitting room where she dressed. In a bureau, she found headed notepaper and a pen and she wrote him a note:

Dear Bobby,
Thank you for being fabulous. I will always

remember you for teaching me so much. I will always remember four times! FOUR TIMES!

Your loving pupil, Kate.

19

Bobby's father was waiting for her in the reception room. He still had a whisky glass in his hand, but he had removed his suit. He wore a white cotton bathrobe with his cowboy boots.

Kate said, 'I've just left your son. You'll be pleased to know he is extremely virile and heterosexual.'

'I know.'

'What do you mean, you know?'

'Little lady, when I agreed to pay DeVille his fee I was not going to take any chances on being fed a line. I had video cameras installed. I've been watching.'

Kate stared at him, surprised at being shocked. After all, she had been commissioned for a fee to provide her body for the man's son. Why should she be shocked if he wanted to watch?

'Then you know your son is no longer a virgin.'

'Hell, a virgin? Four fucking times in two hours. That's some fucking.'

'I'm glad you approve.'

The man grinned at her. 'But you don't approve of me?'

Kate did not respond to the question because the man was still, technically, her employer. Instead, she changed the conversation.

'Might I suggest that you go along with the subterfuge I instigated? I've left him a note. Tell him you were joking about the therapist. Tell him I've gone with my father on a business trip to Africa and that it's unlikely he'll see me again. Let him believe the game we played, at least until he's had some more experience.'

He shrugged. 'Sure.'

She brushed her hair back behind her ear and adjusted her spectacles.

'And now, I'll be leaving.'

'Just a minute, honey.'

'I beg your pardon?'

'When you arrived you promised to fuck my son's brains out.' He toasted her with the whisky glass. 'Mission accomplished. You also said you'd fuck my brains out, too.' He laughed and pointed to the open door that led into his suite of rooms. 'This way, little lady.'

Kate had composed herself to leave and return to the apartment for a bath. This second performance had not been expected but there was no way she could refuse.

She went through the doors and into a sitting room that was similar to Bobby's.

'Straight through to the bedroom,' Prentzel said. 'You know the way.'

Kate went into the bedroom, butterflies of apprehension starting again. She felt unclean because she had not washed for fear of waking up Bobby and, in the presence of the bullying Prentzel, she felt as young as the outfit she wore.

'Are you sure I'm the sort of girl you want, Mr Prentzel? I thought I was too young for you? I'm sure Mr DeVille could arrange for someone far more sophisticated to call round.'

'You're exactly the sort I want, little lady. Young, innocent, and well fucked.'

Prentzel slammed the bedroom door, drained the whisky glass and threw off the bathrobe. He was a big man, barrel-chested and with a gut from living too well. His penis was erect and sticking out in front of him. All he wore were his cowboy boots.

He used a remote control to switch on the television and a video recording of what had happened in Bobby's room came on the screen.

'I've missed out the first hour or so when you were pussy footing around watching movies,' he said. 'We're straight in with the action.'

On the screen, Kate and Bobby were kissing.

Kate stood in front of the television, curious about her performance and thinking how young she looked in the darkened room.

Prentzel stepped close behind her and put his hands around her to grip her breasts.

'You've got great tits, Kate. You know that? I don't think the little shit in there appreciated them enough.'

He gripped the dress where it buttoned down the front and ripped it apart. The violence of the act caused her to gasp and arch backwards against him, so that his penis pressed against her buttocks.

'You like it a little rough, Kate?'

He pulled the dress from her shoulders and it fell to the floor.

'No,' she said.

He unfastened the bra, pulled it from her and threw it across the room. He pushed down the panties and pushed his penis between her thighs, one hand groping her breasts and the other going to her vagina.

'Is my boy's spunk still in there?'

'Yes.'

He pushed a finger inside her wetness.

'He gave it to you good, didn't he?'

'Yes.'

'So will I.'

He pushed her without warning towards the bed and she fell across it. Prentzel rolled her onto her back and ripped down the panties, dropping them on the floor. He pulled apart her legs without preliminaries.

'Now *I'm* gonna fuck you, little lady. A grown up fuck. For adults only.'

Prentzel pushed his erection into her in one easy motion, her wetness enhanced by Bobby's sperm, his penis digging in to the hilt. He heaved up her legs over his arms and pushed deeper and she groaned.

'Did you like fucking my son, Kate? Did you like his cock?'

'Yes.'

'Tell me about it. Tell me how much you liked it. Tell me what you did.'

'I liked fucking him. His cock was big and it never went soft. He was full of spunk and I enjoyed tasting it. I sucked his cock and swallowed his spunk when he came. He fucked me from the front and from behind. He liked it from behind; he liked my bottom.'

Prentzel continued thrusting harshly in and out while she spoke, and then pushed her legs back further still until her feet were by her head and she was almost doubled on the bed.

The position gave him deeper penetration still and his thrusts became harsher and she could not stop herself from yelling out loud with every down stroke.

Squelching sounds came from their union.

'This is a real fuck, little lady. You hear me?'

Abruptly, he rolled off and she let her legs flop back on the bed with relief.

'Now, suck it!'

He lay back against the raised pillows and she went down onto his belly and took his penis in her mouth, tasting herself and Bobby and Prentzel on it. She sucked and guzzled at it, to speed up his orgasm, but he held it in check. He lay back and enjoyed it and worked the remote control to speed up the video to a part with more action.

Kate sucked him for fifteen minutes while he watched the video, occasionally passing comment about what was happening on the screen.

'That's enough,' he said, moving her head. 'Why don't you watch some television.'

He turned her around on the bed so she was lying

on her stomach facing the TV screen where Bobby was climbing onto her back. Behind her, Prentzel did the same. He pulled her hips up and shoved his penis into her from behind.

'You've got a great ass, you know that?' he said, moving so fast that his hips slapped loudly against the quivering flesh of her bottom.

He kept it up until, on the screen, Bobby came.

Prentzel moved again and turned Kate onto her back. He used the remote control to rewind the tape to another favourite part: where Kate fellated his son. She was still wearing her glasses and she could see the upside down images on the screen by tilting her head backwards.

'Tell me, Kate? How old are you, really?'

He straddled her waist, stroking his penis in his hand.

'How old do you want me to be, Mr Prentzel?'

'In these socks and this cotton underwear, sixteen, I guess.'

'You guessed it. I'm sixteen.'

'You're a hell of a whore, little lady.'

He pushed himself up onto her breasts and held them so he could push his penis between the mounds of flesh. Every few strokes he raised himself and pushed the head of his weapon into her mouth.

Soon, the channel he had made was wet with his secretions and her saliva.

His mouth was open and the air rasped in his throat. He watched the television and seemed to be timing himself. Out of the corner of her eye, Kate glimpsed the screen and guessed what he was waiting for: the image of her face after Bobby had come, with her mouth sticky with his sperm.

The moment on screen was getting closer and so was Prentzel. His grip on her breasts was hurting and his weight was heavy but his casual brutishness had aroused Kate. She was frustrated because she could not reach her clitoris to stroke herself to orgasm.

Prentzel heaved one more time and knelt up above her breasts. He held his penis at its base, pressing hard on the shaft with finger and thumb, and directed his discharge into her face.

The sperm shot out in huge globules as Kate stared at the throbbing purple head through her spectacles. The first salvo hit her on the cheek and slid down towards her neck, the second splashed onto the glass of her spectacles, the third went into her open mouth and the rest dribbled out across her lips and chin.

Kate licked up what she could reach with her tongue and swallowed it.

Prentzel got off her but he still hadn't finished. He removed her spectacles, upon which was a large pool of incandescent sperm. He knelt between her legs and scooped it up on the first two fingers of his right hand.

The American raised the fingers to show Kate before lowering his hand. He held apart the lips of her vagina with his left hand and pushed the fingers of his right inside her.

'Now you got me and my boy's spunk up there.'

He climbed off the bed and walked across the room.

He picked up the bathrobe and put it on. Kate's presence now seemed to embarrass him.

'Use the bathroom,' he said. 'Make yourself a coffee.' He picked up the empty whisky glass. 'I'll call DeVille to come and get you.'

Kate remained in the position in which he had left her, sprawled on her back with her head almost over the end of the bed.

'Tell him to bring something for me to wear,' she said.

He waved a hand and left the room.

Kate moved until she was more comfortable, and wiped the sperm from her cheek and neck with her fingers. She looked at how sticky they were and noticed through the wet webs that the video was still running on the television.

The remote control was alongside her and she fast forwarded the video until Bobby was about to lose his virginity.

She lay back on the bed, propped up on the pillows, and watched the television. Of their own accord, her sticky fingers went between her legs. Now she had the freedom to pleasure herself.

Her fingers slipped inside into the wetness. She was so well used that three went in past their knuckles. They slurped disgustingly as she moved them in and out. She tried four fingers and they filled her and she squirmed against them, at the same time using her thumb to rub her clitoris.

Kate watched herself on the screen as she sucked the virginity from sixteen-year-old Bobby Prentzel, reliv ing the moment and the sensations.

On the screen, she and the boy had reached the point of no return and she moaned and pushed her hips against her hand. She came at the same moment as she came in full colour on television, at the same moment that Bobby came with that look of wonder on his face.

20

DeVille brought the ever-useful cape to cover her nakedness and escorted her from the hotel to the chauffeur-driven limousine. They headed back to the apartment.

'How are you standing up to the abuse, Mrs Lewis?' he asked, as the vehicle nosed its way through the early evening London traffic.

'Most often, I'm lying down for it.'

'Well said.'

All things considered, Kate was standing up to it very well, except that she did not consider it abuse; she considered it an education.

She had enjoyed the games she had played with Bobby Prentzel, enjoyed manipulating him into taking action he would otherwise have been incapable of taking. She had enjoyed the feeling of being in control.

Even the obnoxious Prentzel senior had not given her a hard time; well, not emotionally.

Whilst lying back and taking it, she had gained a pretty good insight into the man's character, failings and insecurities. Maybe she should write a book about her experiences, when the two weeks were up.

DeVille escorted her to the front door of the apartment but did not enter.

'Tomorrow is a free day, Mrs Lewis. Relax, enjoy yourself. You have completed your first week. But I shall attempt to arrange something special for your second.'

'I can hardly wait,' she said.

Chloe was out and Kate had the apartment to herself. She dropped the cape, beneath which she was naked, and pulled off the shoes and socks. In the bathroom, she turned on the taps to run a bath.

Whilst she waited for it to fill, she got a bottle of Chablis from the refrigerator, opened it and poured herself a glass. The wine was cold and delicious and she drank it quickly. She took the glass and the bottle with her into the bathroom and continued to sip wine whilst she soaked in the hot water.

When, she wondered, would she get bored with sex?

Perhaps it was all those years of frustration, but right now, she felt she could go on fucking for ever. She even liked the word because it was a taboo word from her childhood. It had also been a taboo word in her polite society of country living, coffee mornings, dull dinner parties and a husband whose libido was raised more successfully by the half-clothed anonymous ladies he found in magazines than by his wife.

Yes, she liked the word.

Fuck. To fuck. Fucking.

Kate loved to think it, to say it, and to do it.

She had submitted to so much in this first week that

she could not envisage what more there was to try. But whatever DeVille came up with, she would be more than willing: she would be eager.

But what would she do when the two weeks of her enforced employment were complete?

Kate did not see herself continuing to live a life of high class prostitution. This was a two-week commission to save her home with the added bonus of freeing her from all responsibility for what was happening to her.

That was being controlled by outside influences; by ringmaster DeVille and the whims of the men and women he chose to give her to. No, not give her to, sell her to.

She was determined not to shirk the truth, but rather to wallow in it: DeVille did not give her to people, he sold her.

This marvellous lack of responsibility was a large part of the attraction of their arrangement.

She laughed.

At least she had exorcised that great childhood fear from her psyche: she would never feel guilt again for her sexual desires or indulgences.

Those deliciously sinful indulgences at school . . .

Where was Gina now, she wondered?

Maybe, when this was all over, she would go and find her and see if the magic was still there that had led them to spend nights of orgasm in each other's arms. Maybe they would pay a return visit to their old school and find that private place in the woods.

Thinking about it rekindled desire between her legs.

Kate got out of the bath and dried herself but did not put on any clothes. She walked about the apartment naked, another freedom she had previously been unable to enjoy. In the kitchen, she nibbled at a piece of cheese and a chunk of bread, but her appetite was not for food; it was still for sex.

When would Chloe return?

Until she did, Kate still had her friend's book to read. It never failed to excite her.

She wondered if she could write her own book, and began to be taken over by the idea, more and more. It could be an exposé of the fantasies of men and the desires of women.

Or perhaps she would write a potboiler of sex in the country in which she herself could star as the lady of the house who has an insatiable appetite for stable lads like Billy.

When she returned to her home, always accepting she would raise the required sum to retrieve her husband's promissory note, it might be nice to seduce Billy amidst the hay.

Kate squirmed as the itch between her legs again became insistent.

Big, strong, handsome Billy, who looked at her with shaded eyes and a slow smile as if he had already fucked her in a fantasy of his own.

What a marvellous thought: to be featured in Billy's wet dreams, to be twisted to his will as he stroked his prick. To be bent over the stable-gate as he took her from behind like a horse in stud, or made to kneel at his feet and worship his weapon with her mouth in a role reversal of their positions of power.

And all in his head as he pulled at his prick with those big heavy hands; all in his head as he made love to her, and fucked her until he came alone into the hay.

Kate resolved to do two things: to seduce Billy at the earliest opportunity when she returned to the country, and to record her experiences in a diary.

Meanwhile, she had another book to read.

She went to the bedroom and took Chloe's story from a bedside drawer.

21

Chloe wrote:

Lessons with uncle were exciting because they were often spontaneous. He took advantage of situations. Like the time at the bistro.

We were dining there late, in a booth near the back of the restaurant, which was still busy. The tablecloths reached to the floor, a fact that uncle pointed out to me.

'How enterprising of the management,' he said, 'to provide such discreet privacy.'

I did not know what he meant until we were sitting side by side on the velvet plush of the bench seat and he slid his hand beneath my skirt.

It was summer, the evening warm, and I wore a blue silk dress with a full skirt, matching underwear and backless high heels.

The silk slid back easily until it was bunched around uncle's wrist at my waist. His hand held the inside of my left thigh above the tan stocking top and his thumb lightly stroked the ruched strap of a suspender.

He kept his hand there when the waiter came, a

young Frenchman who sensed something was going on although he could not see what. Uncle's fingers stroked me between the legs as he ordered food and wine, and the waiter left with a smile twitching his lips.

My panties were loose-legged and he pushed my thighs apart and stroked my slit until the lips opened. I was breathing through my mouth as I stared down the restaurant with eyes that sparkled with excitement.

At the other tables, people ate and talked and laughed, unaware that I had a finger moving rhythmically in and out of my vagina.

Two middle-aged men sat at the nearest table, one facing us at an angle, his companion with his back to us. My stare had become fixed because I now had two fingers inside me and could feel my juices beginning to wet the insides of my thighs; my stare caused the man to return my gaze.

His conversation stumbled and he said something to his dinner partner, causing him to turn in his chair to stare at me as well. I gave them a small smile before looking away.

Uncle's fingers slid out and along to my clitoris, which he brushed with the tip of his forefinger. The contact sent a quiver through me and I closed my eyes and lowered my head. I was extremely close to orgasm.

'Ah, wine,' uncle said.

I looked up, my face flushed, my eyes now glazed because of the desire I felt, my features heavy with want. The waiter's smile froze and he caught his breath. My excitement was causing his excitement.

The waiter showed uncle the bottle.

'My niece will taste it,' uncle said.

The waiter poured a small amount in my glass and waited for my opinion.

Uncle smiled, unaffected by the havoc he was causing between my legs, and I shakily picked up the glass in my right hand. As I sipped, his finger stroked my clitoris. I groaned as the wine went down my throat.

Uncle said, 'I think she likes it.'

He indicated that the waiter should continue pouring, and while the man did so, uncle continued to roll my clitoris like an oiled ball-bearing beneath his finger.

My breathing became ragged and the waiter hesitated. 'Is Mademoiselle feeling all right?'

Uncle said, 'She's fine. She suffers from hay fever.'

The waiter looked quizzically into my face and I stared back with blank features as uncle's finger flicked and rubbed and I came.

I attempted to restrict the sounds of orgasm in my throat and clenched my mouth shut but my breasts heaved against the silk and my nostrils flared.

Uncle sipped the wine and raised his glass to the waiter. 'Very nice, thank you.'

Reluctantly, the waiter departed, not quite able to believe what he thought he might have witnessed.

As my senses regained their equilibrium, I noticed the man at the next table who faced me. He, too, had watched the wine tasting and my sudden seizure. His expression left me in no doubt that he knew I had just orgasmed.

Uncle removed his fingers and he wiped the wet and glistening juices that were upon them around the rim of his glass. He raised the glass to his nose and inhaled, then sipped delicately.

'Beautiful,' he said. 'You make an ordinary wine exquisite.'

The waiter served the food and we ate, although my appetite was now impaired by desire. The man at the other table continued to stare over the shoulder of his friend. He was a fat man in a business suit, the sort of man who could be entertaining a client on behalf of his company, but now his attention had wandered from corporate affairs as he waited to see what would happen next.

My skirt remained at the top of my thighs and, periodically throughout the meal, uncle would stroke my leg or slip a finger between them and stoke the lust that burned there in the hot wetness of my vagina.

He picked up an asparagus tip and regarded it for a moment. Then he handed it to me, almost as if it were a love token. I held it between fingers and thumb.

Uncle said, 'It needs a sauce, Chloe. Revitalise it for me.'

A few yards away, I was aware that the fat man at the next table continued to watch and I was sure that uncle was cognisant of the fact.

I held the asparagus before me and focused upon it; then shifted my gaze slightly until I made eye contact with the fat man. He was so enthralled he did not blush or look away.

With my eyes still upon him, I leaned back on the bench seat and lowered both my hands out of his sight. I pivoted my hips a little and held open my labia with the fingers of my left hand. Slowly, carefully, I slid the asparagus tip into my slit and across my clitoris.

Its contours teased that most sensitive bud and reactivated my passion to the highest level. My mouth opened and a sigh escaped and all the time I kept staring at the fat man.

I moved it backwards and forwards upon my clitoris and the sensation was sweet and gentle and electrifying. Then I moved it further down and into my pink cavern where my juices flowed like hot soup.

The feeling was incredible; not just the physical sensation of pushing an asparagus tip inside my vagina, but the fact that I was doing so in a crowded restaurant amidst the noise of patrons and waiters, and particularly because the eyes of the fat man stared with such intensity that his companion had again turned round in his seat to see what had stolen his attention.

I held the asparagus between two fingers and my thumb and as I moved it around inside me I used the back of my thumb to nudge my clitoris.

My tongue now peeked between my lips as my rhythms took over of their own accord.

'Chloe,' uncle said, 'I'm waiting.'

'Please,' I whispered.

My fingers worked the contours of the asparagus to their best advantage, my thumb rubbed more insistently upon the pleasure bud. I turned eyes to him that were once more beginning to glaze.

'Please?'

He smiled and sipped wine.

'Go ahead. Do it,' he said.

I looked back at the next table where the fat man's companion had now moved his chair so that the two of them could watch. My fingers dipped, the back of my thumb rubbed, breathing began to become more difficult and the faces of the two men slipped out of focus.

Nothing was real now except the asparagus tip that slurped between my legs and the rising charge of electricity that shot out from my clitoris.

I came, and this time I could not control all the noise.

My moans escaped, trickling from my lips like spilt sperm, and my body shook. For a moment, I had no idea where I was, the noise and the lights becoming a distant backdrop. Slowly, the spasms subsided. Slowly, I returned to reality.

At the next table, the fat man's jaw hung slackly and his companion, a man with stern grey hair and moustache, stared in disbelief.

Uncle said, 'Was that good?'

'Very.'

'Then let me taste it.'

I removed my hands from between my legs and put my elbows on the table. In the fingers of my right hand, I held up the asparagus tip: it glistened like a snail, marinated in my juices. I was tempted to put it in my mouth and licked my lips but this was uncle's treat.

My focus shifted and fixed on the two men. The fat one remained slack-jawed, the other now mopped his brow with a handkerchief.

I handed the tip to uncle.

He took it reverently, as if it were a host, and raised it to his nose, flaring his nostrils to enjoy the aroma. He licked it sparingly and enjoyed the taste.

'A most precious gift, Chloe. Thank you.'

He moistened his lips, inspected it closely for several more seconds, opened his mouth and bit off the end.

At the next table, the fat man closed his mouth and salivated. The man with grey hair held his handkerchief as if he had forgotten it was in his hand.

Uncle masticated with great deliberation, swallowed and put the remainder of the asparagus tip into his mouth. He ate that with equal relish. I felt proud at making him so pleased.

'You have acquired two admirers,' he said.

'I noticed.'

'Go to the powder room. And as you leave the table, display yourself to them.'

It was the natural progression of the game and I was happy to oblige.

As I prepared to move, uncle leant across and whispered further instructions.

I moved from behind the table onto the bench seat at the side, making no attempt to push down my skirt. My legs were on display from the tips of my high heeled shoes to the tops of my thighs. They were, I knew, an extremely pretty sight, being encased in tan stockings that were held taut by pale blue suspender straps.

The only people in the restaurant who could see were the two men at the next table. I ignored them, stood up and allowed the skirt to fall into place, and made my way to the ladies' powder room. Walking between the tables and being so close to other people whilst being so wet was another thrill.

In the powder room, I locked myself in a cubicle and removed my pale blue silk panties. With my skirt held up I could smell myself and I pushed the material of the panties into my vagina to soak up some of the juices. Without being aware of what I was doing, my hips began to rotate against them and I felt another surge of pleasure.

It was with a great effort that I stopped myself from masturbating to another orgasm. I held the panties in my right hand, and my bag in my left, and went back into the restaurant.

Once again, the nearness of other customers was exciting and I wondered if they could smell me. The fat man and his business associate watched my progress and as I went past their table, I dropped the panties on the floor.

Uncle appeared to be preoccupied and took no notice and I heard someone scrambling behind me. When I had regained my seat in the booth, I saw the fat man had the panties in his hand, unsure what to do with them now that he had realised what they were.

I smiled at him, in the sort of casual way one diner

exchanges glances with another.

After an age of indecision, he raised the pale blue silk to his face. He sniffed and then held them closer to his nose. His companion said something to him urgently and he reluctantly held them out, although he did not relinquish his grip upon them. The man with silver hair also smelled them.

The waiter returned and uncle ordered coffee for us both and a brandy for himself. After the man had gone to fill the order, uncle looked at me.

'You have been very good, Chloe. You deserve a pudding. A special dessert.' He unfastened his belt and unzipped his trousers. 'Go beneath the table. I will provide the cream for your coffee.'

I glanced at the fat man and the man with grey hair to make sure they were still watching, and then slid from the bench seat beneath the table and beneath the protection of the cloth.

Sounds were muted in this shadow land and I remembered playing beneath a table and its cloth as a child. Then, I had pretended it was a fairytale castle or an indian wigwam; a place of mystery and imagination in which to play childish games. Now, it was a place of tingling excitement in which to indulge in very adult games.

I knelt on the carpet between uncle's feet. He had positioned the tablecloth across his waist and had already released his penis. It was as firm as a cannon, jutting out from his clothing ready to fire a salvo into my mouth.

As I moved my face closer to it, I could smell it. I smiled. The smell and the strength of the erection were the only indications that uncle had been highly aroused himself.

My fingers stroked it and it twitched. I gripped it and moved the sheath of flesh gently up and down. Uncle's legs straightened and his feet stiffened. I heard the waiter returning and dipped my head and sucked the end of his weapon into my mouth.

His foreskin slid back under the pressure of my lips and my tongue dug into the eyepiece of his cannon and his voice no longer sounded so totally in control as he spoke to the waiter.

I sucked and heard his soft groans and wondered what the two men at the nearby table were thinking. The thought of them watching and speculating, with stiff cocks imprisoned in their business suits, made me squirm my thighs. I held the base of uncle's weapon in the fingers of my left hand as my head went up and down, sucking and slurping with the wet friction, and slipped my right beneath my dress to bury it up to my knuckles in my vagina.

He tasted delicious, a savoury complement to the meal, and my senses were once more at the start of a tidal wave, overcome with the power of my mouth, the publicness of our surroundings, and that two men watched and wondered so close to where I was sucking cock.

Uncle came before I could. He made no sound but I sensed the approach of his orgasm and gripped the base of his prick tightly between thumb and forefinger, to increase the pressure of the ejaculation and heighten his pleasure.

His first burst splashed into the back of my mouth, and he continued to shoot decreasing amounts of sperm between my lips as his loins shook for many, many seconds afterwards.

The tension went from his body and his penis began to grow flaccid before I eased my lips from its end and re-emerged from beneath the cover and resumed my seat next to him in the booth.

He lay back, still unfastened beneath the table, and smiled at me.

'Superb,' he said.

I smiled back, tight-lipped from necessity, before turning my gaze to the next table.

The men were still sitting as if at a show, eyes glued to me to drink in any indication of what I had been doing. I smiled at them, too, and slipped my right hand beneath my dress once more, to rub my clitoris and regain lost momentum.

Before me on the table was a cup of black coffee. I picked it up with my left hand and raised it to my face; over its rim I stared again at the two men and saw the lust in their faces and my fingers worked feverishly between my legs.

I raised the cup to my mouth, parted my lips and allowed the full discharge of uncle's sperm to dribble into the hot liquid.

The fat man groaned and clutched himself beneath

his own table cloth and the eyes of the man with the grey hair fluttered as if he was having a stroke, and my tidal wave arrived and swept me into ecstasy.

My left hand shook with the power of the orgasm and I felt uncle take the cup from my hand and replace it in its saucer. I gulped air and leaned over the table for support and stared into the coffee, now streaked with grey globules of semen.

Beside me, I heard uncle sighing with approval and I composed myself and sat upright, picked up the cup, toasted the two men opposite, and drank.

Uncle fastened his clothing and called the waiter. He paid the bill and we left the privacy of the booth, walked past the two men and left the restaurant.

The car was parked outside: a maroon Rolls Royce. He unlocked it and opened a rear door for me. I stepped into the luxury of the deep-pile carpet and sank into the middle of the wide cream leather seats.

'One moment,' he said. 'I have forgotten something.'

He closed the door and went back into the restaurant and I stretched my legs and stroked, through the silk of my dress, the itch that still inhabited my groin.

A minute later, he reappeared – accompanied by the two businessmen from the next table. He opened the rear door again and looked in at me with a smile.

'You remember our friends,' he said. 'They are quite desperate for dessert. I told them you would be happy to oblige.'

He stepped away and the two men climbed into the back of the car, and sat on either side of me. Uncle got behind the driving wheel, started the engine and drove the car along the road.

There was little traffic, the night was dark and the rear windows of the Rolls Royce were tinted black. We could see out but no one could see in.

From the front, uncle said, 'Gentlemen, feel free!'

They were both tentative. The fat man was on my right and he still clutched my panties. There was so much space in the back of the car that their thighs did not even touch mine.

While they hesitated, there was still time for me to take the lead. I decided they might prefer me to be demure and subservient rather than a hussy, and I lowered my eyes. 'If uncle says I must please you, then I will. Do you wish me to . . .' I hesitated as if embarrassed '. . . suck your cocks?'

The fat man groaned and put a fat hand on my knee. He pushed up the dress until his palm crossed stocking top and found warm flesh and he groaned again.

On the other side, the one with grey hair was prompted into action at the sight and he, too, pushed up the dress until it was around my waist and my triangle of black pubic underbrush was exposed.

The fat man's fingers dug between my legs and I opened my thighs; his fingers found the wetness and two slurped inside me and I slid further down the seat.

His companion pulled at the buttons at the front of my dress until he had it open. I wore no brassiere and my small breasts jiggled and bounced beneath his hands, the nipples hard and pointed.

Now they had started and realised uncle would simply drive the car in a leisurely circuit and would not intervene, they grabbed and groped every part of my body until I began to believe it was not my own.

Zips were released, trousers pushed down, breath was ragged, the smell of sex filled the back of the car and I wallowed in the trough of lust and fulfilment.

I was turned over so that I knelt on the thick carpet, my dress around my waist and my bottom bared. The dress hung open at the front and the grey haired man pushed my head into his lap and I found his erection, short and stubby, and held it in my hands and sucked it into my mouth.

His cries filled the car as the fat man positioned himself behind me and guided his penis into my vagina. He fed it in slowly until I thought it would never end; a huge, pulsating prick that filled me. He gripped my hips with his hands and began to fuck me; slow strokes that picked up speed.

Each thrust was accompanied by a gasp; each thrust made me shudder at its power and drove my head deeper into the grey haired man's lap, taking his cock deeper down my throat.

Both were making the noises that preluded the inevitable and their hands were greedy in trying to grab every sensation they could before it was too late.

They were riding fast towards their own conclusions and I wanted mine first. I slipped one hand between my legs and flicked my clitoris in time to the pounding the fat man was giving me, a pounding that made the flesh of my buttocks quiver. I felt myself winning in the race to finish.

This time, I let the rush of sensations take me without any attempt at control, and I moaned despite the cock in my mouth and I shook despite the giant cock in my vagina, and my coming was all the two businessmen in their smart city suits needed to tip them into orgasm.

They came.

The fat man violently, his weight in spasm dislodging the prick from my mouth although I still gripped it in my fingers. Sperm splashed into my face before I could push it back between my lips where it pulsed away the rest of its life force.

Afterwards, they were flushed and unsure what sort of situation they had become involved in. I did not reassure them.

I lay sprawled in the back of the car, sitting on the floor, my skirt around my waist and my legs splayed. The wetness at my vagina now seeped with the flood that the fat man had released inside me. My head rested limply against the seat, the dress open from neck to waist and my breasts exposed. Semen trickled down my cheek.

They had gloriously abused me and I had loved every minute of it.

Perhaps they thought they had raped me, perhaps they thought they had gone too far. They said nothing, but fastened their trousers and exchanged nervous glances.

The man with grey hair said to uncle, 'This is fine. Drop us here.'

'Are you sure? It's a long walk back.'

'No, really. This is fine. It really is.'

Uncle stopped the car and they pushed open both rear doors and tumbled out.

'Thank you,' the grey haired man said hesitantly, first to uncle and then, as he looked into the back of the car, to me. 'Thank you.'

He shut the door and we drove into the night. Uncle had adjusted the interior mirror so that he had been able to watch all that had happened and now his eyes sought mine as he manoeuvred the car.

'Enjoy it?' he said.

'Yes.'

'Why?'

'It was unexpected.'

We drove on in silence and I moved an arm.

He said, 'Don't move. Stay like that. You look delicious and I am getting hungry again.'

Further up the road, he parked the car near a common, got into the back, and fucked me.

22

Kate confessed to Chloe that she was intimidated by the size and pace of London.

'You shouldn't think of London as one big entity,' Chloe said. 'It's really a series of small villages that just happen to be very close together. I'll show you.'

The two girls spent Kate's day off sightseeing, shopping and wandering the streets of Britain's capital city. Kate enjoyed discovering the human side of the metropolis and Chloe enjoyed being her guide.

They had a pub lunch near the Tower of London and took afternoon tea at Harrods before finally returning, tired but relaxed, to the apartment.

DeVille was waiting for them.

'Uncle,' Chloe said.

She gave him a kiss on the cheek.

'Mr DeVille,' Kate said.

He smiled at her formality.

Chloe said, 'Are you staying for dinner?'

'No. I have only called to inform Mrs Lewis of her next commission.'

Kate said, 'Which is?'

DeVille continued to smile as he looked at her. 'My dear Mrs Lewis,' he said. 'You are going to be a birthday present.'

Kate had visions of old Hollywood films.

'What exactly will this entail?' she said. 'I won't have to jump out of a cake, will I?'

'Nothing as silly as that. The father of the Honourable Peregrine Simpson wants to mark his son's twenty-first birthday in a manner that the young man will remember. I take it you can drive?'

'Of course.'

'Then be ready by seven in the morning. I will collect you and take you to the rendezvous in Buckinghamshire. You will have a car to deliver. It is blue, so wear something that matches.'

DeVille left and Kate felt cheated at having her day off spoilt.

Chloe understood and put her arm around her. 'We'll have something to eat and then choose your clothes.' She gave her a squeeze and a mischievous grin. 'And when you try them on we will christen them before the Honourable Peregrine gets his hands on them.'

That evening, they went through the extensive selection of clothes in the cupboards and drawers in the bedroom and chose a pale blue taffeta cocktail dress.

It was cut low at the front and was fitted to the waist from where the crisp material flared out in a full skirt that ended above the knee.

Chloe found a satin basque in a matching shade but withheld the panties that went with it.

'You won't need these tonight,' she said.

Tan stockings and blue high heels completed the outfit and Kate wore her hair around her shoulders.

The result pleased her and she admired her reflection in the mirror in the bedroom. She only had to lean forward slightly for her cleavage to show, whilst the same manoeuvre lifted the stiff skirt at the rear to display her legs all the way to the tops of the stockings.

Chloe showed her approval by running her hands up the back of Kate's legs and between her thighs.

'I think you need a rehearsal,' she whispered into Kate's ear. 'Come to bed.'

The two girls kissed and embraced and Chloe slowly removed the clothes Kate had so recently put on, and they lay on the satin sheet and made love until they fell asleep.

Chloe, who was used to rising early for her modelling assignments, awakened Kate with a cup of tea at six the next morning.

Kate showered, applied her make-up and got dressed, this time also slipping on the matching panties, and was ready when DeVille arrived at seven.

He escorted her to the limousine, behind whose wheel was the same chauffeur who had been witness to the sexual encounter she had had with DeVille in the apartment a few days before.

The chauffeur met her eyes in the rear-view mirror

as she sat in the back seat. He nodded a greeting.

They drove for almost two hours and were deep in the heart of the English countryside when DeVille leaned forward to instruct the chauffeur. 'The gates on the left,' he said.

They turned off the road into a private estate. Gravel crunched beneath the wheels of the car. There was a wood on their right, and sweeping lawns on the left. The sun was bright and the sky blue.

Kate thought they should have been going for a picnic rather than to deliver a birthday surprise.

The drive curved around the trees and, ahead of them, a substantial country house came into sight.

'To the left,' DeVille said, and the chauffeur drove the car onto a paved courtyard. 'Here.'

They stopped by a side door. In front of them was an outbuilding that had been converted to garages; to the left a stable block.

The door opened and a tall, middle-aged man whose face was creased with a severe expression came down the four stone steps to the courtyard. He wore a three piece business suit, a stiff collar, and a tie with a pinched knot at his neck.

DeVille got out of the car to meet him and they shook hands and exchanged words. When DeVille raised a finger, Kate climbed out of the car to join them, stooping to afford the businessman a view down the front of her dress as she did so.

'This is Kate, Sir Ernest,' said DeVille. 'I'm sure she will add the finishing touch to your son's gift.'

Sir Ernest's expression did not change. He stared at Kate as if assessing a race horse.

'I hope so. I will take charge of her now. You may wait here for her return.' He looked back at Kate. 'Come with me, young lady.'

He walked across the courtyard to the garages, with Kate following behind, and entered through an unlocked door. As she followed into the huge and gloomy building, he closed the door behind them. There were four vehicles, one of them draped in a dust sheet. The three cars on view were expensive and rare.

'There,' he said, indicating the vehicle that was covered.

Kate walked towards it. She could see that its shape was low and long. Sir Ernest pulled the sheet clear with one theatrical gesture, to reveal the gleaming blue paintwork and shining chrome of a restored E-type Jaguar.

'It's beautiful,' she said, her breath taken in admiration for this classic car of the 1960s.

'Yes. It is.'

Sir Ernest's voice changed for the first time and he stroked the bodywork gently.

'Listen,' he said suddenly, and, opening the door, he slipped behind the wheel and started the engine.

It roared into life, the bonnet vibrating with the power. Kate leaned forward to touch the metal.

Sir Ernest climbed out of the car and joined her.

'She's a wonderful beast,' he said. 'Can you feel the power?'

'Yes.'

'Feel it properly.'

He pushed her from behind and she leaned forward to hold the car with both hands. He pushed again, forcing her forward until she lay face down across the bonnet, the engine purring beneath her body, the metal's rhythm oscillating into her limbs and particularly her groin.

Sir Ernest threw up her skirt from behind and, without preliminaries, tugged down her panties to mid-thigh. His fingers pushed between her legs, opened the lips of her sex, and went into her vagina.

She gasped at the unexpectedness of the assault but swiftly adjusted to the movement of his hand and felt herself becoming wet.

'Do you feel the power?' he said, his voice hoarse in her ear. 'Do you feel it?'

'Yes. I feel it.'

And she did, too, lying splayed across the throbbing bonnet of this beautiful and expensive machine.

Sir Ernest shifted position behind her and unfastened his trousers. He pushed her legs apart with his knee and thrust his rock hard penis inside her in one movement.

'Do you feel the power?'

'I feel it! I feel it!'

His penis throbbed like the engine upon which she lay and he gripped her hips, rocked against her buttocks, and came inside her with a juddering heave.

Kate was breathless and disorientated as he lifted

himself from her. She heard him refastening his clothes behind her and pushed herself away from the car and stood upright.

Sir Ernest was as stern-faced as when they had met a few minutes before, his tie still pinched in a knot, his suit immaculate. He ignored her and what had just taken place and went back to the driver's door and climbed behind the wheel once more. She pulled up her panties and smoothed down her skirt.

'Get in,' he called.

She opened the passenger door and climbed in beside him.

He pressed a switch and a door at the rear of the garage rolled up electronically. He put the car in gear and drove it out into the sunshine. To the right, there was a narrow paved road that led down the hill towards a lake.

Sir Ernest drove carefully down the road. Round a bend was a summerhouse with a veranda that overlooked the lake. He stopped, took the car out of gear and turned off the engine.

'My son celebrated his birthday last night with friends. He will probably be asleep. You will guide the car down the hill from here and stop it outside the house. You will not need to start the engine or put it in gear or use the accelerator. You will simply have to use the brake. Do you understand?'

'I understand.'

'Good. Then I shall leave you here.'

Sir Ernest got out of the car and began to walk back

up the hill without another glance at Kate, the car or the house ahead. She got out of the passenger seat, walked around the vehicle, and slipped in behind the wheel.

She stretched with her foot and found the brake and made sure she could reach it with ease, before releasing the handbrake and allowing the car to slowly roll down the hill.

When she was outside the front door of the summer house, she applied the footbrake and the car stopped smoothly. She secured it with the handbrake and pressed hard on the horn.

Its noise shocked her and she removed her hand, but no one emerged onto the veranda. She pressed the horn again, giving three sharp blasts.

A young man appeared at a window and stared out. He disappeared briefly and, when he returned to the window, he was accompanied by a second young man.

Kate climbed out of the car and leaned against the bonnet. She had thought she was to be the birthday present for a twenty-one-year-old, but already his father had used his seigneurial rights to claim first thrust, and it now looked as if she would be required to administer to the needs of more than a solitary young man with a hangover.

How many, for goodness sake?

She remembered, from the limited socialising she had been allowed as a teenager, how crass young men from the privileged classes could be, particularly when they were part of a group.

Her accent, which was distinctly public school, would be a handicap and a possible embarrassment if they questioned her about where it had been acquired.

Kate decided to say as little as possible and, when she did speak, to make her accent as nondescript as possible. She removed her spectacles and, reaching through the open window, put them on the dashboard of the car.

The front door opened and the two young men she had seen at the window came onto the veranda. One was tall and had a head of unruly blond curls, the other was small and dark with the sharp expression of a weasel. Both were still blinking sleep from their eyes.

Kate said, 'Who's the birthday boy?'

The blond said, 'He's inside. He's still blotto.'

'What a shame,' Kate said. She held out her arms to indicate both herself and the car. 'This is his present.'

'Good God!' said the blond. 'Sir Ernest does it again! That bastard Perry has all the luck!'

He came down the steps of the veranda and walked past Kate to inspect the car.

The dark haired young man stared at Kate rather than the car. 'Are you part of the present?'

Kate did not like the way he was staring or the way he had asked the question, but her services had been bought and paid for by Sir Ernest.

She returned his look steadily. 'Yes. I am.'

He smiled. 'Good. The party was beginning to flag. You had better come in and meet Perry.'

Kate climbed the steps of the veranda. He opened the

door for her and she stepped past him into the house. The curtains in the front room were open and the debris of a drunken night was clear to see, with empty brandy and champagne bottles lying on the floor, alongside chintzy furniture.

'This way.'

He pushed open the door to another room. Two bunk beds were against one wall, the top bunk occupied by a sleeping figure beneath a coverlet. On the floor was a mattress and, asleep on his back on top of a duvet, was another young man, whose slim body was totally naked and only partially covered across his groin by a sheet.

Kate's guide pointed to the naked body and said, 'That is Perry.'

'He looks as if he could sleep for a week.'

'Perhaps. But you are his birthday present. You should wake him up.'

The figure on the bunk bed groaned and moved. It rolled over and stared down at them.

'What's going on?' The voice was a lazy drawl.

'As yet, nothing, old boy. But it will. Perry's father has delivered the goods this time. There's an E-type outside, and this racy beauty inside.' He smiled superciliously at Kate. 'My name is Simon, by the way,' he said. 'The chap up there is Dorian and the ugly duckling outside is Rupert. I do hope we are all going to be friends?'

Kate felt threatened for the first time since she had been in DeVille's employ. It was a different experience

to when she had gone prepared for rape and bondage
to the house of the Japanese, and it provided a new edge
to her feelings.

But whatever happened in this house, it was still only
sex, a subject whose boundaries she knew well by now,
and these were young men who had only just left adoles-
cence.

Whatever they wanted, she would deliver because that
was her role, and if she was to be true to her own
commitment, she should endeavour to enjoy the experience to the full, including that edge of fear that made
everything sharper, fuller and more real.

From the top bunk, Dorian said, 'Why the tart?'

Simon chuckled. 'For filial enjoyment, old boy. Damn
considerate of Sir Ernest, don't you think?'

Kate realised that part of her trepidation was because
of the cold and calculated way Simon had first greeted
her. He and his friend were continuing in the same vein,
talking about her as if she were not there, as if her only
use was to be used, which, of course, it was.

They were behaving like landed gentry with a servant
girl they intended to enjoy as a plaything; aristocrats
exercising their rights of privilege over someone from
a lower class.

She was reminded of her own designs on Billy the
stable lad back at her own house in the country; the
situation was similar, except that there were four of
them here, and they were in control. The situation, again
unexpected, was also another release from responsibility. Whatever happened, whatever they did, was

beyond her control. She would just have to endure –
and enjoy – it.

Rupert, with the unruly curly blond hair, stepped into
the doorway.

'The car is brilliant.' He stared around, suddenly
aware of the tension in the air. 'What's happening?'

Simon stroked a hand down Kate's back, running it
over the curve of her hip and finding a suspender strap
which he traced through the material with one finger.

'This little girl has come gift-wrapped and ready,
haven't you, dearie?' His hand gripped the softness of
her buttock but she did not pull away. 'So we are going
to have a gang bang, old boy, courtesy of Perry.'

23

Simon turned Kate and pushed her against the side of the bunk beds. When she raised her arms to support herself, Dorian reached over from the top bunk and grabbed her wrists.

'Hold her,' said Simon, his voice suddenly urgent.

He pulled up her skirts from behind to reveal her legs encased in tan stockings and the thin ruched silk of the suspender straps.

'Good God,' said Rupert, from the doorway.

Simon's hands grabbed both her buttocks.

Dorian said, 'What's she wearing?'

'She's dressed for sex,' said Simon. 'And she's going to get it.'

Rupert began pulling off his clothes. 'Who's going to be first?' he said.

Simon's fingers went between her legs and found that she was wet and sticky.

'The old sod!' he said. 'Sir Ernest has beaten us to it. Is that right, dearie? Have you been fucked already?'

'That's right,' Kate said.

She could feel the tension and the heat in the small
room continue to rise. She could feel her nerve ends
being scraped open; her stomach tingled and the muscles
of her vagina spasmed and jumped.

Kate felt vulnerable and available; they wanted to use
and abuse her, and she wanted exactly the same. She
wanted to make all their wet dreams come true, but to
do so, she must play her part and let them believe they
were totally in control, not just of the situation, which
they were, but also of her emotions and sensibilities.

Simon pulled at her panties and they ripped along
the side seam. The sound appeared to galvanise him.
He pulled again, more fiercely, and tore them from her
body. The material dug into Kate's flesh and she yelled.

'Oh God, oh God,' murmured a now naked Rupert.

He joined Simon and his hands went beneath the
skirt, grabbing her flesh, colliding with the fingers of
his friend as he tried to push them into her vagina.

'Get her on the floor,' Dorian said.

He released her wrists and threw back the coverlet
and lowered himself down from the top bunk. He was
already naked.

'Wait,' Simon said.

He gripped the dress at the back and ripped it apart
along the seam of the zip. It snagged and he ripped
again, all the way to the waist.

'Get it off her,' he said, 'get it off her.'

They pushed her backwards onto the mattress, alongside the still sleeping Perry, at the same time tugging
the dress down her legs.

Dorian pushed Perry unceremoniously to one side, and the birthday boy rolled across the mattress until he came to rest against the wall.

The dress was pulled from her feet and she was pinned on her back. Dorian was between her legs and Rupert held her arms above her head.

'Bastards,' Simon said, now struggling to shed his own clothes. 'Wait for me.'

He ripped his shirt as he had ripped Kate's dress, and he tore the zip on his trousers as he tried to get rid of the encumbrance of the garments, frustrated that the other two had no intention of waiting.

'Hold her, hold her,' said Dorian, even though Kate did not need holding, and Rupert obliged.

Dorian spread her thighs and pushed two fingers inside her.

'She's hot as hell!' His face was flushed, his eyes wild. 'She's begging for it.'

He removed the fingers and replaced them with his penis. He shifted his angle, pushed experimentally, and drove it inside with a gush of breath.

Dorian was not interested in technique or making it last; he wanted orgasm.

'You want fucking, don't you, girl? You want fucking, don't you?'

Kate stared up at him, her eyes as wild as his. 'Yes. I want fucking. Come on, do it.' She raised her hips to meet his. 'Fuck me.'

Rupert was close to gibbering with excitement. He let go of her hands and reached to pull her breasts from the basque and his erection brushed against her face.

'Oh my God, oh my God,' he said, suddenly realising the availability of Kate's mouth.

He took hold of her head with his right hand and turned it towards his penis, which he held in his left. 'Suck it!' he said. 'Suck it!'

Kate willingly opened her mouth and sucked it inside and was gratified to hear Rupert's loud groan of pleasure.

'Bastards!'

Simon swore at his friends. He was now finally naked but had to wait for an opening. His hands groped her thighs and his prick rubbed against her leg.

Kate sucked and was fucked and closed her eyes. Hands were everywhere upon her and she responded totally.

Dorian came first.

He yelled and his back straightened upright away from her as he emptied his seed inside. He shuddered for several seconds, rocking her.

As Dorian withdrew, Rupert began to come in her mouth, his spasm so great that it dislodged his penis from between her lips so that he shed most of his sperm upon her face.

'Move!' said Simon.

He urgently pulled Dorian out of the way and knelt between her open and raised thighs, but he could no longer contain his excitement before he entered.

Simon knelt there, so close and yet so far, holding his weapon in his right hand, and shot his juices onto

Kate's stomach and between her legs.

He sank back on his haunches in anguish, swearing softly to himself, while Kate marvelled at the speed and ferocity of the attack, and how quickly it was over, leaving her without an orgasm and still on fire.

Dorian sat on the floor, his back against the bunk beds, regaining his breath.

'I think it only courteous for her to wake up Perry.'

He spoke to no one in particular, but particularly not to Kate.

She had already decided that Perry would not be left out and she rolled over of her own volition to kneel alongside him. He lay on his back and she pulled away the sheet that covered the lower part of his body, to reveal that, in his sleep, he held his penis in his right hand.

Kate moved his hand and took his penis in her own. It was half erect, even in slumber, and she stroked it gently in her palm and Perry grunted and shifted slightly into a more comfortable position.

His penis was stiffening already and now she bent forward and took it in her mouth and sucked it, taking it deep in her throat, using her lips and tongue around the head, rubbing and gripping the sensitive underside, as Chloe had taught her.

The penis became full grown and took on a life of its own and she was inordinately proud of her achievement. She continued to suck the head and masturbate the base and Perry began to moan in his sleep, and his hips began to move regularly in time to her ministrations.

Someone moved to kneel behind her and hands began

to touch her body again, taking their time now that the urgency had been exorcised. Palms groped her breasts that had spilled free from the basque and a freshly rampant penis pushed between her legs.

She moved backwards onto it, pushing herself down against its root, against the groin from which it sprouted, causing its owner to groan.

The person behind her began to move in and out, and her head kept pace with it, as it dipped and sucked, dipped and sucked, and she felt Perry was being brought to the brink despite his unconscious state.

This was going to be the ultimate of wet dreams.

Perry's penis pulsed and exploded in her mouth, as the young man himself sat up, his eyes wide and staring in shock, unaware of where he was or what was happening.

His yell echoed around the room and his body went rigid and shook.

'Oh, you beautiful bitch,' Dorian said, pushing himself deeper into her from behind. 'You beautiful bitch.'

Kate finally relinquished the drained penis from her mouth, as Perry lay back, and she licked the remnants of its spillage from her lips and swallowed it. She smiled to herself.

Dorian had finally spoken directly to her in a warped compliment of love.

'Move her here,' said Simon, and, because no one was in a hurry any more, Dorian obliged.

Perry half turned to face the wall, and slipped back to sleep.

Kate was positioned on her hands and knees in front of Simon while Dorian continued to take her from behind. The dark-haired young man was breathing through pursed lips in anticipation, and he weighed her breasts in his palms, feeling them, squeezing them, pinching the nipples to make her yelp.

Then he took her head and pulled it down into his lap and pushed his penis between her lips. It was not fully hard but it soon stiffened in the soft wetness of her mouth.

He held her head between his hands and bucked with increasing violence as he fulfilled his fantasy of fucking her face.

Kate sucked and slobbered, her senses surrendered to delicious degeneracy, the fingers of one hand scratching his testicles, the fingers of the other gripping and releasing the base of his weapon.

Behind her, Dorian sighed, almost sadly because it was almost over, and came for a second time, gripping her hips as he pulsed out his pleasure.

As he moved, she felt the hands of Rupert, the ugly duckling with the curly hair, caressing her body in preparation for taking his second turn.

'On her back,' said Simon.

Kate was moved again and placed on her back on the mattress. Rupert knelt between her open legs and Simon straddled her face and replaced his penis in her mouth so that he could watch her reaction, and see the stains of the earlier sperm that trailed her skin.

She stared up at him as she sucked, her wide blue

eyes ablaze with sex, her expression urging him to come.

Beyond him, she could see nothing, but she could feel Rupert preparing to enter her and she raised her hips to facilitate the movement. His prick slid into her and she moved against it, groaning in her throat, groaning around the thickness of Simon's prick that was in her mouth.

She was being ridden as if she were a tandem and it was now her turn to buck and raise her own pleasure threshold.

Her actions caused fresh excitement in the two men who thrust into her, and Rupert raised her legs until they rested over his shoulders, and thrust so hard she could hear the slap of his groin against her buttocks.

Simon's eyes began to widen and she realised the balance of power had changed from when she had first entered the house. Now it was her who was in control, the sexuality of her body that was driving and beating the two men who laboured upon her, so far, without giving her satisfaction.

'You bitch, you bitch,' whispered Simon.

His voice had lost its early aggression and now held wonder at her stamina and eagerness.

'Oh!'

She stared as he began to come, and kept on staring as he pulled his penis from between her lips so that he could ejaculate into her face, watching it splash onto her cheeks and neck and into her open mouth.

Another fantasy fulfilled.

As he finished, she smiled, and licked the pools of sperm that had gathered at the corners of her lips.

Simon rolled from her and she concentrated on Rupert who now, with the extra freedom of movement, pushed her legs higher and bent her almost double as he pounded her vagina.

He leaned forward on top of her and stared at her face, at all the sperm that lay in rivers upon her features, at the tributary that ran lazily across her cheek and down her neck, and he reached the point of no return.

Kate yelled, 'Bastard!'

She freed her legs and planted her feet on the floor and heaved back at him, amazed at her own strength, for in her desperate search for her own coming, she lifted him on her raised hips.

Rupert twisted upon her, and his voice roared as he came, and she hit the peak in time and went soaring into her own orgasm.

They lay like broken bodies in a war zone aid station, in the heat and smell of the small room. Perry, the twenty-one-year-old who had still not seen his present, snored gently.

Kate got to her feet. She felt both drained and revitalised by the experience, a warrior with her vanquished foes around her feet.

Dorian lay in the bottom bunk, flat upon his back, a sheet pulled across his lower limbs, eyes staring blankly above him. Rupert lay curled at the bottom of the mattress in a foetal position. Simon sat in a corner, his knees up to his chin as if for protection, and watched her warily.

She unfastened the stockings and dropped them across Perry. Reaching behind her, she unclipped the basque and laid that, too, upon his body. Kate picked up her shoes and stepped over Rupert to reach the door.

'Tell Perry he had a good time,' she said to Simon.

The young man did not respond.

Kate opened the door, stepped past him, and closed it behind her.

The other room was cooler but not cool enough.

She went outside, walked barefoot across the paved road and onto the soft grass, and followed its slope to the edge of the lake. She dropped her shoes on the bank and walked into the water.

Kate swam and floated and let the coldness wash away the stains from her body, and reduce her still burning desires. When she emerged, she felt reborn.

She put on the shoes, collected her spectacles from the beautiful car, and walked up the hillside towards the house and the waiting DeVille, naked and content.

24

DeVille noticed the change in Kate.

As she emerged from the garage and began to walk across the courtyard, slowly and at ease with her nakedness, he climbed out of the limousine.

He held the cape ready for her but she shook her head.

She climbed into the back of the car, stretched her legs and relaxed. He joined her and the chauffeur began to drive back to London.

DeVille said, 'If these two weeks were viewed as a series of tests, then I think you have just graduated, Mrs Lewis.'

'Thank you.'

'It only remains for you to attend a suitable graduation ceremony.'

'I'm sure you can arrange it.'

'I already have. In three days' time. It will be your final assignment.'

'What is the event?'

'A reception that is being given by an Arab oil sheikh for a few select business associates.'

'Where is the venue?'

'A London hotel.'

'Won't they object?'

'Hardly. The sheikh owns it.'

'How many people will be at the reception?'

'Ten. Plus you.'

'I take it that all the others are male?'

'I would imagine so.'

Kate thought about how ten into one might go. It
seemed like hard work.

'How close am I to raising the money I need?'

'The sheikh is generous. Money means little to him
because he has so much. What he has agreed to pay wil
take your total earnings to a level that will match you
debt.'

'This is in three days?' she asked.

'Yes.'

'What do I do until then?'

'Anything you like, Mrs Lewis.'

For no apparent reason, an image of Billy the stabl
lad came into her mind.

Kate made the trip back to her home in the country th
next day. She took Chloe with her.

They rented a car and made the journey an adver
ture. The weather remained fine, and Kate became
guide to the countryside they drove through, as Chlo
had been guide around the city of London that they ha
traversed on foot and by bus and underground.

At lunchtime, they stopped at a country pub for a me

and a glass of wine and renewed their intimacy in new surroundings.

In early afternoon, Kate turned into the long drive that led to her home and Chloe whistled her admiration.

'I can see why you didn't want to lose it,' Chloe said.

They parked at the front and Kate was pleased that her husband's vehicle was not there. Her solicitor had carried out her instructions to change the locks and had issued a legal restraint upon Roger that barred him from the house.

At the moment, at least, it appeared as if Roger was taking the legal threat seriously. Kate hoped her husband had learned what other enquiries the solicitor was making into his business conduct. If he had, it might have tempted him to leave the country.

Kate unlocked the door with a new key and they went inside.

Kate said, 'A lady from the village comes in three times a week as housekeeper. I called her last night and asked her to bring us some fresh food.' She pointed. 'The kitchen is this way.'

The refrigerator was stocked with salad, sliced cooked ham and turkey, bacon and eggs.

Chloe picked up a cucumber. She said, 'If nothing else, we can amuse ourselves.'

'We can do better than that. A good ride in the country will blow the city dust away.'

'I've never been known to turn down a good ride.'

'I'll tell Billy to get the horses ready.'

They went out of the kitchen door and walked around the side of the house to the old stone barn that had been converted into stables. Billy was in the yard, wearing blue jeans, a checked shirt and cowboy-style work-boots. He was grooming the grey, Smokey.

'Hello, Billy.'

'Hello, Miss Kate.' He smiled and she thought she detected a blush beneath the ruddiness of his complexion. 'It's nice to see you back.'

'Nice to be back. This is Chloe.'

Chloe said, 'Hello, Billy.'

The young man blushed deeper and put a finger to his forehead.

'Morning, Miss Chloe.'

Kate said, 'Will you saddle both horses for us. We'll be out in half an hour.'

'They'll be ready.'

The girls went back towards the house and as soon as they turned the corner and were out of sight, Chloe grabbed Kate's arm.

'What a dishy man,' she said. 'So innocent. So lustful!'

'Lustful?'

'Didn't you see it in his eyes? I'll bet he has dreams about you.'

'Do you think so?'

They went into the kitchen and Chloe picked up the cucumber again.

'Maybe we won't need this, after all,' she said. 'Maybe it's time for his dreams to come true.'

They discarded the jeans and sweatshirts in which

272

they had travelled from London, and put on tight cream jodhpurs that showed every curve of their thighs and posteriors.

Kate pulled on brown leather riding boots, while Chloe had brought ankle-high jodhpur boots. They were both naked to the waist when Kate caught Chloe looking at her speculatively.

Chloe said, 'You look good enough to eat.'

'Eat me later.'

'I will.'

The dark girl embraced her and kissed her neck; the flesh of their breasts moulded together and Kate's nipples became immediately erect. Chloe moved a leg between hers and they rubbed themselves against each other.

They kissed, their tongues beginning to make love, before Kate pushed Chloe away gently. 'Don't spoil your appetite.'

Chloe laughed and picked up a cream silk blouse and put it on.

Kate said, 'What about a bra?'

She smiled. 'It's time for Billy to get his first treat.'

The blouse was see-through and left little to the imagination. She tucked it into the waistband of the jodhpurs, pulling it taut across her nipples. The points looked as if they might rip the material open.

Kate said, 'I like it. But my breasts are too big to go riding without support.'

She put on a low-cut white lace bra, which enhanced rather than confined her bosom, and a tan silk shirt with diaphanous properties. She left the few buttons of the blouse unfastened.

'Let's go and see Billy,' she said.

Both horses were saddled and tied up outside the stables. Billy was inside the building and saw them crossing the yard over the top of the stable door.

His eyes widened and this time Kate definitely identified the blush that started in his neck and coloured his face. He remained in the stable, not knowing where to look, his gaze darting from face to face, bosom to bosom, and down to the floor in embarrassment.

'Thank you, Billy,' Kate said.

She heaved herself onto the back of Smokey.

Chloe said, 'Could you give me a hand?'

He reluctantly left the cover of the stable and Chloe smiled at him sweetly.

She said, 'If you make a stirrup with your hands, you will be able to lift me on.'

He linked the fingers of his hands and bent alongside her, so that his face was level with her breasts. She put her left foot in his hands and then took her time sorting out the reins to give him longer to stare at the way her breasts jiggled beneath the silk and how the nipples were hard and pointed.

At last, she pulled herself upwards and he lifted her with ease onto the back of the roan.

'Ooh, Billy.' She smiled at him girlishly. 'You are so strong.'

He coughed, and went redder still.

Kate said, 'We'll be back in a couple of hours.'

They walked the horses out of the yard and onto a track that led away from the house and into the country.

'I'll show you the bottom meadow,' Kate said. 'It's where I used to go to be alone with my fantasy.'

'I can't wait.'

The ride was stimulating. The breeze caressed their breasts and the saddles rubbed their vaginas. Kate again enjoyed the power of the horse between her legs.

They took a circuitous route around the land that she owned and visited a nearby lake, before heading back to their real destination.

Chloe said, 'I'm enjoying this too much. If we don't stop soon, I'm going to come.'

Kate smiled and touched her heels against the flank of her horse to put it into a trot, and led the way to the copse in the bottom meadow.

They dismounted and tied the horses to a tree and Kate led Chloe into the privacy of the clearing in the bushes. The grass was soft and inviting and she sat down. She removed her spectacles and placed them alongside her.

'This is the place I used to visit,' she said. 'This is where I could be alone with my fantasy and remember that day long ago.'

Chloe came to stand alongside her and Kate caressed her thigh.

'What did you do, here?' Chloe asked in a low voice.

'I masturbated. I pushed my fingers inside myself and rubbed my clitoris until I came.'

Kate pushed her head between Chloe's thighs and

275

began to bite the girl's vagina through the jodhpurs. Her hands felt her buttocks through the cloth. A seam ran down the crotch of the breeches and she worked it against Chloe's clitoris.

The girl held Kate's head and moved her hips against her.

'You delicious bitch,' she said. 'You bitch, you bitch . . .'

The words turned into a moan and she held herself tight against Kate's face and came.

When the shaking had stopped, she dropped onto the grass alongside her and Kate held Chloe in her arms. Slowly, their kisses of tenderness began to change into something more urgent until their tongues were fighting each other.

Now it was Chloe's turn to take command and she abruptly ripped open the tan silk shirt, sending those buttons that were fastened pinging into the undergrowth.

Her hands pulled Kate's breasts from the bra cups and her mouth sought their softness, suckling at the nipples in turn. Her fingers now moved to the jodhpurs and Kate pulled in her stomach so that Chloe could unclip the waistband and pull down the zip.

Chloe's right hand slid across the flatness of her friend's stomach and beneath the panties as stealthy as a snake. The hand continued heading for the hot, dark, wet cave between her legs.

She moved up to kiss Kate's neck and pushed her tongue in her ear, its tip digging in and out in a rapid, wet, fucking rhythm that had the blonde girl gasping open mouthed. And all the time, the fingers moved closer and closer to the centre of her universe.

Chloe's middle finger dipped into the moist channel and found Kate's clitoris and she called out an unintelligible cry. The finger worked with tense fury as Chloe's mouth slid back to the breasts that heaved on the platform of the bra cups and she sucked again at the nipples.

Kate felt the edge of the orgasm approaching like the pre-tremors of an earthquake. Chloe sensed it, too, as Kate's legs began to stiffen and her body adopted the position for an overload of pleasure. And she came.

Her cry was long and strained and loud; the quivers that shook her body went on and on as if she had gone over the edge and was refusing to return.

At last, her limbs began to relax and her eyes became normal and she rolled into Chloe's arms. The two girls lay together in the grass; Kate held Chloe's breast gently, and Chloe sucked her fingers clean as languid as a contented cat.

Kate said, 'That was so good.'

Chloe kissed her forehead. 'So was mine. Swift, unexpected and undeniable. It must be this place.'

Kate said, 'It is a special place.'

Chloe smiled.

'You've been here so many times and given yourself so much pleasure that the trees remember. The ground is fertile from your juices. And the crop you have sown is sex and sensuality in large abundance.'

Kate laughed softly.

'You are very poetic, Chloe.'

'But it is true. I will not be able to come to this place again without wanting to fuck and be fucked, to love and be loved. Or to simply lie down and stroke the tinder of my dreams into flames with my fingers between my legs.'

Kate stared up into the blue sky. 'We'll come back soon,' she said. 'But now we have to get back. Billy will be waiting.'

They got to their feet slowly, reluctant to be leaving this open air temple to the senses.

Chloe said, 'What are you going to do about your blouse?'

Kate looked down at herself and laughed. She removed it and dropped it on the ground. Her breasts looked larger and more succulent than ever as they rested in the half-cups of delicate white lace.

'When we come back we will see it and remember.'

'And in the meantime?'

Kate adjusted her breasts in the bra cups. 'In the meantime, Billy will have something else to be embarrassed about.'

Chloe laughed.

'Then I guess I'm over-dressed.' She tore open the blouse and took it off; she dropped it next to Kate's. 'Another memory,' she said, and stretched her arms high into the air. 'It feels good.'

Kate said, 'I'm feeling hot and sticky. When we get back, I'll ask Billy to cool me down.'

'I thought the idea was to get hotter and stickier?'
She smiled. 'All in good time.'

25

The ride back was exhilarating and the two girls were still more highly aroused by the time they reached the house and rode back into the stable yard, their breasts moving deliciously to the motion of their mounts.

'Billy!' Kate called.

He came out of the barn where he had been working. Because of the heat, he had removed his shirt and was naked to the waist, wearing only blue jeans and work boots. His body was well muscled and tanned. It was obvious he had not expected to see the two young women also naked, or almost naked, to the waist.

The young man stared, open-mouthed, at Chloe's bare breasts and Kate's only partially concealed ones. The shock, and the stare, lasted for several seconds before he regained control of his wits.

'What happened? Was there an accident?'

Kate said, 'We got too hot.' She swung herself off the horse. 'I'm still hot. Will you fetch a bucket of water, please, Billy?'

'Yes, Miss Kate. Straight away.'

He went for buckets, still casting glances back, but relieved to be able to escape the stares of the four exposed nipples.

Kate and Chloe took the horses into the paddock at the back of the stables, tied them to the fence and began to unsaddle them.

Billy joined them.

'I'll do that, ma'am.'

'Almost done,' Kate said. 'Never mind, you can help us cool down.'

The girls removed the saddles and carried them into the tack room at the side of the barn while Billy unfastened the bridles and let the horses loose into the paddock.

When they were alone in the tack room, Kate whispered to Chloe, 'Give me a few minutes alone with him. Let's see what happens.'

Kate went back into the barn that was alongside the stables. Billy was waiting, still stripped to the waist, with two buckets of water at his feet.

'Will there be anything more, Miss Kate?'

'Yes.'

Kate walked across the straw-littered stone floor until she was standing close to him. She looked up into his face, which now seemed to be permanently red.

She said, 'I would be very much obliged if you would take off my bra. I can't work the clip.' She held up her hands in explanation. 'My fingers are too sweaty.'

'Take it off?' His voice was small and shaky.

'Yes, please. The clip is at the front. See?'

She pointed and his eyes followed her finger to the valley between her breasts. Both of them had escaped the cups and were resting upon the white lace. The nipples had been erect with desire ever since she and Chloe had gone to the bedroom to get changed and had been unable to stop themselves from fondling each other.

'Here?'

Billy pointed and she nodded.

He reached forward, the fingers and thumbs of each hand poised, edging closer to the thin band of material that held the cups together.

Then he hesitated and looked into her face. 'Are you sure, Miss Kate?'

'I'm sure.' She dropped her voice. His closeness and his maleness were turning her on far more than she had expected. 'Take it off for me.'

Billy touched the lace and tried to work the fastening but his grip was too tentative. Kate's breasts now heaved slowly and seductively. They ached for his caress.

'You have to be much firmer than that, Billy. Don't be afraid to touch me.'

He gulped but this time his fingers did not hesitate and they pushed inside the bra and against her flesh and the clip came apart all too quickly. He lifted the bra from her shoulders and she let it slip down her arms until he was left standing in front of her, holding it in his hand.

Kate took it from him and dropped it to the floor.

'You have a lovely touch, Billy.' She took hold of his hands and slowly placed them over her breasts. 'You are so big and strong and gentle.'

He was still nervous and did not attempt to flex his fingers to grip her nakedness. He was simply allowing her to push his hands against her body.

'Billy, wash the sweat from my breasts.'

'Yes, Miss Kate.'

He picked a sponge from one of the buckets and squeezed it against her left breast. The water was cold and she shuddered and stepped closer still and put her arms around his torso.

'I'm sorry, Billy. But the water was a shock. And you feel so safe and reliable.'

She moved away again and let him continue to use the sponge upon her upper body, the coldness making her skin tingle and her nipples bulge even more. Then she took the sponge from him and wiped his chest where she had pressed against him and made him wet.

Billy was trembling with nervousness but there was now a strange look in his eyes.

Kate looked down at herself. 'The water has soaked my jodhpurs. I'd better take them off.'

She sat on a bale of hay and lifted up one of her legs and he responded. He turned his back to her, took the riding boot between his legs and held the heel, while she pushed with the other foot against his buttock until it came off. He repeated the process with the other boot and placed them out of the way against the wall of the barn.

Kate stood up and unfastened the waistband of her jodhpurs and released the zip.

'Pull these off as well,' she said. 'They are so tight, they're difficult to remove.'

Kate sat back on the bale of hay and pushed the jodhpurs down her thighs, revealing the white triangle of her panties. She leaned back and raised her feet.

He hesitated again.

'It's all right, Billy. You can touch. I like your touch.'

His hands held her hips and slid down over her curves until they reached the jodhpurs. He tugged and they came down and she lifted her feet off the ground so he could remove them completely.

'My panties are wet, too.' She licked her lips because the tension she was feeling was causing a drought in her mouth. 'Take them off.'

Billy no longer hesitated. He put his large hands around her waist and she lifted her hips. His palms slid beneath her, over her buttocks, feeling the soft flesh as they slid the brief lace panties downwards. His fingers hooked round them and he tugged them down her thighs and clear of her feet.

Kate licked her lips again. She lay naked on the hay, except for her spectacles and a pair of white knee socks.

'Your trousers are all wet.' She gulped softly. 'If you take them off, you can put them to dry in the sun.'

Billy was breathing heavily, causing his chest to expand. Kate admired how slim his waist was, and how his stomach muscles were taut and knotted.

'My trousers, Miss Kate?'

'Yes. Take off your trousers, Billy. That's an order.'
She was breathing through her mouth now. 'Do as
your mistress says.'

Billy reached down and pulled off the cowboy work-
boots, which he placed tidily alongside Kate's riding
boots. He hesitated, staring at Kate's nakedness, still,
perhaps, not believing that this was happening, or
thinking it would end in a cruel joke.

'Take them off, Billy,' Kate hissed.

He unfastened the jeans and pushed them past his
thighs. They slid down his legs and he stepped out of
them and left them lying on the floor.

All he wore were white socks and white boxer shorts
that, Kate noticed, bulged.

She sat up on the bale of hay.

'Come here,' she said.

He stepped in front of her and his body trembled.

Kate ran her fingers slowly down his chest and the
bulge in the boxer shorts twitched.

'You have a beautiful body, Billy.'

Her fingers hooked into the waistband of the shorts.
He gulped.

'So have you, Miss Kate. You're so beautiful.'

She scratched his stomach beneath the waistband and
moved her other hand up the inside of his thigh.

'Have you thought about me, Billy?' The hand moved
higher up his thigh. 'Have you thought about my body?'

'Yes, miss. I have.'

Her hand slipped beneath the leg of the shorts and
burrowed its way across the pubic hair at his groin. She

moved her fingers tantalisingly close to his erection without actually taking hold of it.

'Have you thought about touching me, Billy?'

'Yes, miss.'

'Of holding my breasts?'

'Yes, miss.'

'Of making love to me?'

His voice was a whisper. 'Yes, miss.'

She looked up the length of his body and smiled at him with parted lips as her fingers finally slid around his penis. He shuddered and, for a moment, she thought he might come immediately.

'I've had the same thoughts, Billy. The same dream. I've thought about you fucking me.'

She fed the erection through the slit at the front of the shorts so that it protruded as hard and firm as an iron club. It throbbed in front of her face and she dropped her gaze momentarily to look at it. She could not resist leaning forward to lick the purple head.

Kate felt it tremble in her hand and stopped licking. She looked back up into his face.

'I want you, Billy. Do you want me?'

'Yes, miss.'

She moved her fingers around the base of the penis, in a slow masturbatory pattern, and felt it tremble again and knew he could no longer hold himself in check.

'Come for me, Billy! Come for me!'

The young man's mouth opened and his eyes widened and he cried out as his penis jerked and shook in her

287

hand and the bulbous head spat out its milky secretions into her face.

He shook for a long time after he had stopped ejaculating and it seemed as if it were only Kate's hand at the base of his weapon that held him upright.

When she released his penis the young man staggered sideways to collapse upon a bale of hay.

Kate had been watching his reactions so intently she had not been aware that Chloe, now stark naked, had emerged from her hiding place, and was now alongside her.

'Delicious,' whispered the dark-haired girl.

She brushed the long blonde hair from Kate's face with her fingers and leaned over and, with a delicate tongue, began to lick the sperm from Kate's face. When her mouth was full she put her lips to Kate's lips and they kissed and shared the elixir of lust.

They lay upon the hay bales and kissed and touched and their legs entwined and their hips thrust against each other for several minutes, until Kate touched Chloe's shoulder and they stopped and looked across at Billy.

He had discarded the shorts and now sat wide-eyed in the hay, watching the two young women whilst he stroked his fresh erection.

'Your turn, Billy,' Kate said. 'Do you want to fuck me?'

'Yes.'

Chloe moved to one side and Kate held her arms open.

'Do whatever you want. Use me any way you wish. Make your dreams come true.'

He stood up and walked towards her, his penis upright

and swaying from its root. Alongside her, he stared down at her body, devouring it first with his eyes, and then with his hands. They felt her breasts and stroked her face before slowly trailing down to her hips.

His left hand caressed her flank, his right stroked through the bush at the juncture of her open legs, and those big, strong fingers slid across her clitoris, causing her to move her hips in desire.

Billy kept his hand there and she moved against it. At last, he pushed a finger inside the hot wetness and she moaned. He pushed two fingers inside and she writhed against them.

Suddenly, he removed the fingers, stepped between her splayed thighs, and pulled her forward on the hay bale and straight onto his iron-rampant penis.

He held her hips as he thrust within her. His strength was phenomenal and his passion furious and her limbs flopped around under his attack.

As swiftly as he had entered her, he withdrew, and flipped her over onto her stomach in one easy motion. He pulled her towards him again, the hay scratching her thighs, and onto his iron rod from behind. His hips smacked against her buttocks with the harshness of a spanking.

Chloe climbed onto Kate's back, straddling her so that she faced Billy. As he continued his rhythm, she hung around his neck and licked his face, trailing her tongue across his skin and into his mouth.

The kiss was as harsh and uncompromising as the way he was pounding into Kate, whose moans were now a mixture of pleasure and pain. Billy did not want tenderness, he wanted sex.

Chloe slid back onto the floor, crawling around his body as if she were a snake descending a tree.

She licked and scratched and bit her way downwards and between his powerful legs, until she sat with her back against the bale of hay over which Kate lay. Above her face, his iron rod pistoned in and out, and the sack of his balls swung with the rhythm.

Chloe pushed her mouth into the sweating and aromatic area between his thighs, and licked and sucked at the sack. At the same time, she held his buttocks in both hands, and dug her fingernails deep enough to break the skin. She felt him shudder and groan and she dug deeper with her fingernails, and raked the flesh.

Billy began to roar, the sexual anger of his voice echoing around the stone barn. The roar changed into a chant that was timed to the thrusts that appeared to be climbing to a far crescendo.

The chant was: 'Fuck! Fuck! Fuck!'

Kate's moans and squeals and Chloe's slurping provided the accompaniment until the chant slurred back into a meaningless shout, and he came, juddering his love juices deep inside his mistress as Chloe's fingernails dug deeper still.

He collapsed on top of Kate and his bulk was such that she could not move until Chloe had extricated herself from his thighs and rolled him from her back.

Chloe helped Kate to her feet but after such treatment she found it difficult to stand. The two girls held on to each other and stared down at the stablehand who lay supine on the hay with blood trails on his lacerated buttocks.

Kate composed herself and spoke with as much dignity as she could muster. 'Thank you, Billy. That was most satisfactory. I shall not want you again today.' She paused and took a deep breath. 'But be here in the morning. Both Miss Chloe and I will be riding again.'

She moved slowly and carefully, still leaning on Chloe, out of the barn and across the yard. The fresh air made her straighten and she rubbed herself against her friend and lover as they walked.

Chloe's left arm was about her shoulders to give support, but her right hand had slipped between Kate's legs and was keeping the fires of desire burning at her vagina.

'Next time,' Chloe said, 'I shall have him.'

'He's a stallion. He'll break you in half.'

'I'll risk it.' Her fingers slipped inside Kate. 'In the meantime, I'll lick him from you. When I get you upstairs, I shall wash you with my tongue.'

The two naked young women kissed in the middle of the yard; their mouths lascivious, their hands groping each other's bodies. When they continued walking they still touched and licked, all the way to the house.

They went directly upstairs and into Kate's bedroom where they spent the rest of the afternoon fucking and making love and planning what to do with Billy the following day.

26

For her graduation, Kate wore all white. Her underwear, stockings, high-heeled shoes, and the knee length linen suit were all pure white.

Around her neck was a white pearl necklace and her hair was held high upon her head with a white silk ribbon. This time, because of the numbers that would possibly be involved, and under the advice of DeVille, she wore contact lenses instead of spectacles.

The affect was stunning, although she felt she had been prepared more as a sacrifice than a graduate.

DeVille accompanied her in the chauffeur-driven limousine to one of London's most famous hotels, where a man in a uniform and top hat opened the door for her with deference. But as she walked through the heavy glass doors, his air of respect slipped and he was unable to stop himself from staring after her in open appreciation.

The linen of her suit was so fine that it was close to being transparent in the strong sunlight.

Eyes followed her as she crossed the lobby with

DeVille to the bank of lifts and she reflected that less than two weeks ago she could have crossed the same lobby in total anonymity in her safe tweed skirt and flat shoes.

Kate straightened her shoulders and basked in the admiration that came from the men, and the jealousy that came from the women. She preferred this to tweed skirt anonymity, any day.

They ascended four floors and when the lift doors opened they were met by two heavy men in suits who inspected a card that DeVille handed to them. Kate was impressed by the security and by the wealth it implied.

The men allowed them to leave the lift, and they were directed down a corridor to where another plain clothes security man maintained a position by the entrance to a suite of rooms.

DeVille showed the card again and the man knocked on the door. It opened and an Arab in white robes stared at Kate. Finally, he nodded to DeVille and opened the door wider.

DeVille said, 'This is where I leave you, Mrs Lewis. I shall see you later. I hope you enjoy yourself.'

Kate was surprised to feel calm and in control of her emotions, despite the fact that she was stepping through a door into the unknown.

She smiled at DeVille. 'Thank you,' she said. 'I shall do my best.'

Kate stepped forward and left DeVille in the corridor. The Arab closed the door, shutting her off from the outside world and admitting her to her final assignment

294

They were in a reception room and the Arab indicated with a raised finger that she should wait. He opened sliding double doors, through which she could hear the chatter of conversation, went through and closed them behind him.

He returned soon after, this time pushing the double doors wide open. Beyond him, the conversation had stopped. The guests, it seemed, were awaiting her entrance.

Kate took a deep breath and walked into the room. The Arab exited and closed the doors behind him. She stopped and looked around.

Three black men in suits were to her immediate left, holding drinks and appraising her appearance. Two men who could have been Arabs or at least from the Middle East were sitting at a bar at the other side of the room, and a group of four Europeans were nearby to her right, again holding drinks.

Nine in all, all soberly dressed and middle-aged, and of various races, sizes and physiques.

The room itself was furnished with a chaise longue, two low sofas and a wide and well-padded seat that had no sides or back. Fitted on wall brackets around the room were giant television screens; she counted six of them. And while there was carpet around the sides of the room where the furniture was located, the space in the middle was a small but glittering dance floor.

Kate looked again and realised why it glittered so much: the dance floor was a mirror.

Although she had made her entrance, the guests

still appeared to be waiting. Light background music started, coming from hidden speakers, and the television screens flickered into life.

The attention of Kate and the nine men transferred to the giant screens. Each one showed a different film, and yet they were all the same: pornographic.

A couple copulated on one, a large naked group writhed upon another, a giant negro was being fellated by a young white girl on a third, three men all entered one woman simultaneously on the fourth, and on the fifth, two women penetrated each other with rubber dildoes.

The sixth was a shock. The screen showed Kate and the men nearest to her.

As the party developed, she imagined that she would be vying for video stardom with the other performers already involved in sexual activity on the giant television sets.

A door across the room opened and their host entered. He was elderly and small and wore white flowing robes. A murmur of greeting went up from the nine men and he smiled and inclined his head to them diffidently, before stepping onto the mirrored floor.

He held his hand out as an invitation to Kate and she walked forward, stepped onto the reflective surface, and approached him. They shook hands and his touch was gentle and moist, his fingers moving slowly like worms in her palm, sensing her flesh.

The sheikh said, 'Welcome, Kate. You are a beautiful lady and you honour us with your presence.'

'The honour is mine.'

'My guests have heard a lot about you and have been eager to meet you.'

'I hope I do not disappoint them.'

'And I hope you will enjoy my little party.'

She smiled and squeezed the worm fingers gently. 'How could I not enjoy it,' she glanced around, her gaze taking in the men, the television screens and the floor upon which they were standing, 'when you have gone to so much trouble?'

He smiled happily at her reply, let go of her hand and called to one of the men at the bar. 'The young lady needs a drink.'

A slim swarthy man said, 'Of course.'

He poured a glass of champagne and brought it to her, first smiling into her face as she accepted it, and then lowering his eyes to the floor.

The skirt of the suit was slightly flared and she knew he would be able to see all that was beneath it as well as if he were lying on the floor looking up.

Kate sipped the champagne and smiled around the room. Three other men strolled onto the floor to surround her. They started an inconsequential but polite conversation, calling her by her name. She participated in the chat, and all the time they blatantly alternated their gaze between her face and the floor.

She swayed from one leg to the other, did small spins that flared the skirt further as she turned to answer questions, and the mood began to change.

The other men had joined them and the group fluctuated, some going to the bar to replenish their drinks, others taking their places to talk and stare beneath her skirt in the reflective floor.

Their host, the sheikh, moved away from the central group and sat in the room's solitary armchair and watched.

On the screen, an underfloor camera was relaying the pictures that it took as it peered directly up her skirt: her thighs, suspenders, buttocks, and the narrow wisp of loose white silk beneath her legs that was the crotch of her French panties, were being shown in full colour and larger than life on the giant screen.

The heat in the room was rising; the men themselves were generating it, and she drank her third glass of champagne and wondered how and when it would start.

It started with a question.

Perhaps the sheikh had given a signal that she had missed, but the same slim and swarthy man who had handed her the first drink, began.

'Do you like being fucked, Kate?'

She smiled at him and touched her top lip with her tongue before replying.

'I love being fucked.'

The other men fell silent and she realised that the music had died and that her words were being picked up by a microphone and were being played through the speakers of the room's sound system.

'Do you . . .' The swarthy man coughed before continuing.

Perhaps, she thought, he was the one with nerves? 'Do you like sucking cock?'

This time she ran her tongue around the inside of her open mouth. 'I love to suck cock. I would love to suck your cock.' She glanced at the man next to him. 'And yours.' And the man next to him. 'And yours.' She sipped her champagne. 'I want to suck all your cocks, and be fucked and sodomised and have you spray your sperm upon my body and in my face.'

The room was silent except for their breathing. The nine men had stopped drinking and now circled her, some staring at her body through the linen suit, the others gazing at the mirror upon which she stood to see beneath her skirt.

Kate handed the empty champagne glass to the slim and swarthy man. She said softly, 'Who is going to be first?'

Three or four of the men who had already got rid of their drinks moved together. Their hands took possession of her body, gripping her breasts, raising her skirt and grabbing at her buttocks; pushing between her thighs and invading her vagina with demanding and impatient fingers.

She tilted back her head and let herself go. She was theirs and it was a glorious release not to have to think or make decisions but simply to respond.

The jacket of the suit was torn because of the greedy hands, and then it was ripped open and pulled halfway down her shoulders. The bra's front fastening was unclipped and the white lace material was left hanging, trapped by the remnants of the jacket.

Her naked breasts were mauled and pulled. A mouth sucked on one and she felt erect staffs of male flesh pushing against her through the material of their suits.

'Over here,' someone said.

She was half carried, half led to the low but well-padded bench that had no sides or back. Along the way, the jacket and the bra were dragged from her arms leaving her naked to the waist.

Kate was laid upon the bench, and the skirt was unbuttoned at the waist but, when the zip became stuck, two men simply ripped it apart, pulled it from her and threw it to one side.

The panties were hauled down her legs and the men paused to survey their handiwork as she lay spread upon the upholstery, wearing only high heeled shoes, white stockings and suspender belt, a string of pearls and a smile.

She could not believe the fire between her legs or the excitement that was being generated in this room.

'Who,' she whispered hoarsely, 'is going to be first?'

The men began to pull their clothes off, expensive suit jackets were discarded carelessly, zips were forced in the rush to shed their trousers.

First was the swarthy man from the Middle East and he did not wait to undress.

He pushed his trousers down his thighs and climbed between her legs, opened the lips of her sex with his fingers and pushed his stiffness into her.

Kate heaved her hips back at him and contracted the

muscles inside her vagina to tease him into swift ejaculation. When she saw the surprise in his eyes she knew she had succeeded. He held himself upright on his arms, his upper torso still respectable in shirt, tie, waistcoat and jacket, and shuddered into orgasm.

Then her view was blocked by another man who had not bothered to undress, a black man who pushed the penis that protruded from his trousers into her mouth.

Kate used her techniques again, remembering all she had learned from Chloe and DeVille, and brought the man in her mouth to an equally swift conclusion with her fingers and tongue, gulping down his semen.

Naked and semi-naked men now took the place of the first two and she was again taken between the legs and had another penis thrust into her mouth at the same time. Once again, the owners of the erections did not feel as if they would last long. The atmosphere was volatile and she knew it would not take much to entice any of the waiting pricks to shoot their sperm.

As the second pair finished they were pulled from her body. Another penis was presented to her face and she was turned on her side as two men climbed upon the bench at front and rear.

She took hold of the weapon near her mouth, masturbated it swiftly and expertly as she licked the head, and it exploded into her face.

The sight was too much for the man who had pushed himself close behind her and whose own penis was against the cushion of her buttocks. He shuddered and yelled in dismay as his own orgasm caught him out and he shed his juices into the crease between the soft globes.

Hands still clutched and groped and she was turned and twisted and, this time, a penis that approached her from behind used the discharge that oiled her flesh as lubrication to force a way into her anus.

The penetration was sharp and caused her to cry out as another erection smeared its secretions across her face before dipping into the warm, wetness of her mouth.

Her vagina waited and was not disappointed and a third entry was made and she moved in a daze, dimly aware that all the noise they were making was being picked up by a microphone and magnified through the speakers.

Her anus proved too deliciously tight for sustained pleasure and the man behind her ejaculated with a shudder. It caused a chain reaction and his two companions followed suit, releasing their lust into her vagina and mouth.

The bodies rolled away and she was left alone and unfulfilled. She had been concentrating on servicing the nine men rather than on her own enjoyment and still had to achieve her own first orgasm.

She raised herself on the bench on one arm and surveyed the room. The businessmen no longer looked impressive. Some sat on the floor or on the sofas, partially dressed, as they recovered from the intensity of the first bout.

A black man was standing alone by the bar, totally

naked apart from black socks and shoes. He grinned and toasted her with his drink.

Across the room, the sheikh remained in his armchair. He was able to watch the action live or on the giant television screens. Each one now showed a different angle of the proceedings with pictures furnished by hidden cameras.

The sheikh smiled at her and politely applauded.

Around her, men were recovering and preparing for the second assault. This time, they would last longer.

They started simply, with one being fellated while a second penetrated her vagina from the rear, but their stamina made the others impatient. Hands groped her breasts and thighs and, after those first two had finished, she was again taken by three at the same time, while a fourth insinuated himself onto her chest where he pushed his penis between the valley of her breasts.

Her hands felt other naked thighs of men who were waiting and she reached up, although she could not see, and took two more revitalised weapons in her hands and masturbated them steadily until a point of entry became available.

All their bodies now shimmered with sweat whilst hers also shimmered with the juices that they shed. Some of the men came and fell away, others took their place, her position was changed and they experimented still further in how to use her flesh in the ways that were most conducive to their enjoyment.

The penis between her breasts weeped its passion onto her neck whilst another slipped from between her lips prematurely and discharged its liquid into her face.

More sperm was pistoned into her vagina and her anus and the insides of her thighs became sticky and slippery with excretions, as if she had been coated with grease.

Activity lapsed again and because Kate did not know whether she could stand, she did not try but remained lying upon the bench and waited.

Three or four of the men looked as if they could manage no more and quietly slipped from the room with their clothes, presumably to nearby bedrooms where they could shower and once again become respectable.

Finally, only three remained. The slim and swarthy man, a European with a beard and a large belly, and a tall bald black man with a hairless chest.

All were totally naked and watched her from the bar where they drank while they discussed what they were going to do. They eventually approached with their weapons half erect. Kate lay on her back, her body spreadeagled for their pleasure: they chose her mouth.

One at a time, they used her mouth and she sucked them into full size. As they grew and became firm, they rubbed the heads of their pricks upon her breasts, holding the flesh to make a cushion, using the nipples as targets for their thrusts.

Kate lay in total submission and allowed them to do all the work: one in her mouth, one on each breast, until she sensed from the noises that they made and the jerkiness of their strokes that they were building to yet another climax.

They came, not all together, but in reasonably quick succession; each one showering into her face the remnants of his juices, the sperm now thin and watery.

She lay with her head tilted back and her mouth open as the centrepiece of their male fantasy.

The men staggered away, gathered their clothing and a last drink, and left the room.

Kate was thirsty and ached but, more than that, she was frustrated for she had still had no orgasm. She turned her head and stared around the room and saw her image large upon all the screens. The sheikh, still in his armchair, nodded to her and applauded once more.

And then he raised his arm in a signal to a hidden aide.

The doors through which she had entered slid open, and Kate tilted her head backwards off the bench to look. Even with a view that was upside down she recognised the small darkly tanned girl who entered: it was Chloe.

Her friend wore the outfit she had worn when they first met: a short pleated tennis skirt and polo shirt in white, ankle socks and tennis shoes. She looked young and fresh and innocent.

Chloe walked into the centre of the mirrored floor and waited, one knee turned in and her right foot raised onto its toe, in a pose calculated to make her look a juvenile.

The sheikh got out of the armchair and joined Chloe on the glittering floor. He walked around her, looking at her slim, tanned body from every angle, gazing frequently at the image reflected by the mirror beneath their feet.

He completed his inspection and gestured towards Kate. 'It is time to join your friend,' he said.

Chloe walked to the side of the bench and stared at Kate with wide eyes that took in the stains and the sweat and secretions and the way the lips of her sex were swollen and open from over-use.

The sheikh explained, 'She gave so much pleasure. Now it is time she received pleasure. Please.'

He indicated that Chloe should kneel on the floor between Kate's legs and she did so.

Kate closed her eyes as she felt the hands of her lover caressing her wet thighs and gently touching her between her legs.

She felt her breath on her flesh and then a tongue upon her exposed clitoris and she groaned out loud. Chloe's tongue licked along the sex lips, probed inside and played with her bud of sensitivity.

Kate lifted her head and looked down her body and Chloe stared back, her eyes gleaming with sensuality and the sperm of many men spread across her youthful features.

Behind her, the sheikh knelt and pushed up the pleated skirt. He tugged down the virgin panties to mid-thigh and slid his fingers into the pleasure trench between her legs.

Chloe's eyes widened and she moaned and dipped her head to lick and suck with still more passion at Kate's vagina.

The sheikh opened his robes and rubbed the tip of his thin but firm penis in the wetness and heat between the young girl's legs. Then he changed his angle of attack, circled her anus, probed it with a prod, and pushed himself slowly inside.

Again Chloe lifted her head from between Kate's thighs, her eyes wider and a scream upon her lips, and the sheikh thrust fiercely from behind: three, four, five strokes, and came.

Chloe twisted her body to make her bottom even softer and more tender against his loins, and joined her cry with his gasp, her fingers playing all the time at Kate's clitoris, a stimulus that in conjunction with everything else caused Kate to finally find her orgasm.

Her cries were still being relayed through the speakers and as her head rolled in ecstasy, her distorted features stared back at her from the giant television screens around the room, giving added power to the peak of pleasure that she rode.

Kate passed out.

When her senses re-focused and she was able to become aware of who she was and where she was, Chloe was kneeling by her side and stroking her face.

The television screens were blank, the speakers silent and the sheikh had gone.

Chloe said, 'It's just us, now. Just us.'

27

The sheikh had been thoughtful as to the welfare and entertainment of his guests; he was similarly considerate about Kate. In the reception room he had provided a wheelchair.

DeVille was summoned by Chloe, and he covered Kate once more with the ubiquitous cape. Chloe pushed the chair across the mirrored floor and Kate laughed.

'Is this really necessary?'

DeVille said, 'Probably not. But you have earned a rest and there is no point straining muscles that are already aching.'

He had a point. When she moved, she felt as if she had been playing an extremely strenuous sport non-stop for two hours.

Kate allowed herself to be helped into the wheelchair and was then perambulated along the corridor to the lift by DeVille. Chloe walked alongside like an attentive nurse.

The limousine was waiting and the chauffeur picked her from the chair and placed her in the back of the vehicle.

When they were underway, DeVille said, 'You may need tomorrow to recover. Perhaps you would care to call at my office the day after, when we can conclude our business.'

'Successfully?' Kate asked.

'Very successfully.'

She sank back in the upholstery, content with reclaiming her home and life, tired with her recent sexual exertion, and, in a way, sad to be ending a two-week period where guilt and responsibility had had no meaning.

The chauffeur carried her from the basement car park into the lift and held her easily in his arms until they reached the correct floor. Chloe unlocked the apartment door and the chauffeur laid Kate gently on a couch.

'Thank you,' she said, wishing she felt more like giving him a more personal thank you that he would remember.

He smiled into her eyes for the first time, as if the rules that had held him at a distance had now been dissolved.

'Any time you need me.'

DeVille and the chauffeur left and Chloe ran her a bath, helped her undress and then led her into the bathroom and eased her into the foaming water.

Kate lay back and let the water take the weight and ease the strain. She relaxed and smiled at her friend and lover.

Chloe said, 'Any regrets?'

'None. It should have happened years ago. I will never be afraid of sex and men again.' She touched Chloe's hand. 'But perhaps there is one regret.'

'Tell me.'

'That I will be moving back to the country, and you will be staying here.'

Chloe leaned forward and kissed her on the mouth.

'There are always weekends. I always wanted a retreat in the country, somewhere I could escape to.'

'You'll come?'

Chloe laughed. 'Every time I'm there.'

Kate laughed with her and then became more serious. 'I think I love you, Chloe.'

'Good. Because I know I love you.'

They kissed again and then Chloe stood up and took off her clothes and slid into the bath with Kate, and they touched and held each other as gently as the suds that floated on the water.

Chloe said, 'We have tonight and all day tomorrow to do nothing but indulge ourselves. We shall eat, drink, watch movies and make love.'

'In that order?'

'No.' She smiled. 'Perhaps we will forget about the food and the drink and the videos.'

Two days later, Kate went to DeVille's office. She wore the same clothes as she'd had on that first day she had reported for duty two weeks before.

Miss Sheldon gave her a warm smile of welcome and showed her into DeVille's room with the river view. He handed her documents that once more gave her the total ownership of her home. She put them in the handbag that looked like a briefcase.

He said, 'I will be sorry to lose your services, Mrs Lewis. You are a remarkable woman.'

'So I have discovered. I think that I should thank you for the opportunity you provided.'

'An opportunity you took so well. We remain, of course, business partners, but if I can ever be of personal service, please do not hesitate to ask.'

She smiled. 'It is I who should be making such an offer. I enjoyed the work and I think I have a talent for it. If, in the future, you have a request for something particularly special or challenging, perhaps you will bear me in mind?'

'With pleasure, Mrs Lewis. Now, if there is anything else I can do?'

'One last thing. I would be extremely grateful for the use of your car and chauffeur to take me back to the country. After my recent exertions, I do not yet feel ready to face public transport.'

'Of course. No problem at all.'

They shook hands.

'Goodbye, Mr DeVille. Or should I say, until we meet again.'

'Precisely. Au revoir, Mrs Lewis.'

Kate relaxed in the back of the limousine as it headed out of London's urban sprawl and counted herself fortunate.

She had got rid of her husband, taken and passed with flying colours a two-week degree course in advanced erotica, discovered inner strength and personality of which she had been unaware, gained control of her life for the first time, and fallen in love with a beautiful young woman.

Chloe would be joining her in the country at the weekend and until then she would just have to amuse herself.

There was Billy, of course, who would be happy to be a discreet working stud for his mistress. And the young curate had possibilities, while the new doctor had been particularly friendly when they had met in the village.

Perhaps she would seek spiritual guidance from the handsome young cleric to whom she could confess all manner of arousing things, and it really was about time that she had a full medical examination.

She wondered if they both did house calls?

In the meantime . . .

Kate spoke to the chauffeur. 'I never did discover your name.'

'It's George, madam.'

'Well, stop the car for a moment, if you will, George.'

'Certainly, madam.'

He pulled into the side of the country road and Kate got out of the back and climbed into the passenger seat alongside him.

'You may proceed.'

'Yes, madam.'

The car continued taking her home.

'You have been very considerate, George, and I wish to thank you properly.'

She put her hand onto his lap and stroked the inside of his thigh. A bulge began to become apparent that brushed against the back of her fingers. The bulge got larger and she unfastened his trousers and pulled down the zip. Her fingers dipped into the underpants and released a virile prick.

'Tipping is so vulgar, George. Don't you agree?'

'Extremely vulgar, madam.'

'I would much rather express my appreciation verbally. Or, at least, orally, if you see what I mean.' She squeezed his prick. 'Do you see what I mean, George?'

'Clearly, madam.'

'And do you think that would be a satisfactory remuneration?'

The prick throbbed in her hand.

'Totally satisfying, madam.'

'Good.'

Kate dipped her head and went to work.